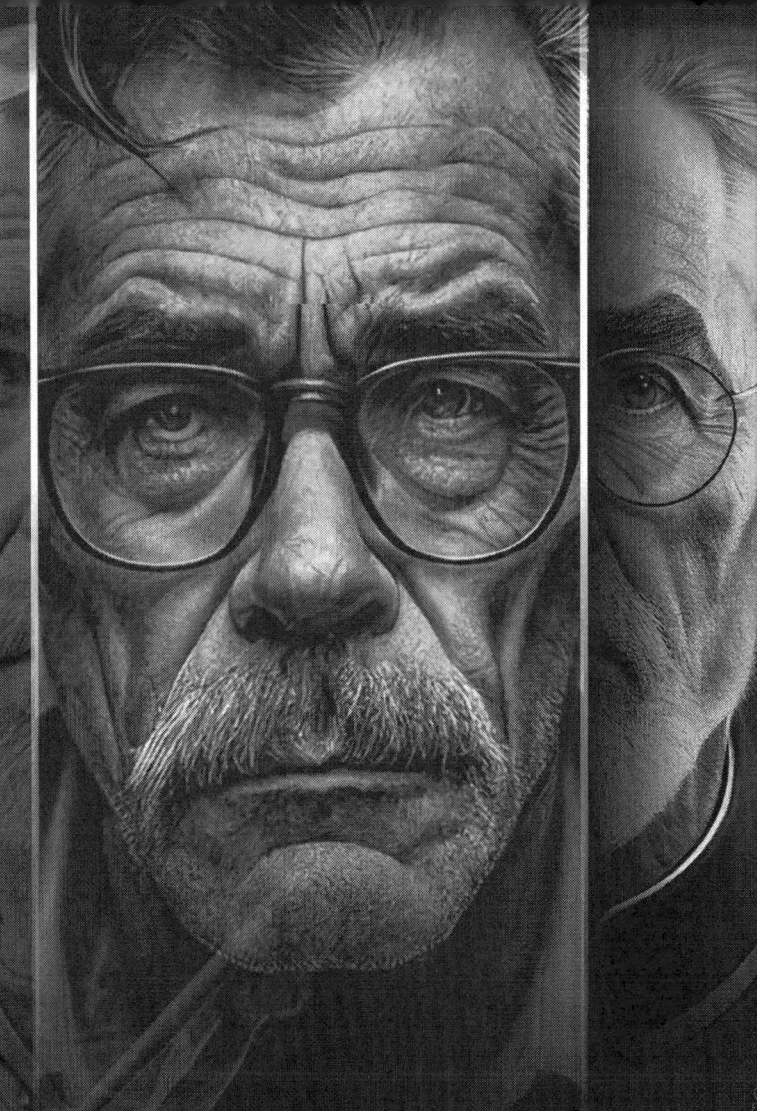

FORGER

A PSYCHOLOGICAL THRILLER

MARK SPIVAK

For Carolann

"The highest problem of any art is to cause by appearance the illusion of a higher reality."

JOHANN WOLFGANG VON GOETHE

"There is nothing either good or bad, but thinking makes it so."

WHOEVER WROTE HAMLET

CHAPTER 1

New York City, Present Day

Cheryl Weissberg had been in a police station only once before, during a class trip in middle school—"a half-assed version of *Scared Straight*," she confided to her diary. The girls weren't even supposed to go, but they were included at the last minute after someone got nabbed for shoplifting. She remembered the peeling paint, the drabness and the chill: it wasn't a cold day, but there was something about the air that was thin and piercing. As she trudged behind her classmates, a door cracked open and she glanced down the corridor into a cell. The young man sat in a corner, bearded and unwashed, a cross between Charles Manson and Jesus Christ. She dreamed about him for months.

"You're his psychiatrist?" asked Detective Larry Westerfeld.

"Clinical psychologist. Lester has been seeing me on and off for about a year."

"Well, you did a hell of a job." The detective yawned and glanced at Assistant District Attorney Sherri Brancacci. "I love it when the shrink shows up before the lawyer. Tells you exactly where you're heading."

"Lester has been extremely mild-mannered throughout therapy." Weissberg perched on the edge of a chair, trying to avoid looking at the detective. She was afraid she would stare at his shirt cuffs, which were fraying. "At no time did he seem to present any danger to anyone."

Westerfeld chuckled. "A regular Boy Scout."

"So you believe he just snapped?" asked Brancacci.

"It looks that way. Could you fill me in on the details of what happened?" asked Weissberg. "I rushed over here as soon as I heard the news, but I can't say that I'm up to speed."

"There was supposed to be an auction of a famous painting at the Cantwell Gallery today," said Westerfeld. "I'm sure you heard about it. It apparently was a hot ticket, a thousand bucks per head. What happened was that your boy here walked up to Phillip Cantwell right before the auction was supposed to start and shot him twice at close range."

"He actually had a ticket to the auction?"

"Why are you surprised?" asked the detective.

"I know they were expensive, and I didn't think he could afford it. But didn't they have a metal detector at the auction?"

Westerfeld ran his fingers through his hair. "Does it sound like it?"

"Larry," said Brancacci.

"I'm just trying to understand what happened," said Weissberg.

"He used an old army service revolver," said Westerfeld. "1960s issue. Any idea where he might have gotten that from?"

"His father was a retired master sergeant. He died about six or seven years ago, and Lester inherited his rent-controlled apartment."

"Ah," said Westerfeld. "Okay."

"Can you tell us what he was doing in therapy?" asked Brancacci. "Since he's murdered someone, the confidentiality rules are out the window."

"Lester was in and out of therapy for most of his life, and he was institutionalized several times. I started treating him after he was committed to Bellevue following an incident at the Museum of Modern Art—I was finishing my residency at the time. I diagnosed him as having Dissociative Identity Disorder, or DID. It's what used to be called multiple personality disorder."

"Like Sybil?" asked Brancacci.

"More or less, yes."

"What was the incident at the museum?"

"He was at an opening reception for an exhibit of Neo-Dada works. It's a type of art he really hates. He had been protesting the exhibit for some time, calling the museum, circulating petitions, that type of thing. He took out a box cutter and approached one of the paintings in an agitated state. The security guards thought he was going to slash the painting, so they tackled him. The police referred him to Bellevue."

"Let me get this straight," said Westerfeld. "This guy goes to a reception at MOMA, waves a box cutter around and gets himself arrested. But to you, he's harmless?"

"Lester is really a very gentle person. And he's an artist himself. He wouldn't have harmed a painting, no matter how much he hated it."

"No offense, doctor, but you sound a little naïve."

"I'd prefer to think of myself as idealistic."

"So what was he doing at the Cantwell Gallery?" asked Brancacci. "Why was he upset?"

"He was actually the one who painted the canvas they were auctioning off."

"I thought the painting was supposed to be some undiscovered French masterpiece," said Westerfeld.

"It was supposed to be, yes. But it was actually painted by one of Lester's alters, a man named Louis Bétancourt. Another alter, a Jesuit priest named Gordon Humphries, donated it to the Palmetto State Art Museum in honor of his parents. I was working in therapy to reunite Lester's personality and thought we had reached the point where he was a whole person. But apparently the decision to sell the painting reopened some very painful childhood trauma for him."

"So he shoots the gallery owner?" asked Brancacci. "That doesn't make much sense."

"She's right," said the detective. "And if he was pissed off at his parents, why would he want to donate the painting in their memory? And why would he care if it were sold?"

"That type of behavior is typical. It allows the patient to maintain a connection to the abuser."

"Well, you lost me," said Westerfeld. "To be honest, I don't care why he shot Cantwell. Motive is only useful to me before the crime is solved."

"And you never had any inkling that this man might be dangerous?" asked Brancacci.

"Not at all. If I had the slightest suspicion, I would have reported it immediately."

"He never threatened anyone, or talked about committing violence?"

"Never." She paused. "There was one occasion when the Louis Bétancourt alter was very upset about a painting he didn't like. He said that in the old days, he would have been obligated to challenge the artist to a duel."

"A duel?" asked Westerfeld. "You mean, with pistols?"

"Yes. Part of Louis's persona was that he was French, descended from a famous Impressionist painter. He wore ridiculous costumes—embroidered vests, sashes, berets. He said he was an expert marksman. It was all play acting, so of course I didn't take the talk of a duel very seriously."

"Well," he said, "it doesn't take an expert marksman to walk up to an unarmed man and shoot him from two feet away."

"What we don't know, detective, is who actually pulled the trigger in this situation. It could have been Lester, although that wouldn't be my guess. I think it's more likely to have been Bétancourt, who actually painted the canvas, or Father Humphries, who was outraged because he donated the picture in memory of his parents."

"Here we go," said Westerfeld. "I feel an insanity defense coming around the bend."

"I'm not an attorney, sir, as you said. I just feel badly for Lester."

"If you want to feel badly for someone," said the detective, "try Phillip Cantwell's wife and children."

"Larry, please," said Brancacci. "This isn't useful."

"You're right. The fact that he was neglected as a child gives him the right to murder people in cold blood." He stood up. "If you ladies will excuse me, I have bullshit coming out of my ears. I need to go rinse them out."

"What's going to happen?" asked Weissberg after Westerfeld left the room.

"We're going to charge him with premeditated murder," said the ADA. "His attorney can sort out whether to use an insanity defense. I imagine he'll have the best lawyer money can buy."

"I doubt it. Lester is a person of limited means. I'm sure he'll need the public defender."

"Well, he could afford a thousand dollars for a ticket to the Cantwell auction, as you pointed out. But if he needs an attorney, one will certainly be provided for him."

"May I speak with him?"

"Unfortunately, no. As you say, you're not a lawyer. He'll be arraigned, and you can visit with him after that."

"Lester really is a very gentle person. I can't imagine that he was the one who consciously pulled the trigger."

"Sorry, doctor. I don't make the law—I just enforce it."

Brancacci stared at the therapist, not without sympathy. They were around the same age, at the beginning stages of establishing their careers. "I know this is difficult for you, and I'm sorry. I'll make sure he gets a commitment for psychiatric evaluation, which will at least make the early stages of incarceration easier on him."

"Thank you."

"I'll admit that I'm curious about one thing, though. You say he actually painted the canvas that was up for sale at the Cantwell Gallery."

"That's my understanding, yes."

"And as far as anyone knew, that picture was an undiscovered work by Seurat. So Lester must be an incredibly gifted painter."

"I can't say. I'm not an art expert."

"Why would someone like that create forgeries? If he had that much talent, wouldn't he want to be recognized as a genius in his own right?"

"God, I don't know." Weissberg shook her head, resisting the tears that fought their way to her eyes. "I guess there wasn't any current market for what he wanted to do. A hundred years ago, I'm sure he would have been famous. Today, it's like he's just wearing his grandfather's shoes."

CHAPTER 2

Fourteen Months Earlier

Weissberg was assisting on psychiatric rounds at Bellevue when she felt her cell phone vibrate. She stepped away from the patient and glanced at the text. It was from Jensen: *Intake, right now.* She shook her head and put the phone back in her pocket. *Three days left, and it doesn't stop. There's an endless parade of drooling lunatics in my karma. I should have listened to my mother and become a dermatologist.* It was nearly eleven, and she was scheduled to go off shift at midnight. Now she knew she was guaranteed to stay until at least two in the morning.

"I'm sorry," she told the lead psychiatrist. "I've just been paged by Dr. Jensen. He needs me in intake."

The psychiatrist dismissed her with a wave of the hand. When she arrived downstairs, Jensen was actually smiling.

"Well, this is your lucky day."

"How so?"

"We have a patient who hasn't been medicated."

"Praise the Lord. I've been waiting nearly a year."

"Plus, I think you'll find the case interesting."

She looked at the man through the one-way glass. He seemed calm and serene as he stared at the wall.

"What's his story?"

"His name is Lester Gordon. He was arrested earlier this evening at the Museum of Modern Art."

"What happened?"

"Tonight was the opening of their show about the Neo-Dada movement, whatever that is. I gather that our boy here has been very vocal in his opposition to the exhibition, doing a lot of pissing and moaning. So they have the opening reception, and he gets in because he's on some sort of VIP guest list. According to the police report, he was hostile and acting strangely. Then he took a box cutter out of his pocket and approached one of the paintings." Jensen glance down at the file. "Robert Rauschenberg. Are you familiar with him?"

"I've heard the name."

"Art isn't my strong point. But I gather he lunged toward it in a threatening manner, and everyone thought he was going to slash the painting. The security guards tackled him, then the cops took him away. When they got him down to the precinct, they realized they were out of their depth."

"Have you spoken with him?"

"Briefly. He may not be medicated, but he doesn't make a hell of a lot of sense." Jensen grinned. "I had a gut feeling that this might be your type of case."

"Okay. Let me review the file, and I'll go in and talk to him."

When she entered the room there was a single guard standing to Gordon's right, but he hardly seemed necessary: the patient was extremely docile. His expression was dreamlike, and he appeared to be in a trance. She sat down across from him and smiled.

"Good evening. I'm Dr. Cheryl Weissberg. How are you doing tonight?"

His reverie broken, Gordon followed her voice and stared at her. His expression reminded Weissberg of a camera lens coming into focus. He looked at her with a benign expression.

"It's a pleasure to meet you. Obviously, I'm hoping you can help me."

"How so?"

"I have no idea what I'm doing here. I suspect there's been a terrible mistake."

"I see. Why do you think you're here?"

"To be perfectly frank, doctor, I don't have a clue. Perhaps the long arm of the Protestant clergy is at work, trying to suppress me."

"I beg your pardon?"

"Roman Catholics have been persecuted since the very beginning of the modern era. It's nothing new, and those of us in the Society of Jesus have sadly grown accustomed to it. But much as I hate to say it, this borders on garden variety harassment."

"Well, let's start from the beginning. Can you give me your name?"

"Father Gordon Humphries."

"And your occupation?"

"I work in a supervisory capacity for the Jesuit diocese. My duties are many and varied. Primarily I travel around the Eastern United States, and file compliance reports on our major educational and spiritual facilities."

"I see. Can you tell me what you were doing at the Museum of Modern Art tonight?"

"My dear, I wasn't at the museum tonight, although I certainly consider it to be a delightful place—a home away from home, if you will. I dined with a friend earlier this evening, and I suspect I must have passed out. I have a heart condition, you see, which has been getting slightly worse as I've grown older. Thankfully you're too young to know about any of this, but I sadly have to tell you that it's inevitable. The human body is one of the finest pieces of machinery on earth, but it cannot stand the ravages of time."

"Then you have no recollection of being at the museum tonight?"

"None at all. I've been asked this a few times, and I know that everyone is just doing their job. But still, there's no reason why someone in my position should be subjected to this type of persecution."

"I have to tell you, Father, that someone matching your description was arrested earlier this evening at the museum. This person took a box cutter out of his pocket and approached one of the Rauschenbergs. The security guards restrained him and called the police. They were convinced that his intention was to slash the painting."

"Goodness, that certainly wasn't me." His skin was pale and dry, like an old piece of parchment that might crack in sudden movement. "I'm a great devotee of the arts—you might even call me a patron of the arts. My parents were prominent collectors, with a large collection of significant canvasses. While I'm definitely not a fan of Robert Rauschenberg, I would never harm a work of art. As God is my witness, I pledge that to you. For this reason and many others, I'm certain that a terrible mistake has been made."

"You could be right. I'm just trying to get to the bottom of all this."

"Of course. You're also just doing your job. I understand that."

"Very good. Would you excuse me for a moment?"

"Certainly."

She closed the door and sat down next to Jensen, who had been watching the interview through the one-way mirror.

"Well?"

"Well what?" Jensen looked at his watch. "I guess he's not a fan of modern art. Neither am I, to tell you the truth."

"Any reactions to what you just heard?"

"He sounds schizophrenic to me."

"Every patient sounds schizophrenic to you. But before we medicate this man into oblivion, I'd appreciate the chance to find out what's really going on with him."

"I admire your dedication, especially considering that your time is short." He looked at his watch again. "I thought you were becoming more compliant with the system, but I realize you just can't leave here without saving someone. It's your nature."

Just like it's your nature to throw them on the trash heap. She almost said it.

"How about this? Once—just once—instead of filling someone full of drugs, then releasing them back out onto the street and hoping they don't kill an innocent passerby, maybe we try to help them. Like we even ask this guy some questions and see what his problem is."

"I'll tell you what I'm going to do. I'll book Mr. Gordon, or whatever he calls himself, into a 72-hour stay with us. During that time, feel free to converse with him to your heart's content. At the end of the three days he'll be released, and your time with us will also be up."

"That sounds fair. I'll go back in and tell him."

"Very good. I'll make the arrangements, and then I'm heading for the barn. I'll see you tomorrow."

Weissberg walked back into the room, where the patient was glaring at her. He seemed agitated and slightly hostile.

"Who are you?" he asked.

"I beg your pardon?"

"Maybe you didn't hear me. Who the hell are you?"

"I'm Dr. Cheryl Weissberg. You have no recollection of speaking to me before?"

"You look familiar." He stared at her. "I think we've met

before, but I can't remember where. The real question is, what am I doing here?"

"Well, let's take it from the top." She settled in across from him and consulted the file. "What's your name?"

"Lester Gordon."

"And why do you think you're here, Mr. Gordon?"

"I don't know. The last thing I remember was lying on the marble floor at the MOMA."

"Apparently you were arrested because the guards thought you were going to deface one of the paintings. Do you remember brandishing a box cutter and approaching one of the Rauschenbergs?"

"Vaguely, yes. But I wouldn't have harmed the painting—I would never cause any damage to a work of art. I was simply trying to register a protest. This sort of thing can't continue."

"What sort of thing?"

"Pandering to the thoughtless creators of so-called modern art, while the great Impressionist masters go neglected."

"Ah, I see. For what it's worth, I happen to agree with you."

"Really?"

"I'm a fan of Impressionism myself. So here's what we're going to do, Mr. Gordon. We're going to keep you here for a few days, until I can get this whole episode sorted out with the police. Obviously it's been a misunderstanding."

"I don't want to be forced to take medication."

"You won't have to, if I have anything to do with it. But keeping you here will allow me to straighten out the authorities on your behalf. You can get some rest, and the two of us will have a chance to talk. Does that sound agreeable to you?"

"If it goes the way you say, fair enough."

"Very well. We'll make sure that you're comfortable, and I'll see you in the morning. Look for me around ten."

CHAPTER 3

Phillip Cantwell shifted in his chair, scratched his forehead and patted the wave of his silver-flecked hair. He played with his cufflinks and fondled the sleeve of his dark blue suit. It was a Zegna, one of his auction suits bought several years before as part of his continuing effort to look the part of a well-heeled Upper East Side gallery owner. Sitting at the back of the room, he scanned the crowd relentlessly, looking for the familiar signs of relaxed affluence that might foreshadow a bidding war.

"This is it," he said to his director George Portius. "Hold your breath."

"And now for Lot #29, our final lot of the day." The auctioneer lowered his voice and leaned in toward the microphone, trying to create an aura of drama. "This is the one that everyone has been waiting for:

"*The Dance Hall at Noon,* by the acclaimed post-Impressionist painter Georges Seurat. Once described as 'the most beautiful painter's drawings in existence,' this particular series was created toward the end of Seurat's life as part of a depiction of the Parisian entertainment scene. His stark and dramatic rendering of the dance hall environment gives us a precise sense of what life was like in the French capital at the end of the 19th century.

"This remarkable work consists of Conté crayon and white gouache on paper. The lighting is subdued, bridging the gap between the darkness of the evening and the squalid greyness of the morning after. We see a janitor on a deserted stage, mopping the floor with a sense of resignation; he is surrounded by the scenery that forms the backdrop for the show, threadbare and desolate in the dim light of day.

"This stellar piece came to the Cantwell gallery as part of a recent estate sale. It is a classic example of the Seurat style, and we are honored to present it to you today. We will start the bidding at one million dollars.

"I am looking for an opening bid of one million dollars. Do I have one million dollars." The auctioneer surveyed the room. "One million dollars in the rear," he said, pointing the gavel toward the back of the hall.

A dozen pairs of eyes looked back to see the bidder, but he had already lowered his paddle. In fact, no one had raised their hand at all. It was an example of "chandelier bidding," a ploy used to quickly surpass the reserve and create a sense of momentum.

"Do I hear one million two? I'm looking for one million two." He pointed to the left side, where a prim dowager held up her paddle. "One million two from the young lady on my left."

A bell rang from the bank of agents sitting at laptops behind him, and he turned to face the sound.

"One million four from an anonymous bidder in Singapore," said the auctioneer. "Do I have one million six?"

The elderly woman raised her paddle again.

"One million six, and we're just getting started." He beamed. "I'm looking for one million eight. One million eight." As his eyes scanned the room, the bell sounded again. "One million eight from the gentleman in Singapore. "Can we ask for two million?"

There was a pause of ten to fifteen seconds as the auctioneer looked back and forth around the hall. For Phillip Cantwell, the interval was agonizing: this was the moment when either the bidding would explode or fizzle out completely. Portius heard his boss's stomach rumble and put his hand on Cantwell's shoulder.

"It's against you, ma'am," he said to the dowager. "A once in a lifetime chance to own a seminal drawing from one of the most prominent post-Impressionists." The woman raised her paddle without expression.

"Two million—thank you!" exclaimed the auctioneer. "Do we have two million two?"

In the second row, a skinny man with bleached blond hair raised his paddle and smiled.

"There we go—two million two down in front. Remember that this is still a bargain. Drawings from this series have fetched as much as three and a half million within the past few years."

The bell sounded again, and the auctioneer turned to the computer bank.

"Two million four from the gentleman in Singapore. He will not be denied. What about you, folks? Do you want to see this extraordinary piece leave the country, or do you want the bragging rights for yourself?" He looked at the elderly woman, who shook her head. The man in the second row raised his paddle again.

"Two million six! Are we heading for a record? Could this be the moment when we make history here in Manhattan? We're looking for two million eight."

There was another fifteen-second pause.

"Two million eight," he chanted. "Can I have two million eight?" The bell sounded once again, and he pounded the podium with excitement. "There we go—two million eight. We're closing in on it now. It's against you, sir." He pointed to the man in the second row. "I'm looking for three million. Can I have three million? It's only money, after all."

An appreciative chuckle swept across the room, but the skinny man did not budge.

"Three million. I'm looking for three million."

The interval stretched to thirty seconds.

"We have two million eight from Singapore. I'm looking for three million. Do I hear three million?" He paused. "Fair warning, folks. The bidding stands at two million eight. Do I have three million?"

The auctioneer banged the gavel on the podium.

"Sold to the gentleman from Singapore for two million eight hundred thousand dollars. We thank you for being here today, and we appreciate the patronage that makes Cantwell Gallery the premier boutique auction venue in the city."

"God, that was close." Phillip Cantwell slumped in his chair. "I was afraid we weren't going to make it."

"It was a no-brainer," said Portius. "It's not like opportunities like this come along every day."

"Still." He shook his head. "Tell me you weren't worried during those pauses."

"Everything worked out. And I believe we made some money. How much were the incentives?"

"No buyer's premium, as usual. And we're rebating fifteen per cent in lieu of a seller's premium. On top of that, we gave him his discount. But we're into it for one million four, so we should be okay even after giving away the store."

"Sounds fine to me."

"I don't care if we make a dime," said Cantwell. "The publicity from this should serve as a magnet for other major consignments. That's the game here."

The anonymous electronic bidder had been Charles Wong, owner of the largest chemical manufacturing company in Asia and one of the region's biggest collectors. Cantwell had met him five years earlier, during a sweep through the peninsula trolling for customers. The men shook hands at the end of a Cognac-drenched dinner. This time, there was no seller's premium since the piece had come from an estate sale. Rebating the 15% to the businessman was not totally legal and the usual $100K discount was blatant bribery, but it was the price of luring the high-bidding collector away from Sotheby's. Wong's participation in the Cantwell sales had helped propel them into the top of the second tier of New York auction houses.

"Drawings are fine," said Portius, "but we need a major Impressionist canvas. We can assume that Monet, Renoir and Degas will go to Sotheby's and Christies, but we could use one of the Pointillists. Pissarro, Signac, or a major work from Seurat."

"God," said Cantwell dreamily. "A Seurat canvas. I would kill for a Seurat."

CHAPTER 4

When Cheryl Weissberg walked into the examining room the next morning she saw Lester Gordon chained to the table, flanked by two guards.

"What's going on here?"

"He got a little rambunctious during the night, ma'am," said the guard on the left. "We had to restrain him."

"Take them off, please."

"We don't recommend that. No offense, ma'am, but you don't look like you weigh more than a hundred pounds."

"One hundred four. But you look like you can handle yourself, so please do it anyway." She looked at Gordon, who seemed as docile as a sleepy puppy. "How are you today, Mr. Gordon?"

"Who are you?"

"Dr. Cheryl Weissberg. We spoke last night. Do you remember?"

"Maybe."

As the guards removed the handcuffs and legs restraints, Gordon seemed to implode into himself. He folded his legs underneath him, his arms crossed against his chest, and he curled up into a ball toward the back of the chair.

"So." Weissberg's heart was racing with anticipation. "How are you today?"

"Dunno."

"What's your name?"

"Les."

"Are you Lester Gordon? We were speaking last night."

"I'm Baby Les." His voice was high-pitched and breathless. "That's what Mommy and Daddy call me."

"I see. So Baby Les, did you sleep well last night?"

"No! I don't know where I am."

"Did Mommy and Daddy leave you here?"

"I don't know. I don't remember." Tears welled up in his eyes and fell down on his hospital gown. "They're never here."

"What do you mean?"

"They go out all the time. They leave me with the babysitter."

"Do you like the babysitter?"

"She's okay sometimes. But she doesn't care about me."

"Why do you say that?"

"She doesn't read to me. She makes me go to bed early. And then she has her friends."

"What kind of friends?"

"Men like Daddy. Sometimes Daddy."

"I see. How old are you, Lester?"

"I'll be seven in August."

"So you're not really a baby, are you? You're probably in the first grade."

"I just finished kindergarten."

"Did you like that? What was your favorite part?"

"It was okay I guess. I liked the finger painting."

"Why do you think they call you Baby Les, if you're not really a baby?"

"I don't know." Gordon started to sob. "I don't know what I'm doing here. Where are Mommy and Daddy?"

"I'll tell you what I'll do. I'll go try and find them for you, if you act like a big boy." She glanced at the security guards, who were rolling their eyes. "Can you do that for me?"

"I guess."

"You do your best, and I'll try to find them for you. I'll even try to find you a lollipop. How does that sound?"

"It sounds okay."

"Good. I'll be right back."

Weissberg retreated into the next room and scribbled furiously into the case file. It was coming at her faster than she could sort it out, so she simply tried to record her stream of consciousness impressions. There had been three distinct personalities so far: Father Humphries, Lester Gordon and Baby Les. *Could it be? Is this my first real case of DID?* She flashed back to all the cautions Dr. Brillstein had drilled into them in graduate school. The patient may try on these personalities to get the therapist's approval, because it has worked in the past. Once the personalities emerge and the patient gets encouraging feedback for them, the tendency will exaggerate. Look for the underlying childhood trauma, the evidence of abuse and neglect.

She was still writing a few minutes later when Dr. Jensen walked into the room.

"Top of the morning." He glanced at Weissberg, but she did not look up. "You seem quite absorbed by Mr. Gordon. Care to share your thoughts with me?"

"You don't want to know what I think. Or what I suspect."

"You're probably right about that, if it's related to that New Age crap that Brillstein drilled onto you in graduate school."

"This is a complicated case. I'm not sure what's going on yet, but I can tell you it's not simple."

"Whatever. Regardless of what's going on, you that you have two and a half days to figure it out."

"I hope that's enough time."

"It has to be. Your clock is ticking."

"Do me a favor?"

"Name it."

"Find me a lollipop."

CHAPTER 5

Weissberg wandered down Spring Street, stopping to investigate the boutiques and restaurants that occupied the ground floor of the street's three-story brownstones. In a single block she saw a retro barbershop, an eatery with a fern-filled outdoor garden run by a husband- and-wife team, a shop dedicated to selling handicrafts made within the borough, and a yarn store where local knitters gathered to "stitch and bitch."

She loved Boerum Hill and regretted that she hadn't moved to the area before real estate prices in Brooklyn escalated. The explosion had occurred relatively late: for many years the neighborhood served as a bedroom community for the ironworkers who built the city's skyscrapers, and the stately brownstones were run as boarding houses. The district hadn't been added to the National Register of Historic Places until the 1980s, but by now it was out of her financial reach. She contented herself by setting up her office on nearby Atlantic Avenue, on the edge of Boerum Hill, and spending her free time shopping and daydreaming. The area was filled with artists, and brought back memories of weekends in Cheryl's childhood, when her parents had taken her on outings to the city's museums.

Passing an art store, she decided to go in and see if she could pick up some reproductions for her office. The launch date for her practice was only several weeks away, but the walls of her consulting room and small reception area were still bare.

"Morning, ma'am." The clerk looked up from his paperwork. "Can I help you find something?"

"I'll just look around, thanks." She smiled. "Although I hope I'm really not old enough to be called ma'am."

"Not at all." The clerk grinned. "Figure of speech. I was just being polite."

She realized the store was basically an art supply shop, but she spotted a selection of posters in one corner. She flipped through them quickly. They were almost entirely examples of the different phases of modern art, with Cubism the oldest period represented. She wasn't opposed to them on aesthetic grounds but felt they would be too jarring for her purposes.

The clerk walked over to her.

"So, young lady. See anything you like?"

"To be honest, I was looking for something a little bit more soothing."

"Ah. What kind of art do you prefer?"

"I've always had a soft spot for the Impressionists. My parents used to take to see their canvases when I was little. I'd like an original, of course, but I don't have a few extra million laying around."

"I'm afraid a few million wouldn't do it anymore. But I can always order something for you. I have a catalog, if you'd like to look at it. I gather this is for your residence?"

"Actually, I'm opening an office nearby. I'd like to create a calming effect, but I also have to look at the art all day long, so it has to be something I like."

"What kind of business is it?"

"I'm a shrink."

"Really? Psychiatrist or psychologist?"

"Licensed psychologist. I'm just opening my own practice."

"You should do very well around here. I don't think there's a well-adjusted person in the entire neighborhood."

"Excellent. Maybe you can send some cases my way."

"I have another thought. We might be able to get one of the local artists to do a copy for you. It might not cost much and would be a lot nicer to look at than a poster."

"That sounds like a great idea. Could you suggest someone?"

"That's where it gets tricky. To be honest, Impressionism isn't the favorite style around here." He hesitated. "There's one guy that might do it. He seems to be into that whole period."

"What's his name?"

"Bétancourt. I believe the first name is Louis."

"Well, he's French, anyway."

"He's got a story about being descended from Camille Corot, the painter. I have no idea if it's true, but he goes around wearing a beret and a phony 19th-century outfit. He tells me the story every time he's here. Corot wasn't an Impressionist, of course, but he was one of the godfathers of that whole movement."

"Sounds like my kind of guy. Can you put me in touch with him?"

"I don't have his contact information, but he comes in from time to time—usually complaining about some antique paint or canvas that we can't find for him. I think he has a studio around here. The next time he comes in, I'll tell him about you and find out how much he would charge."

"Do you have any idea what the cost might be?"

"No, but I know a lot of these guys are just trying to scratch out a living. I doubt that most of them are in a position to turn down work."

"Excellent." She took a scrap of paper from her purse and scribbled on it. "Here's how to reach me. I'm afraid I don't have business cards made up just yet."

"I'll let you know if I hear anything."

"Thank you so much. You've been really helpful."

"No worries." The clerk grinned again. "If you want to kickstart your practice, just hang around this place. You'll meet enough whack jobs to keep you going for years."

*

"So how are things going?" asked Dr. Karen Brillstein, settling in behind her desk. "You must be nearly finished with the residency by now."

"I'm holding up," said Cheryl Weissberg. "I have just a few days to go, but it seems like an eternity. It hasn't been a pleasant experience."

Brillstein smiled. "Bellevue seldom is."

"At some point you stop and ask yourself, what was the

point of all that training? You'd never be able to help any of those people in a million years."

"Well, you know the theory: you have to see the extremes of dysfunction before you develop a sense of how to treat the mild cases, the ones that can be salvaged. And remember, those are the majority. I'm sure it doesn't seem that way at the moment, given what you've been exposed to."

"It definitely proves something you told us more than once—that sanity is relative."

Brillstein had been a supportive and nurturing figure to Weissberg throughout graduate school. She was well-known in the psychology field, both at Columbia and nationally: the leading researcher into Dissociative Identity Disorder, or what lay people would call multiple personality. Despite the fact that the disorder had been officially recognized in the DSM-IV, or the fourth edition of the Diagnostic and Statistical Manual of Mental Disorders, many mental health practitioners felt it was a fairy tale. The skeptics believed that when the secondary personalities (or "alters") surfaced, the patient was rewarded by a show of attention from the therapist, and this led to the emergence of more alters. And since DID was largely based on childhood trauma, therapists who diagnosed the disorder were frequently accused of planting those memories in patients during hypnosis.

"And how's my good friend Dr. Jensen?"

"He's a piece of work. At his best, he's insensitive to patient suffering. At his worst, he's a painful example of how twisted you can get if you spend a career in that system."

"Sounds like nothing's changed."

"And he thinks you're a complete quack."

"I've heard that before." She was affable, even cheerful. "From a lot of people, in fact, most of them far more influential than Jensen."

"I'm sure."

"The truth is he's not a bad clinician. He's just been overwhelmed by the system, as you point out."

"To be honest, sometimes I can't blame him. You look at these people and the shape they're in, and it's just awful. If you let it get to you, you probably couldn't function."

"True." She removed her glasses and wiped them with a tissue. "I assume you haven't run into any cases of DID at Bellevue?"

"Most of the patients I see don't even know their own names. They're medicated into another planetary system."

"I'm not sure what I'd do in that situation, to be honest. If they're not highly medicated, they'd likely pose a threat to everyone's safety."

"But I did see a case the other day that seemed to show most of the signs."

"Hmm." Brillstein leaned back and removed her glasses. "Let's hear it."

Until she met Lester Gordon, the closest she had come to the disorder was reading Brillstein's book, *Multiple Personality and the Search for Self*. She appreciated her mentor's sense of humor, which had helped to brighten the graduate school experience for her. Brillstein often described DID skeptics as "people who threw up on their popcorn while watching *Sybil*." The reference was to a 1976 movie starring Joanne Woodward and Sally Field, which described the plight of a DID patient who harbored 15 distinct personalities. Unfortunately, the movie comprised most of what the public knew about DID.

"It certainly sounds like a possibility," said Brillstein when her student was finished. "I think it's too early to tell, but I'd like you to keep me posted on this one."

"I will. Promise."

"We'll see how it unfolds, but I don't want you to get in over your head."

"Thanks. I appreciate it."

"Now let's focus on happier things. What's your plan following the residency? Are you still going into practice?"

"Absolutely. I've signed a lease on a small space in South Brooklyn, near Boerum Hill. I wanted to be in Boerum Hill but couldn't afford it—the rents have skyrocketed in the past few years."

"Yes, it's trendy now. All those artists. They call it the poor man's SoHo."

"But I'll be near the subway line, so it should work out. For the first few years, if I have to, I'll pick up some shifts at Bellevue to make ends meet."

"Well, you're starting small, which is a good thing. And you've obviously given the plan a lot of thought. Good for you."

"It's scary, but I think I can make it work."

"Hopefully I'll be able to send some referrals your way." She smiled. "Just remember, if you hit any rough spots or run into a situation you can't handle, pick up the phone."

CHAPTER 6

The man walked into the art shop in the Boerum Hill neighborhood of Brooklyn. He appeared to be in his mid-fifties, thin and pale, with blanched white skin. He was dressed in the manner of a Parisian bohemian of the late 19th century: his vest was embroidered to resemble a frocked waistcoat, his head was crowned with a beret, and he wore a thin, penciled moustache that curled up at the corners. He strode toward the counter.

"Afternoon, sir. How can I help you?"

"I am Louis Bétancourt. Perhaps we have met before."

"Yes, we certainly have. What can I do for you?"

"This establishment was actively involved in sourcing some brushes for me. Kolinsky sable hair brushes."

"Ah, yes." The clerk skimmed through a black loose-leaf notebook. "No luck so far, Mr. Bétancourt. And to be honest, it doesn't look encouraging."

"May I ask what is the problem?"

"We've explained it to you, sir. The U.S. Fish and Wildlife Service has halted shipments of those brushes into the country. Some are still getting through, of course, but we don't have access to them."

"This is very strange indeed. I have seen advertisements for such brushes on the Internet."

"I understand. And the brushes could be real, or they might not be. That's the problem with the Internet: you can't inspect the brush beforehand and make sure it's legitimate."

"I find this very hard to believe." The man stood up straight, affected a haughty manner, and stared at the clerk. "May I remind you that I am the great-great-grandson of Jean-Baptiste-Camille Corot, one of the most celebrated painters of the 19th century?"

"That may well be, sir." The clerk grinned. "But that doesn't get you a Kolinsky sable brush today."

"This is no laughing matter, young man. My great-great-grandfather was one of the seminal artists of 19th century France. He taught many of the Impressionists how to paint, including Camille Pissarro."

"I understand."

"And now you're telling me that I cannot even purchase artistic materials for my own career?"

"Mr. Bétancourt." The clerk tried to be patient. "I don't mean to offend you, sir, but I have to ask. If you can buy these brushes from Internet sources, why wouldn't you do that?"

"I would prefer to patronize my local merchants. I'm sure my great-great-grandfather did exactly that. There is a thriving arts community here in Boerum Hill, as you know, and I believe it should be nurtured."

"I appreciate that, sir. But I can't sell you those brushes if I can't source them."

"Very well. I will continue my quest as best I can. I can assure you that the rich Bétancourt tradition will not be stifled. I thank you for your time."

"I'll tell you what—as a consolation prize, I might have some work for you."

"*Vraiment?*" The artist straightened up, a look of excitement in his eyes. "You are referring to an artistic commission?"

"Possibly. There's a doctor setting up an office in the neighborhood, and she wants a picture for her consulting room. It wouldn't be a fortune, but it might lead to other work."

"I will not paint a portrait of a soup can, young man."

"That's not what she's interested in. She wants something soothing. She says she's a fan of the Impressionists."

"Well, well." Bétancourt stroked his moustache. "This is very intriguing indeed. I am greatly in your debt."

"No problem. Do you have a number where I can reach you?"

"I don't patronize the telephone system." He dismissed the entire communications grid with a wave of the hand. "But I shall be in touch. I will take the liberty of checking back with you every few days."

"Sounds good."

He turned and walked out of the store, striding down Smith Street toward his studio, passing clusters of restaurant and cafes filled with young people. He knew the type. When he first rented the living room of Lester Gordon's apartment and turned it into his *atelier*, he had attempted to insert himself into the local art community. It was pointless. Boerum Hill might be overrun with youths who called themselves artists, but they were frauds. He recalled one long afternoon spent at a sidewalk café similar to the ones that dotted the street. There had been a handful of Abstract painters, and two young men who assembled performance art. One of them used materials from a nearby junkyard; the other focused on toilet fixtures. When they asked him what type of work he did, he explained his background and detailed his quest to recreate the glorified era of Impressionism. One of the young men had sniggered. He never went back.

*

On the day before his scheduled release, the patient seemed clear-headed and alert. Cheryl Weissberg walked into the consulting room shortly after her shift began at 3 p.m., fingering the lollipop in her pocket.

"Please take off the restraints," she said to the guard.

"Once again, ma'am, we don't recommend it."

"Please do it anyway."

"Thank you," said the patient, rubbing his hands after the handcuffs were removed. "I appreciate it. Thank you for recognizing that I'm harmless."

She sat down across from him.

"How are you doing today?"

"Not too bad under the circumstances."

"What's your name?"

"Lester Gordon." He looked at Weissberg with suspicion. "Why would you ask me that? We went through this yesterday, and the day before that."

"Sorry, I'm terrible on names. Do you remember mine?"

"Weissberg, I think."

"Mr. Gordon, have you been hospitalized before?"

"A few times, yes."

"Can you tell me when, and for what reasons?"

"I could, but I'm not going to. It makes me uncomfortable. I'd rather keep the conversation on a higher level, if that's all right with you."

"Then let's talk about why you're here this time. According to the police report, you were brandishing a box cutter at the Museum of Modern Art. You approached one of the paintings, and the guards were afraid you were going to slash it. That's when you were wrestled to the ground."

"As I told you, I had no intention of harming the painting. I just wanted to make a statement. No one would listen to me."

"What was it you wanted to say that they wouldn't listen to?"

"I've been trying to alert the world the dangers of degenerate art for years—decades, actually. A place like the MOMA has a tremendous impact on the artistic community. They never should have put on a show like that. It goes way beyond being coarse entertainment for the masses. Art students go to those exhibitions. They see work like that being celebrated, and they think it's okay to paint that way. They think that they can become famous if they crank out garbage like that."

"Why does that type of art upset you so much?"

"Painters are supposed to depict the beauty of the universe, to hold a mirror up to the glories of nature. They are the ones who should pull reality together and present it to the public, rather than presenting the chaos and disorder of their own minds."

"In other words, they should paint like the Impressionists?"

"Exactly. Didn't you day you were a fan of Impressionism?"

"I don't know a great deal about art, but I do like that particular style. Why did you go to the exhibition if the Neo-Dada movement bothered you that much?"

"I needed to see it first-hand. I wanted to see who was there, and what kind of effect it was having on them. What I saw disgusted me."

"How so?"

"Almost everyone was oohing and aahing over that crap, as if it were real art. As if it was something worthy of their admiration."

"And you thought you would stop that by attacking the Rauschenberg?"

"I told you, I wasn't going to attack it. I was trying to make a statement."

"A little earlier, you said that painters should present the beauty of nature, rather than the chaos and disorder of their own minds. Is that what your mind is like? Chaotic and disorderly?"

"Sure. Like most peoples', I guess. To me, the beauty of nature is an escape from all that."

"Mr. Gordon, I assume you've been in therapy before."

"Yes."

"For how long?"

"On and off for a number of years. I'm not seeing anyone at the present time."

"Why is that?"

"My therapist abandoned me."

"Abandoned you?" She quickly replaced the surprise on her face with an empathetic expression. "You mean he or she terminated therapy?"

"He died, actually. He was killed in a boating accident."

"That's an awful thing. I can see how it must have felt like abandonment."

"It was stupid. He was white water rafting out West. People like that are supposed to be smarter than me."

"What was his name, may I ask?"

"Dr. Hannity. Peter Hannity. My father died shortly after that."

"Well, my condolences to you. That sounds terrible." She rose and straightened her skirt. "Would you excuse me for a moment?"

Gordon nodded, and she walked into the adjoin room where Jensen was waiting.

"Did you hear all of that?"

"Most of it." He yawned. "I still don't get why he wanted to attack the painting."

"He says he wasn't going to."

"Whatever. Either way, we're releasing this guy tomorrow. And coincidentally, we're releasing you as well. If I don't see you, congratulations."

"I'd like to continue treating this man."

"That's up to you."

"Can we make continued therapy a condition of his release? I'm not sure he would do it otherwise."

"Do you think that's ethical?"

"Why not? We're not releasing him with the usual supply of medication, but he clearly needs help."

"I've seen much worse," said Jensen. "So have you."

"I was always told that sanity is relative, and it is. But that doesn't mean that we should give up on people who need treatment."

"Well, what's your plan of treatment?"

"First I want to find out who has Dr. Hannity's records, so I can learn more about him. He's obviously disturbed, not to mention dissociative."

"Here we go. It sounds like a Brillstein diagnosis to me."

"Yesterday he said he was seven years old and called himself Baby Les. The day before that, he told me he was a Jesuit priest named Gordon Humphries. How does that sound to you?"

"You know, I played a lot of basketball when I was

younger—made the varsity in high school, although I didn't start. But I always had the fantasy of playing in the NBA. I was going to be the next Michael Jordan." He chuckled. "Then one day, I looked in the mirror and saw a 6'1" white guy. I realized I might be better off listening to my mother and becoming a doctor."

"Is there a point to this?"

"I suggest you give Mr. Gordon, or whoever he is, a mirror. That might be an effective course of treatment."

"I'd still like to give it a shot."

He shrugged and scribbled something on the clipboard. "We'll release him with the proviso that he continues therapy with you."

"Thank you."

"Don't mention it. And if I don't see you tomorrow, I do wish you the best."

Weissberg walked back into the room where Gordon sat.

"Sorry for the wait, Mr. Gordon. I needed to talk to one of my colleagues."

"I imagine you're trying to figure out what to do with me, since I'm going home tomorrow."

"Actually, we've figured it out. My opinion is that you need further therapy, so we've made that a condition of your release. You'll have to see me at least once a week in my office."

"Where is that?"

"I'm starting a practice in Brooklyn, on Atlantic Avenue. Right near Boerum Hill."

"Really? That's right near my apartment. I can probably walk."

"Excellent. Where exactly do you live?"

"Nearby, as I told you. All of my information should be in the record here."

"So does that sound agreeable to you? Coming to see me on a weekly basis?"

"I can't afford to pay you."

"I'm not asking you for payment. I just think that therapy would be beneficial for you." She handed him a sheet of paper and a pen. "Would you sign this form for me?"

"What is it?"

"It's an authorization for me to get your records and session notes from your time with Dr. Hannity. I'm not sure who has them."

"I guess so." He scribbled his name on the form. "I gather I don't go home otherwise."

"What's your schedule like next week?"

"It's wide open, as far as I know."

"Good. Why don't you come in Wednesday at three?" She handed him a business card. "I think I can help you."

"That's what they all say."

CHAPTER 7

Cheryl Weissberg was sitting in the break room at Bellevue when her phone vibrated.

"Hello?"

"Dr. Weissberg?"

"Yes?"

"This is Benny from the art store. You and I spoke last week."

"Of course. How are you?"

"Doing great, thanks. I hope I'm not disturbing you."

"No, go ahead. I was just taking a break."

"I had a visit yesterday from Louis Bétancourt, the painter I mentioned to you. I told him about our conversation. It turns out he's been working on a watercolor that sounds like it fits your description perfectly. It depicts a fishing port at dawn, with the harbor filled with boats. I believe he said the city was Dieppe, on the Normandy coast."

"It sounds lovely."

"He said he's almost finished with it. If you're interested, he'd be happy to reserve it for you."

"Did he mention the price to you?"

"He said he'd be willing to let it go for a thousand dollars."

"Wow. I'm afraid that's a lot more than I had in mind."

"How much did you want to spend, if you don't mind me asking?"

"I was thinking more in the range of $400. But I wouldn't want to insult him."

"I could mention that the next time he comes in and see what happens. I'm not sure if it was a firm price or a starting point. I also haven't seen it personally, so I can't say if I think it might be worth it."

"I have no idea what the going rate would be for a painting like that. Could you give me a rough idea?"

"For an unknown artist, probably closer to your figure than to his. But obviously I don't know how much time he's spent on it, or how he values that time. You also need to take into account that Bétancourt isn't likely to become famous anytime soon, so the painting probably won't increase in value."

"Well, I hate to put you out, but would you mind doing a little negotiating for me? If we could get the price down to $500, I'd probably be interested."

"I'll see what I can do the next time he comes in. I have a feeling he'll be back soon, since he thinks he might have a sale."

"Thank you so much. I appreciate it."

"Happy to help. I'll let you know."

*

Obtaining Lester Gordon's patient records turned out to be much easier than Cheryl Weissberg could have imagined. Dr. Peter Hannity had the foresight to execute a professional will that identified a close personal friend, Dr. Kenneth Goren, as the custodian of his files. Weissberg was able to get Dr. Goren on the phone within forty-eight hours of Gordon's release from Bellevue, and he agreed to overnight the records and session notes to her.

They arrived several days in advance of Gordon's first appointment, and they were revealing. Lester Gordon had experienced mental problems for most of his life. His first hospitalization had occurred at 15, following an episode of severe depression. He was institutionalized twice in his late twenties, and once again in his early forties. Throughout his life he had received numerous and varying diagnoses including schizophrenia, bipolar disorder and multiple personality disorder. There were five or six different diagnoses in all, which fit the pattern for DID.

From the session notes, Weissberg was able to glean the following information:

Gordon had grown up as an Army brat, moving from one locale to another every two or three years. This pattern was disruptive in forming close friendships or even patterns of identification with his surroundings. He was always the new kid in the school and was frequently bullied because of his slight physical stature and strange appearance. From adolescence onward, his tendency was to withdraw into himself.

His childhood was traumatic. His parents were neglectful to the point where Gordon never felt he had received a clear and unequivocal feeling of love from them. His father was a serial philanderer. His mother was distant and unemotional, more concerned with her bridge game and social life than relating to her only child. He craved the love of his parents but had never received it.

"Patient is devoid of personal connection in his life," noted Hannity. "He is totally lacking in friendships and only maintains surface contacts with employers, neighbors, and others. There is no evidence he has ever had an intimate relationship with a woman, nor does he appear to want one. He refuses to engage the topic in therapy. There is little doubt that this lack of intimacy with others is directly related to the lack of love and validation he experienced from his parents during childhood.

"The childhood trauma of the patient appears to go beyond parental neglect," he wrote at another point. "Evidence suggests that on one or more occasions he may have accidently witnessed his father having sexual relations with women other than his mother, although he resists exploring the issue. If true, this discovery would likely have been interpreted by the child as a violent encounter and would be the probable cause of his inability to share an intimate relationship with women."

Gordon was precocious from the second or third grade onward, and he demonstrated an obvious talent for drawing. This gift was not nurtured by his parents or encouraged by his teachers. He began copying famous paintings even before puberty, and as an adolescent he ingratiated himself with his classmates by forging fake report cards that were indistinguishable from the real thing. By his own admission he spent most of his later childhood and early adolescence immersed in art books at the various locations where his father was stationed. He developed an obsession with the Impressionist painters of the late 19th century, and he revealed in therapy that he frequently fantasized about growing up in a world where everything was as beautiful and harmonious as it was depicted in their paintings. Hannity felt that his dissociative personality first emerged at this stage.

"Patient yearns for the world of the Impressionists," Hannity observed in one of his session notes, "a universe that is calm, ordered and peaceful, where everything can be rendered and resolved by the artist."

In his late teens Gordon's father was transferred to the New York area, where Lester completed high school. After graduation he enrolled in the Art Students League of New York, where his real problems began. Lester resisted any suggestion to consider painting in a more modern approach. In fact, he was repulsed by the appearance of most modern art: its very formlessness caused him to revisit the disharmony and trauma of his childhood, and he found this to be intolerable. The more his professors tried to nudge him in the direction of modern art, and the more his fellow students made fun of him, the more it hardened his resolve to paint like the Impressionist masters.

It was during this period that his father rented the apartment in Boerum Hill, relying on his army connections to snag a rent-controlled lease. The family was living in Queens at the time. His father used the apartment as a crash pad for liaisons with mistresses and hookers.

Lester Gordon was on a collision course with his own psyche. After 18 months he dropped out of the Art Students League in disgrace and began a downward spiral that ended with his second hospitalization. His father was still in the military, so Lester landed in a reputable facility where the staff was committed to helping him make an adjustment to reality.

They failed miserably. By his early twenties Lester was out on the street, estranged from his parents, making a living by selling watercolors on the Brooklyn pier. He did very well at this, since his faux-Impressionist scenes of Paris and the surrounding countryside reverberated with New Yorkers who had traveled in Europe. Some of them were so good that the buyers displayed them as legitimate period works.

He continued making a living this way until his late twenties, when an urban renewal project obliterated his platform for selling paintings. Lester deteriorated, and eventually became homeless. He had occasional contact with his parents, but his father was inclined to be firm with him and not coddle his only son. He was picked up on the street by the NYPD and transported to Elmhurst.

Toward the end of his hospitalization, he was treated by Dr. Peter Hannity, who continued therapy with Lester after his release. He made progress, reconciled with his parents, and lived near them in Queens. He was employed in an art gallery where he helped restore old paintings and get them ready for sale. In his spare moments he painted familiar Impressionist themes, but he encountered little success in selling his work.

His life remained stable until Dr. Hannity's death. Six months later his father died of cancer. The family sublet the Boerum Hill apartment, and Lester moved in with his mother.

"Patient displays varying degrees of dissociation and dislocation from reality," Hannity wrote. "Episodes range from mild to severe and are not totally dependent on outside stress factors. At his best moments, he disavows his failure to succeed in the art world because of his obsessive attachment to Impressionism. On the other extreme, he comes close to constructing an alternative personality as an Impressionist painter, which is ideally how he would like to see himself. It seems apparent that despite his considerable raw talent, he cannot maintain a persona that allows for the gratification of his self-expression."

The missing link, of course, was the seven years that had elapsed between Dr. Hannity's death and the present. Weissberg suspected that the dual shock of losing his therapist and his father in the same year had catapulted Gordon into a fantasy world, causing him to unconsciously construct different identities as a survival mechanism. Almost certainly one of those identities was the actual forger, who had yet to surface in her conversations with the patient. Weissberg suspected that Gordon's projection of the forger's identity was far more than an attempt by the patient to cope with reality. The forger represented the flowering of Gordon's enormous natural talent, the vehicle to prove once and for all that he was right and the world was wrong.

CHAPTER 8

Cheryl Weissberg was startled by a knock on the door.
Finally liberated from Bellevue, she was spending her
spare time trying to make her new office look as professional
and comforting as possible. The walls were still bare, but she
had shopped around for accessories that would make the
consulting room seem warmer. She was painting the reception
area when she heard the knock.

She went to the peephole and saw a thin, pale man wearing
a beret and an embroidered vest. He was staring at a piece of
paper and glancing around the hallway.

"Who is it, please?"

"My name is Louis Bétancourt. I'm sorry to disturb you,
but the art store told me you might be interested in one of my
paintings."

She opened the door and extended her hand, using her
training to conceal her amusement. In a previous century, the
man would best be described as foppish: the beret was tilted
rakishly on his head, and a luxurious red silk cravat adorned
his skinny neck. His upper lip was adorned with a thin, curling
moustache. He looked like a small child who had raided his
mother's dress-up box.

"Please come in, Mr. Bétancourt."

"Thank you. I hope I'm not disturbing you."

"Not at all. I'm opening the office later this month, and just trying to get everything in order. How did you find me?"

"I took the liberty of doing some research. Benny from the art store mentioned that you were a doctor, and that you were new to the area."

"Yes, I'm a psychologist."

"Aha. A follower of the bearded Viennese demigod."

Weissberg allowed herself a smile. "You could put it that way."

He looked at the walls of the reception room. "I see you're doing some painting. Perhaps I could help."

"Oh, I think this type of job is probably beneath you. Benny told me about your background."

"Yes. I am the great-great-grandson of Jean-Baptiste-Camille Corot, the famous 19th century painter. Perhaps you have heard of him?"

"I've heard of him, but I'm not familiar with his work."

"He specialized in landscapes and portraits, but also did printmaking and etching. He had a long life and was very prolific. I suppose you could describe him as a Neo-Classicist, but much of his work anticipated the Impressionist movement, which is my specialty. In fact, some of the most famous Impressionist painters studied under him."

"Well, I'll definitely have to look him up."

"You're doing a very nice job here. Ecru is an appropriate

color for your *métier*—very calm and peaceful." He cleared his throat. "In any case, I know you're busy, so I'll come to the point. Benny conveyed your offer for the painting. While I am a firm believer in supporting my neighbors, I really couldn't let it go for that price."

"I understand, and I don't want to offend you. I'm sure you put a lot of time and effort into it. But I'm just starting out, and I need to watch my pennies."

In fact, Weissberg was well capitalized for her new venture. She had saved enough money to carry her expenses for six months without attracting any clients, and she could easily maintain the office for a year or more if she had a reasonable patient load. But Benny had made a solid point: Bétancourt was unknown, and the painting was unlikely to appreciate in value.

"Let me make you a proposition." He was obviously uncomfortable with bargaining over his work. "I believe your offer was four hundred, and my asking price was one thousand. Would it be possible to do eight hundred?"

"I'd love to, Mr. Bétancourt, I really would. I just don't want to overextend myself."

"Do you have some flexibility?"

"A little bit."

"Then let's do this. Can we compromise on a figure of six hundred dollars, contingent on your approval of the work? If you're not happy with it, you won't owe me a *sou*."

"Well, that sounds reasonable. I suppose I could stretch

to six hundred. It's going to be the main decoration in my consulting room, after all."

"Could I trouble you to show me the space?"

"Come this way." They walked into the inner office, and she pointed to the wall. "I'll be sitting in that chair, and my patients will be across from me. The picture would be mounted above me, so it's what they will see during a session."

"Wonderful. The painting will fit perfectly, and it should complement the color scheme of the room extremely well. And putting modesty aside for a moment, if I may say so, it's a work of no small artistic achievement. I'm know you'll be very pleased."

"I'm sure I will. I look forward to seeing it."

"Then I shall bring it around for your approval shortly, perhaps in a week or two."

"I'll give you my cell number, so you can let me know when you're coming."

"If you don't mind, I would prefer to simply come by. I dislike telephones—they are a modern intrusion into the mental space of human beings, a place that should be sacrosanct. Given your profession, I'm sure you can appreciate that sentiment. "

"More or less. I regard them as a necessary evil."

"I'm sure you would agree that there is enough evil in society, and probably not much need to seek out more of it. In any case, with your kind permission, I shall call on you when the canvas is completed."

"Please do. I'll be here full-time in a few weeks."

*

One week later, Weissberg was tired but on schedule. She had finally finished painting the interior of the office. The phone lines were installed, and all the furniture was in place. She looked around her with satisfaction as she pondered the cheapest and most effective way to advertise her new practice.

Her daydreaming was interrupted by a knock on the door. She looked through the peephole and saw Louis Bétancourt.

"Mr. Bétancourt, nice to see you again. Thanks for coming by."

"I was here yesterday, but I guess you were out." He held a large package wrapped in butcher paper. "I suppose I really should have phoned."

"Sorry about that—I've only been here on and off. Please come in."

"Thank you. I brought the canvas we discussed." She watched as he carefully placed the picture on the reception desk and unwrapped the paper. "I eagerly await your opinion."

Weissberg glanced at the painting and was transported into the early morning of another century. Fishing boats were anchored at the modest pier; small eddies in the brackish water of the port created the sense that the vessels were bobbing in their berths. Her eye was drawn to the horizon, where a sunburst of yellow and orange seemed to create a limitless vista of light. Beneath that brilliant and awakening sky, boats sailed off into the distance toward the sea.

"Well?" Bétancourt waited patiently, but his anxiety was obvious. "I hope you like it."

"I love it. It's absolutely beautiful."

"You're too kind."

"No, I mean it. I'm amazed—I don't think I've ever see anything like it. Does it have a title?"

"I've called it *Dawn at Dieppe*. It's a watercolor in the style of Paul Signac. Perhaps you're familiar with his work?"

"Not as much as I should be."

"He was an extremely influential painter of the 19th and 20th centuries. He began as an Impressionist and was a friend of Monet. Later on, he worked with Seurat to develop the Pointillist style."

"Well, it's magnificent. Thank you so much. And it will be perfect for the space in my office I told you about."

"I'm very gratified by your enthusiasm. Perhaps you could do me one small favor?"

"Tell me."

"If you could recommend my work to others who might be interested, that would be very helpful indeed."

"I certainly will, no question about it. Let me pay you, before I forget." She rummaged in her handbag and retrieved her checkbook. "On top of everything else, your timing is perfect. I'm hoping to open the office in a week or so. I'm really surprised that you could finish it so quickly."

"The canvas was almost done when we spoke. I just needed to put a few final touches on it." He glanced at the check. "I'm afraid you made a mistake. We agreed on six hundred, and this is for eight hundred."

"It's not a mistake. You originally asked for eight hundred. Now that I see the painting, I realize it's more than worth it."

Bétancourt removed his beret and gave his patron an elaborate bow.

"I thank you. And if you should again require some artwork for your residence or office, I am at your service."

CHAPTER 9

"Good afternoon, Mr. Gordon," said Cheryl Weissberg, trying her best to project a pleasant and cheerful demeanor. "Thank you for coming."

"I didn't have much of a choice, did I?"

"Even so, I appreciate the fact that you're here. Please come in."

"Sure."

Gordon followed her into the consulting room. Weissberg sat down in her chair and pointed to the sofa.

"Please, have a seat. Before we start, I need to ask you something." She took a digital voice recorder from her purse. "With your permission, I'd like to record our sessions. Is that all right with you?"

"I guess so. But why do you want to do that?"

"I have a feeling the material will be useful for us to review together at some point later on. What do you think?"

"I guess it's okay, but I wouldn't want anyone else to hear it."

"Of course not." She shook her head. "Everything we say in here is confidential. But I have a strong feeling that it will come in handy for us."

As he relaxed on the sofa, Gordon glanced up at the painting mounted above the therapist's head. His eyes became glossy, and he seemed to slip into a trancelike state.

"Mr. Gordon?"

He sat for nearly a full minute without responding. Weissberg decided to wait him out. When his eyes came back into focus, he looked at her and smiled.

"Goodness. What on earth am I doing here?"

"This was one of the conditions of your release, if you recall. You agreed to see me on a regular basis."

"Well, I'm deeply grateful to you for arranging my liberation from that place. And I assume this is psychotherapy, which of course is one of the tools that we use in our ministry. There are times when faith alone is not enough to solve problems, and we must call on science to intervene."

She hesitated. "Father Humphries?"

"Yes, and I believe I recall your name. It's Dr. Weissberg, is that correct?"

"Yes, it is."

"Well, I like your office. It's very cozy, and the color scheme is well thought out."

"Thank you."

"The paint looks somewhat fresh."

"I've just opened my own practice, so I had to do all the work myself."

"You've done an admirable job." He looked up at the painting. "And your choice of artwork is very interesting indeed."

"I'm very fond of it, thanks. But I'm wondering why you would find it interesting?"

"Are you familiar with the painting in question?"

"Not really."

"It's a copy of a watercolor by Paul Signac, the famous neo-Impressionist painter," said Humphries. "I'm sure you know his work."

"I've heard of him, but that's about it."

"He was one of the founders of the Pointillist style, along with Seurat. This particular canvas was titled *Dawn at Dieppe*. I believe it was a study for one of his larger seascapes. In any case, I know this work intimately because I own the original."

"Really? What an amazing coincidence."

"Indeed it is. So I can assure you that I've spent many happy hours looking at this canvas in the past."

"And where is the painting now?"

"I'm making some arrangements to give it away as a charitable bequest."

"That's extremely generous of you."

"Perhaps so. You see, my parents were formidable art collectors. My father was in the army and retired as a two-star general. He traveled widely as a result of his position, both professionally and for leisure. He had the opportunity to purchase a great deal of art back when prices were far lower than they are today. It was really a question of being in the right places at the right times."

"I see."

"Unfortunately I have a heart condition, and my health has been deteriorating in recent years. This state of affairs has forced me to consider what might become of my parents' art collection after I'm gone. I wanted to make sure the pieces were displayed in venues where they could be appreciated by the greatest number of people."

"I understand. That's very thoughtful."

"For the ultimate destination of *Dawn at Dieppe,* I'm looking for a small regional museum. My thinking is that the gift would have greater impact there than it would at a larger institution. If I donated it to the Museum of Modern Art here in the city, for example, it would rest in some warehouse away from view, only to be brought out every few years as part of a special exhibition. My only condition is that the painting be identified as having been donated in memory of my parents."

"That's a very touching memorial."

"It was the least I could do, really. I owe a great deal to my parents. My father was a bit taciturn, of course, as you might expect from his choice of profession. But I know he loved me, even though he might not always have been able to show it. My mother, on the other hand, doted on me throughout my childhood. It was very difficult to lose them." Tears welled up in his eyes. "Since you're a therapist, I can tell you that I'm still doing my best to deal with it."

"When did they die?"

"My father passed about six years ago. My mother hung on for three years after that."

"Well, I'm sure whatever museum you decide on will be thrilled by your decision."

"In any case, I don't understand why I've been compelled to come here. I have many contacts in the Church as well as the art community, and I'm sure they would have vouched for me."

"That's really not necessary. But as I said, coming here was a condition of your release. I'll need to see you once a week."

"At least you're an art lover. We have that in common."

"Actually, this painting was done by a local artist by the name of Louis Bétancourt. Have you heard of him?"

"Bétancourt?" He looked puzzled. "No, I don't think so. Is he art student?"

"He's way too old for that. I'd say he's probably in his mid-fifties." She stared at him. "In fact, he bears an uncanny resemblance to you. That's why I asked if you knew him. I thought the two of you might even be related."

"I'm afraid not." He laughed. "But of course, they say that we all have at least one twin we're not aware of. Looking at the painting, though, I can tell he's remarkably gifted. If you want to talk about resemblances, it's an extremely faithful rendition of the original."

"That's good to know. Father Humphries, it sounds like you have more paintings you want to donate? I gather that the Signac wasn't the only one?"

"There are two others, both by Seurat. They were the jewels of my parents' collection. One was a small study for one of his famous canvases, *Circus Sideshow*. Have you seen it?"

"I don't think so."

"The other is a painting titled *Madonna and Heir*, a major work created toward the end of Seurat's short life. There were some provenance issues with all of them, very minor things, and I need to resolve those first."

"What kinds of issues?"

He waved away the question with a sweep of his hand. "Oh, I think that's a discussion for another time."

"Very well." She handed him a card. "I'll see you next Wednesday at three."

"I've enjoyed conversing with you. Hopefully my schedule will permit me to keep the bulk of our appointments. I do travel a great deal, in my supervisory capacity for the Society of Jesus."

"It's very important that you show up regularly. If you have a conflict, please give me a call and let me know."

"I promise to do so." He raised his hand in a benevolent gesture. "*Pax vobiscum.*"

CHAPTER 10

"Mr. Gordon, nice to see you again," said Cheryl Weissberg one week later. "Thanks for coming."

"As I've said, I don't have much choice. I don't want to go back to Bellevue." He looked around the reception area. "I guess I was here last week, but I don't remember much about it."

"Probably not. You had what I would call a blackout."

"That makes sense, because I really don't remember anything that went on." He sat down on the sofa facing Weissberg. "Did I faint?"

"No, you were just hard to reach for a while."

"Your office looks very bare," he said as he looked around the room. "Didn't you have some art on the walls?"

"I did have a painting that hung here, over my head, but I took it down. I thought it was a bit dated."

"What type of painting was it?"

"It was a canvas in the Impressionist style, done by one of the artists in the neighborhood. My understanding was that it was a copy of a watercolor by Paul Signac, although I could be wrong about that. I do like the Impressionists, but I think I need something more modern in here. Maybe a reproduction from the Cubist period of Picasso or Braque."

"No!" He seemed genuinely agitated. "Don't do that."

"Why do you feel so strongly about it? I think something more modern would create a feeling of energy."

"Don't fall into that trap, please. You're obviously an intelligent woman—there's no need to be a slave to the fashions of the moment. I understand how it starts: you want to be in step with everyone else, you want to follow the trends. So you look at things like Cubism and Fauvism. And do you know where that leads?"

"Not really. Where?"

"It leads to the Abstract Expressionist crap turned out by people like Jackson Pollock. And that stuff is a crime against nature. I wouldn't dignify it by calling it art. Do you know how Pollock worked? Have you ever seen the movie about him?"

"There was a movie around 2000 or 2001, I think, but I missed it."

"No, I'm referring to the old documentaries, the ones that showed him at work in his studio. You know what he did? He splashed paint around like a madman, threw it indiscriminately against a long, rectangular canvas, like a small child on crack. And when the paint dried, you know what he did then?"

"What's that, Lester?"

"He took a saw, cut the canvas into sections, and sold each piece individually. For a small fortune, I'm sure. It was insanity masquerading as art."

"So you think real art can only date from the Impressionist period?"

"It's not a question of when the paintings were created. It's all about what they capture, which is the beauty and harmony of nature. To me, that's the most important thing: celebrating order, not creating chaos."

"And is that how you feel sometimes—chaotic? Out of control?"

"Most of the time, yes. But when I look at the Impressionists, the world comes back into focus for me. It's a vision of things that makes life worth living."

"And you don't think it would be worth living otherwise?"

"It depends on how you define being worth living. The world today is an ugly place. If you don't at least strive for beauty, why bother?"

"Well, I see your point. Let's focus on that feeling of chaos you were talking about a minute ago. Does that remind you of something you've felt before? Maybe something from your childhood?"

"Here we go," he said with disgust. "I'm not going to spend the next ten years talking about my childhood. I know how much you people love to do that. Then you'll go and get yourself killed in a rafting accident, and I'll have to start all over again. It's like calling the cable company, where you tell someone your story, then you get put on hold. And when the next person comes on the line, you have to go back and repeat it all. You can send me back to Bellevue if you want, but I'm not going to do it."

"Losing Dr. Hannity must have been very traumatic for you. I'm terribly sorry about that."

Lester Gordon looked like he was struggling to hold back tears. Weissberg gave him a minute to compose himself.

"He was a nice man. He seemed to care about me."

"Do you think your parents cared about you?"

"I told you, I'm not going to talk about it."

"Fair enough. I'll respect that. Let's go back to your love of Impressionism. I'm wondering where it came from. Was that something you learned in art school?"

"You've got to be kidding."

"Why would you say that?"

"I went to the Art Students League, on West 57th Street. They like to say that they sustain the tradition of training great artists. What a bunch of crap."

"Don't they like the Impressionist style?"

"They say they do, sure. They give it lip service. But just try to paint in that style, and their venom comes out. You see what they're really all about."

"And what is that?"

"Making a lot of money by pandering to the taste of the moment, just like the artists they admire the most. It's nothing more than political correctness applied to art. As long as you paint according to modern trends and turn out canvases that look like they were done by a ten-year old, they're happy with you. But just try to depict the beauty of nature—try to paint in the Impressionist style they say they admire—and you get criticized, made fun of. The only legitimate art is what they like. It's an industry."

"Many people think that art and money are intertwined."

"And some people think that art is about vision and message."

"Did they make fun of you?"

"Not directly, no. But they constantly told me that I was out of date, that I had to reflect the times. They said it was the responsibility of an artist to mirror the consciousness of the moment. It's ironic, because that's exactly what the Impressionists were fighting against back in the 19th century. So you know what I did?'

"What was that, Lester?"

"I did a painting blindfolded. Literally. I tied a scarf around my eyes and just slopped paint onto the canvas, without knowing what I was doing or what colors I was using. It was a piece of garbage. And when the paint dried and I brought it in to them, guess what? They were thrilled. They said it was great work, that I was finally making progress. The painting looked like it was done by someone's cat."

"It sounds like it was a very frustrating experience for you."

"After that incident, I knew I was finished. And I realized all over again what I knew in the first place, that I was right and they were wrong. I had more talent in my pinky than the entire school put together."

"If that's the case, and I'm not saying it isn't, why don't you think your paintings were more successful?"

"Because everyone thinks like the idiots in the Art Students League: the critics, the museum curators, the gallery owners. They're all wrapped up in proving to each other that they're knowledgeable and hip. It's like it was back in high school, when everybody was trying to be the coolest kid in the class. And to be cool in the art world, you have to appreciate the modern style. If Monet lived today, he'd be in exactly the same spot I'm in."

"Well, that could be true."

"Do you really agree, or are you just humoring me?"

"To be honest, I really don't know enough about it to offer an opinion. I'm just trying to get to know you, to get an insight into what you think."

"But you say you took down a copy of an Impressionist painting because you thought it was too sedate."

"As I said, I don't have the passion for the subject that you do. I probably see it as room decoration more than anyone else."

"I guess most people feel that way." He leaned forward and spoke with intensity. "And it might be nice room decoration, but more than that it's a window into the soul. Those guys were looking at nature, which is beautiful enough, and pulling the visual elements together to create a harmony that allows the world to make sense."

"Very well put. I see your point."

"I hope so." He stood up to go. "I gather you want me back here at the same time next week."

"Yes, please. Would you like an appointment card?"

"I'll be here."

Insanity masquerading as art, indeed. She watched him leave. *What's the difference?*

She walked to her desk and pulled out a worn copy of *Multiple Personality and the Search for Self,* by Karen Brillstein. The book was nearly ten years old but was still regarded as the definitive work in the field. She flipped through it and came to rest in the section titled "Identifying the Alters."

"In most DID patients, there are complex relationships between the alters. Some of the identities will be aware of the others and frequently interact with them, while some may be unknown to their counterparts. There is generally a personality that exerts significant influence over the others, coordinating their activities and even being aware of their thoughts. We refer to this identity as the transactional alter. The therapist should be careful to remember that the transactional alter is not necessarily the most important: while a stronger personality than the rest, this identity is not always the central figure in the patient's disorder. The transactional alter may or may not be directly linked to the childhood trauma that brought about the patient's condition in the first place. The therapist's challenge is to isolate and treat the alter that lies at the core of that trauma, since he or she is usually the key to healing the patient and uniting the different personalities."

She put the book down. *I have to find a way to override his resistance and deal with Baby Les, or I won't be able to cure him.*

CHAPTER 11

The thin, gaunt man paused at the entrance to the Palmetto State Art Museum in Columbia, South Carolina, holding a rectangular cardboard box. He clutched the box in a protective and loving manner as if it were a beloved household pet, periodically stroking the corrugated top and sides. He was dressed in a simple priest's habit with a Roman collar. His pale and nearly whitewashed skin was dotted with red blotches, and both colors seemed even more prominent against the background of his black suit. His hair was flecked with gray, and his ears protruded from both sides of his head like a pair of taut angel's wings.

He stood in front of the door for five full minutes, oblivious to the stares of passing pedestrians. Some of them hesitated as they skirted around him, uncertain whether the man needed help. They decided to pass him by. Some were hustling on their way to work, others held back because of their inbred Southern reserve, and most founded it incongruous to offer assistance to a priest. One woman stopped briefly and noted the man's dreamy expression: he seemed removed from reality, as if he were in a hypnotic trance.

When he finally opened the heavy museum door, he was

greeted by a smiling young receptionist at the Information Desk.

"Good morning, Father!" Her high-pitched voice was accompanied by a brilliant smile. "You've chosen a beautiful day to visit the Palmetto State Art Museum."

"Thank you," muttered the priest. "You are correct. It may not be Sunday, but it is certainly the Lord's day."

"Can I direct you to one of the exhibits?"

"I have an appointment." He searched the pockets of his habit and retrieved a scrap of paper. "My name is Father Gordon Humphries. I'm here to see Elizabeth Pattinger. I believe she is the Registrar."

"Of course. I'll page her for you."

Less than a minute later the priest was greeted by a middle-aged woman with carefully coifed brown hair, wearing glasses and a tweed suit. She led him past the entrance to the exhibitions and down a hallway to her office.

"Please sit down, Father Humphries. How was your flight?"

"Very pleasant, thank you." He carefully placed the cardboard box on the floor next to his chair. "I came in last night, actually. I'm getting too old to be rushing around at the last minute."

"I know the feeling." She laughed. "Sometimes I feel older than that myself. Is this your first time in Columbia?"

"Yes, it is, although I've traveled around the region a good deal. I function in a supervisory and administrative capacity for the Society of Jesus."

"It sounds like very interesting work."

"Oh, I'm not sure about that. I suspect they're simply finding something for me to do. But I try my best to make sure that everything is running smoothly."

"Well, I must say we were overwhelmed by your generosity. Your gift will be a very significant one for the museum."

"Thank you."

"As you probably know, the Impressionist masters are one of our weakest areas. We do have a work by Monet, but by and large our collection is seriously lacking."

"I'm very happy to help."

"Someday, our dream is to have an Impressionist collection housed in a separate wing."

"With the Lord's guidance, I'm sure you will attain your goal."

"We'll need all the help we can get." She laughed again. "That's why we're so grateful for your gift—it helps fill one of our greatest needs. Can you tell me a bit more about the painting than you revealed in your email?"

"It's a watercolor titled *Dawn at Dieppe*. Many historians believe it was a study for one of Signac's larger seascapes. Most authorities date the work to the mid-1890s, when Signac was beginning to move from Impressionism toward Pointillism. Because it was probably a study, it doesn't appear in any of the major catalogs."

"How did it come into your possession?"

"It was part of my parents' collection, as I might have

mentioned. They traveled widely and bought a great deal of art, back when it was more affordable than it is today. My father tended toward modern and realistic canvasses, but my mother had a soft spot for the Impressionists. It definitely rubbed off on me."

"I can certainly understand why."

"The paintings in their collection have brought me a great deal of joy for many years. But now I'm afraid I'm reaching the stage where I need to look beyond my own lifetime. I'm motivated by a desire to have these canvases bring the same joy to as many others as possible." He hesitated. "I have a heart condition, and I want to find a home for as many of the pieces in my parents' collection as I can. You never know what might happen."

"I'm sure you'll be around for many years to come. And we hope you'll stop in and visit when your schedule brings you to the area. We'd like to consider you part of the family."

"That's very kind." Humphries blushed, making the red blotches on his face even darker. "I appreciate it greatly."

"Well, you're being extraordinarily generous. I'm sure your parents would be very proud."

"I hope so. That's the reason that I've asked this gift to be named in their honor—Theodore and Lillian Humphries."

"Yes, you specified that in your emails. We'd be pleased to do so."

"I appreciate it."

"And you're absolutely correct: this will be a legacy that will live on after them, and it will have a positive effect on many people." She hesitated. "I see you have it with you. Would it be possible for me to get a peek?"

"Of course."

She assisted Humphries as the two of them lifted the painting from the box and removed the Styrofoam brackets from the corners. They rolled back the bubble wrap with great care until a riot of color and sunlight came into view. Dawn was breaking over Dieppe. Fishing boats languished in the harbor, waiting for the crews who would take them out to sea. Light glittered against the masts of the ships, and Liz Pattinger's eyes were drawn into a vortex of yellow and orange that exploded off the sun in the middle distance. She had never seen anything like it.

"Oh, my God. It's absolutely beautiful."

"Yes, it is, thank you. It's a remarkable piece. I hate to part with it, but I know it's the best thing under the circumstances."

"I'll have it placed directly into the vault." With difficulty, she diverted her eyes from the canvass and looked at Father Humphries. "I need to ask you about documentation. I'm sure your parents purchased the painting a long time ago, but did they leave you any certificates of authenticity or proof of sale?"

"Goodness." The priest shook his head. "After they passed on, most of their personal effects were placed in storage. There must be forty or fifty boxes of documents. I don't know how I could go through all of them. I don't think I have the energy, to be honest."

"That's perfectly all right."

"I assume you must have someone on staff who does authentications?"

"Actually, we don't. This is a small operation. But we can have the painting authenticated. It's not a problem."

"I imagine you'll want more than one. I hear that's standard practice in these situations."

"We probably can't afford to have more than one." She laughed. "But it's not something you should worry about. If you have time today, I'd like to introduce you to our Curator, Jeffrey Horshak. He's very anxious to meet you."

"By all means. I've arranged my appointments so that I may spend a day or two in Columbia, since I've never been here before. I'd be delighted to meet him."

"Please follow me."

She picked up the Signac watercolor with both hands and carried it down the hall. Humphries followed her into a corner office, where a large man with a crew-cut and blue blazer rose to meet them.

"Father Humphries?" He extended his hand. "I'm Jeff Horshak, Director of the Palmetto State Art Museum. Welcome, sir, and many thanks to you."

"It's a pleasure to meet you. Are you the Director, or the Curator?"

"Both." Horshak's smile glinted out from behind his wire-rimmed glasses. "We run a skeleton crew here. It's hard enough to compete for artwork, even when you're not wasting money on administrative salaries."

"I would imagine so."

"That's why we're so touched by the magnitude of your gift. It's canvases like these that will help elevate us into the front ranks of America's regional museums."

"I'm pleased to do it. My only stipulation, as I've said, is that the gift be acknowledged as a tribute to my late parents."

"Yes, I have it here." He picked up a sheet of paper from his desk. "Gift of Father Gordon Humphries, in loving memory of Theodore and Lillian Humphries. That's how the annotation will appear when the work is exhibited."

"Thank you very much."

Pattinger held the canvas up, and the Director stepped back a few feet to admire it.

"Remarkable," he said. "You almost feel as though you could step onto one of the boats."

"Yes." The priest nodded. "I've never gotten tired of looking at it."

"You know, before you came here, I looked through most of the catalogs of Signac's work, and I couldn't find this one."

"I was just discussing that with Miss Pattinger," said Humphries. "Signac was a very prolific painter, as we both know. And from everything I can tell, this watercolor was a study for one of his larger seascapes. I assume that's why it doesn't appear in most of the catalogs."

"Hmm. Which seascape was that, I wonder?"

"Who knows?" The priest extended his palms upward in a gesture of humility. "I couldn't begin to project myself into the mind of a genius like Signac. If I can get up in the morning and make myself coffee, I'm grateful for that."

"Amen." Horshak looked at his watch. "Do you have time for lunch, Father? It's almost noon."

"Yes, that would be very nice of you."

"Let's go grab something. After that, I'll give you the five-cent tour of the museum. We may not have the same resources as the major markets, but we do a lot with what we have."

"I look forward to seeing it."

"I'm going to put the painting in the vault," said Pattinger. "It was wonderful to meet you, Father Humphries."

"It was my pleasure as well."

"And God bless you." She smiled. "I imagine you're the one who usually says that, but I'm sure He will."

CHAPTER 12

Father Humphries ended up spending four days in Columbia. This was longer than the museum staff had anticipated, but they quickly realized that their new benefactor required little in the way of entertainment. He refused most of their offers for meals, sightseeing, and free entrance to local attractions. After his initial tour of the museum, he logged most of his time sitting in front of the museum's sole Monet. To Horshak's amazement, the priest spent two or three hours each afternoon staring at the painting with a dreamlike smile on his face.

When he announced he was leaving, Horshak arranged for a docent to drive him to the airport the next morning. The two men had dinner together on Humphries' final night in the city. The Jesuit seemed happy, but his good humor was underlined with thoughtfulness and inner reflection.

"I hope you enjoyed your time with us, Father."

"Very much so. It was a welcome respite from the traffic and noise up in New York City."

"I would imagine." The Director paused. "I believe Liz said that you worked in a supervisory capacity for the Society of Jesus—traveled around, made sure things were shipshape."

"That's correct."

"I gather you're semi-retired, or maybe completely so."

"Why would you think that?" Humphries smiled. "I'm not as old as I might look."

"Actually, you don't seem old at all. But I know there are no Jesuit facilities in this area, so I'm assuming you came here for some rest and relaxation."

"That's exactly right."

"Well, you seem to be quite a fan of Monet."

"I have a passion for the Impressionists in general." The priest's expression was pensive and distracted. "I suppose I inherited that from my parents. It's strange, because I'm not even that fond of nature. But I've never found a group of people who so accurately captured the blessing of being alive."

"Yes, I suppose that's true. That's a very good way of saying it."

"Perhaps it's their use of color, or the way they depict the play of light on objects. But when I look at those paintings, I feel that I'm in freefall, hurtling toward the true meaning of the universe." He patted his mouth with a napkin. "Forgive me. I get a little silly when I discuss the subject."

"Not at all. If everyone had your passion for art, the world would be a far better place."

"I think that's absolutely correct." The priest stared at Horshak. "I have something to tell you, but I've been a bit hesitant to bring it up."

"I'm all ears. Please go ahead."

"This is a slightly delicate topic, and one that might even

sound suspicious if it came from someone other than myself. But the real reason I came to Columbia has to do with the disposition of my parents' art collection. As I told Miss Pattinger, I have a heart condition and have been unwell in recent years. I'm very concerned about making the best possible arrangements for these paintings, so that they may be appreciated by the greatest number of people. I was very close to my parents, and I feel I owe them at least that much."

"I understand. It must be difficult for you to talk about."

"I'm sure you're wondering why I chose to give the Signac to the Palmetto State Art Museum, rather than a larger and more prosperous institution."

"To be honest, that did cross my mind."

"There were several reasons." The priest cleared his throat and took a drink of water. "For one thing, a larger museum might not have appreciated that particular gift, or for that matter any gift I chose to make. Those places have so much artwork that they can't possibly display it all. I don't want the paintings in my parents' collection to sit in storage and be brought out every three years to be hung as part of a special exhibit."

"That's very perceptive, and exactly right."

"I don't want to offend you, but the other reason is that I wanted to concentrate on the area of greatest need. I know that a small regional museum such as yours lacks the funds for major acquisitions."

"Unfortunately, that's true. We're not exactly at the top of many donor lists, either."

"This is what I thought. And so we come to the part that may be delicate." He paused. "My father was a high-ranking army officer—he retired as a two-star general. Right after World War II, he was stationed in Germany and attached to NATO. This was a period when the full range of Nazi art theft was first being discovered."

"I see."

"As you may know, the extent of the theft was enormous. People are still cataloging it today, and what they've discovered fills two volumes the size of telephone books. It was the most disgracefully corrupt regime in history."

"No argument there."

"The Nazis had some very strange concepts about art. They strongly preferred classical pieces and felt that anything modern was a negative influence on society. So in the beginning they restricted themselves to traditional paintings and sculptures from the Medieval period and the Renaissance. But as time went on, they confiscated modern pieces as well. Their excuse was that they wanted to protect the public from the corrupting influence of that type of art, but of course they were in it for the money. After the war, the full extent of their art theft gradually became known."

"Father, are you saying that your parents had some of those pieces in their collection?"

"I'm sure they didn't realize. At the time, there was an active black market in art objects. No one knew where these paintings were coming from, or perhaps they preferred not to know. I have to assume that my father was blameless in this."

"I'm sure he was."

"So here is the situation." The priest spoke slowly and carefully. "I am in possession of two canvases by Seurat. One is fairly small, the other is a reasonable size. They are quite beautiful, breathtaking in fact. They have given me much joy over the years, but also a good deal of guilt. I tried my best to track down the original owners, with the intention of returning their property to them, but it appears that they perished in the war. There are no heirs or descendants I can find, or at least find easily." Humphries stared at Horshak. "I would like to explore the possibility of donating those canvases to the Palmetto State Museum of Art."

"I don't know what to say, other than it's incredibly generous of you. We'd love to have them, provided all the efforts to find the rightful owners have been exhausted."

"I'm at a dead end on that. There are, however, other issues."

"Such as?"

"As you know, Seurat died at the age of 31, so his work is far more abbreviated than other artists. The official catalog lists 240 works, and these paintings do not appear in it." He paused. "I bring this up because we had a similar situation with the Signac, and I understand how it may look. But in this case, I think there was considerable confusion created by the war and the wholesale art theft that resulted."

"Are you certain these are authentic?"

"I haven't had them authenticated, no, because my financial

status doesn't permit me to do so. Authentication would never have been necessary for me unless I was planning on selling them, which is something I would never do. But if we proceed with the donation, I would insist that you have them authenticated, even though the cost may be substantial."

"Well, this is a case where it would certainly be worth it."

"As I'm sure you know, the Pointillists are the toughest painters on earth to forge. The technique was obscure and incredibly time-consuming. Anyone looking to make fast money on a forgery would be very ill-advised to choose an artist such as Seurat—one picture could literally take years to replicate for anyone who is not a master. As to the canvas and the paint, they look quite real to me, but of course I'm not an expert."

"I'd definitely like to see them, and I'm both touched and flattered that you would consider us."

"Why don't we do this? I will likely be returning to Columbia in several months. I'll bring the smaller of the two canvases with me, and we can proceed from there."

*

Jeffrey Horshak reviewed the conversation with Liz Pattinger the day after Father Humphries left town.

"Well?" he asked when he finished relating the story. "What do you think?"

"God, I don't know." She shook her head. "Obviously it would be an enormous coup to get them. But these are murky waters, Jeff. How do we know that one of the heirs won't come out of the woodwork and sue us a few years from now?"

"We could try to track them down, I suppose. But I'm not sure that we have the resources for that, considering the money we'd have to spend on authentication. But we'd have to make sure they were real, so we wouldn't have much of a choice there."

"True."

"To me, the big question isn't whether the pictures are real, but whether this guy is legitimate."

"What do you mean?"

"Well, he comes out of nowhere with a Signac watercolor under his arm. He's from New York City. In my experience, people like that don't consider places like Columbia to be the vacation capital of the world. He says he's a supervising executive for the Jesuits, and there's no Jesuit college or institution here. He says he's a sick old man, but he doesn't look that old to me."

"I'd say he's around fifty. He definitely doesn't look well. A little strange, maybe, but not well."

"He's an eccentric kook, but that's not unusual—most art collectors are. But none of these works appear in the catalogs. And now he's got this story about the two Seurats that were confiscated by the Nazis. He knows very well that we can't verify it."

"Why do you think he came to us, rather than the Columbia Museum of Art?" asked Pattinger. "Columbia is more centrally located and easier to get to."

"Who knows?" Horshak shrugged. "Probably because he

thought this was the official state museum. I'm sure that's what the Board had in mind when they named the place."

"Well, he looks like a nice old man to me." She sighed. "Maybe I'm too gullible."

"And maybe I'm too suspicious. But I can tell you, at this rate we're not going to get the new wing built anytime soon."

"The idea of an Impressionist collection is too ambitious. I'm sure you realize that."

"Forget about an Impressionist collection. This isn't the Musée d'Orsay in Paris. But you and I both know we need more space, and we're no closer to breaking ground."

Five years before, when Horshak had accepted the job at Palmetto State, the Board had made it clear that the construction of a new exhibit wing was one of their top mid-range goals. The Director's progress had been slow and difficult. The project was projected to cost several million dollars, and there were few donors in the community with pockets deep enough to fund that type of dream. The city was surrounded by rural poverty, and charity dollars tended to go toward more realistic programs such as community health centers.

"So what are you going to do?" asked Pattinger.

"I'll get a pre-authentication assessment on the Signac. That should give us something to go on, without spending a fortune. If it seems to check out, we'll take a look at the first Seurat."

*

Several weeks after Father Humphries returned to New York City, Jeffrey Horshak received the following letter by certified mail:

Dear Mr. Horshak:

Thank you for contacting Truth in Art for your authentication needs. We appreciate the trust you have placed in us.

Based on the information provided by you and enhanced by a visual examination of the work in question (*Dawn at Dieppe* by Paul Signac; watercolor, 1893), we are pleased to provide the following pre-authentication assessment:

The work is executed in the style of Signac and appears to be authentic. The materials are representative of the period and historically accurate. One very strong argument in favor of authentication is the fact that the pigments have faded over time, more or less in the correct proportion to the color attrition that is expected in most Impressionist and neo-Impressionist works. In our general experience forgers tend to use the brightest and most vivid colors possible, in ignorance of the fact that most painters of the period employed non-permanent pigments that inevitably fade.

However, please bear in mind that we could only make an outright authentication after the standard battery of spectroscopic tests. The cost would be in the range of $3,000. We're mindful that Palmetto State is a small institution with limited resources, and the fee might not be warranted for a minor work by a major artist.

While the painting certainly looks like an original and was

obviously executed by an artist of extraordinary talent, there are several factors that argue against authentication. Foremost among these is the fact that the canvas does not appear in any of the published catalogs of Signac's work. Given his long life span and prolific tendencies, this is not a major concern by itself.

You also raised the point that the donor doesn't have (or can't locate) any proof of sale or certificate of authenticity. This is more troubling at first, but less so considering your description of the donor and his circumstances. The painting was apparently purchased more than fifty years ago, at a time when documentation was less prevalent and expected than it is today. You also noted that the donor himself was supportive and even encouraging of the authentication process.

If you would like to proceed with the full range of spectroscopic examination, please let us know. As a gesture of good will, we would offer you a 10% discount on our services.

If not, it seems to us that you have every right to hang *Dawn at Dieppe* in one of your galleries and present it to the public as an original work by Paul Signac. We imagine it will provide pleasure to museum visitors for many years to come.

CHAPTER 13

"Thanks for finding time for me. I know you're busy."

"I'm really sorry it took so long." Dr. Karen Brillstein sat down behind her desk and looked at Cheryl Weissberg. "I do apologize, but last week was extremely hectic. We had Ph.D. candidates doing their oral defense of their dissertations. I'm sure you remember what that was like."

"God, don't remind me."

"Anyway, I've read the file. This looks like an interesting case."

"I could really use your help."

"Happy to. Where are you at thus far?"

"As you saw, the patient arrived at Bellevue after he was arrested for disrupting an exhibition at the Museum of Modern Art. I went in to talk to him, and he started dissociating during the initial interview."

"What were his physical indicators?"

"He seemed to go into a dreamlike state prior to switching—his eyes would almost go out of focus. As far as I can tell, there are three alters. One is a Jesuit priest by the name of Gordon Humphries, and the other is a child version of the patient called Baby Les. I haven't actually seen the third alter emerge directly from the patient. He's a painter called Louis Bétancourt."

"How do you know there's a third alter, if he hasn't emerged?"

"Because I actually saw him in person. He sold me a picture that's hanging in my office."

"You can't be serious."

"Absolutely. Before I opened the practice, I was shopping in a neighborhood art store. The manager suggested that rather than buy a reproduction, one of the local artists might be willing to do a painting for me. He put Louis Bétancourt in touch with me, and he came to my office twice."

"That's an amazing coincidence. You actually did business with the patient while he was projecting one of the alters. It's unreal."

"It is. I didn't realize it at the time, of course. But when I saw Bétancourt, I was startled because he looked exactly like Lester Gordon."

"What's the picture like?"

"It's beautiful. If you saw it in a museum, you'd swear it was an Impressionist work."

"Interesting."

"In fact, during one session with Lester Gordon, he looked at the painting and immediately dissociated. The Gordon Humphries alter came out. He said the picture was a copy of an Impressionist canvas by Signac, which he was planning on donating to a museum. He told me an elaborate story about his parents being art collectors, and how he wanted to give away the most important paintings before he died, so that the greatest number of people could appreciate them."

"And so you think the Louis Bétancourt alter is the forger?"

"That's my theory, but this is where it gets complicated."

"Let's hear it. But first, please explain this obsession with Impressionism to me."

"That's an integral part of it," said Weissberg. "I gather Lester Gordon became fixated on the Impressionists for a number of reasons. Most of it had to do with the trauma of his childhood—they represented a soothing, pastoral view of the world. He was extremely talented, but he was practically laughed out of art school because he insisted on painting in the Impressionist style, when all his fellow students were turning out work that looked like Jackson Pollock."

"Makes sense."

"His grip on reality was probably borderline before that, but he went steadily downhill for decades after he left art school. He was institutionalized several times and spent years in therapy and got the usual assortment of diagnoses. Then about seven years ago his therapist and his father died within a year of each other, and that was the one-two punch that put him over the edge."

"Is there evidence of childhood abuse?"

"In the form of extreme neglect, yes. His late therapist felt it was responsible for most of Gordon's later problems. But when I spoke with Humphries during the first session, he made a big deal about the fact that he had donated the painting in memory of his parents. In fact, he almost started crying when he mentioned them."

"All of that is part of the pattern. It allows them to maintain a connection to the abuser. What exactly did he do to get himself arrested at MOMA that night?"

"He was vehemently opposed to the exhibition, which was a collection of work by Neo-Dada artists. I gather he had been agitating against it, circulating petitions, that kind of thing. He seems to view any canvas painted after 1900 to be a threat to his existence. On the night of the opening, he was brandishing a box cutter and moving toward one of the Rauschenbergs when the guards tackled him."

"Let's go back to Father Humphries. You say he's going to donate this painting to a museum? The original of the work that's hanging in your office?"

"Not just that one, apparently. He says he also has two paintings by Seurat."

"Sorry, but I don't know as much about art as I should."

"Neither do I, but I did some research on Seurat. He died at the age of 31, so his work was limited. If those two paintings were legitimate, they'd be priceless."

"But you don't believe they're legitimate?"

"I wouldn't know. But I have a strong gut feeling that they were painted by the Louis Bétancourt alter, even though the evidence argues against it."

"How so?"

"They would have been incredibly time-consuming and

difficult works to forge. If Lester Gordon had that type of talent, he'd be one in a million. Or more like ten or a hundred million. Plus, it would require a level of concentration and perseverance that would be unusual for someone who was mentally disturbed."

"Hmm." Brillstein removed her glasses and regarded them thoughtfully. "But it's possible, I suppose."

"Sure. Just look at Van Gogh."

"Ah." She smiled. "But Van Gogh was an *original* talent. You're telling me that this man is only capable of painting in a derivative style."

"Honestly, I'm not sure how you evaluate these things. I don't have the background, but I intend to do some more research. I need to speak to some experts as well. And I'm going to need your help."

"So you said. What can I do for you?"

"For starters, is this DID?"

"It certainly sounds that way, but of course I couldn't tell unless I examined him. It sounds like all the signs are there. But you always have to be careful that the patient isn't fooling you."

"What do you mean?"

"As I probably told you in graduate school, one of the things that DID skeptics always say is that these patients try out different acts on their therapists, to see what works. Many of us fantasize about being someone else, as you know. With a patient in this situation, they sometimes act out a different personality and find that it gets them more attention, so they continue. There are all sorts of people who crave attention from their doctors."

"Would you be willing to examine him?"

"Down the road, yes. But with this type of patient, it's crucial that you form a bond with him first. If I got involved at this point, he would likely become withdrawn."

"I'll keep you posted on my progress with him."

"If I were you, I'd keep this between us for the moment. This type of case could bring you a great deal of aggravation."

"How so?"

"As you know, DID is still regarded by many clinicians as a bogus disorder, despite its inclusion in the DSM-IV. You're just starting out. Even worse, you were a student of mine. If this case isn't open and shut, people will say that I brainwashed you."

"I'm just following the evidence."

"Good. Then go one step at a time and see where it leads."

Weissberg hesitated. "There's one more problem."

"Yes?"

"I'm not sure exactly where he is at the moment."

"Cheryl, what are you talking about?"

"He's been missing sessions. He came to the first two, then missed one and came to the next. Right now, I don't know where he is."

"You've tried calling him?"

"He doesn't have a cell phone."

"Have the police check his apartment. He might be in some sort of danger."

"Well, actually, I don't know where he lives. I know he's in the neighborhood, but I don't have his exact address."

"Good God. He didn't fill out any paperwork?"

"He did all of that at Bellevue. And I don't want to alert Bellevue that he's missing, because they might lock him up again. And at that point, Jensen would medicate the poor guy into another universe, and his treatment would effectively be over."

"Hmm. Most likely, he's off donating one of the paintings to a museum. I assume you know which ones he was considering?"

"Not really. He was pretty vague about that." She felt herself blushing. "Look, I know this sounds sloppy, but I didn't want to spook him."

"He'll be back in a few days. And when he does return, he'll come and see you. He has nowhere else to go."

"When he comes back, how do I get to talk to Lester Gordon or Baby Les, rather than Gordon Humphries?"

"That's easy. Remove the painting from the wall before he arrives."

"I've already done that."

"Then hang a Jackson Pollock reproduction in its place." She smiled. "Sounds like that should keep him focused."

CHAPTER 14

"Please come in, Lester."

"Sure."

Lester entered Cheryl Weissberg's consulting room and sat down on the sofa, across from the therapist.

"How have you been getting along?"

"Not too bad, thanks."

"It's been a while since I've seen you."

"What do you mean?"

"You missed your session last week. I was a little concerned about you, but I didn't have your address or any way to contact you. And I didn't want to ask Bellevue for it, because they might have recommitted you."

"I appreciate it, thank you." He paused. "To be honest, I don't know where I was."

"Were you out of town?"

"I'm not sure. But I'm sorry if I didn't show."

"Well, just do me a favor and let me know going to be away. That way I won't worry."

"Will do." He glanced up at the wall. "I see your painting isn't framed yet."

"Not yet, no. I'm scouting around for some other pieces. In

the meantime, I have a favor to ask of you."

"Yes?"

"Normally I wouldn't do this, but I have to ask you to wait for a few minutes. I'm expecting a call about a patient who has been hospitalized, and it's important that I take it. Is it all right with you if I do that?"

"I guess so."

"I'll be right outside. I really appreciate your understanding. As I say, I wouldn't do it if it wasn't really important. I don't have a patient after you, so we can make the time up."

"That's okay. Go ahead."

"Thank you. I'll be back as soon as I can."

Weissberg sat down at the desk in the reception area. After a few minutes she walked over to the door of the consulting room, inserted the key in the lock, and turned it as quietly as she could. She sat back down and looked at her watch. If her theory was correct, Gordon would react soon to her absence. She knew from reading Hannity's notes that the patient had felt neglected as a child, and Lester had told her the previous week that Dr. Hannity had "abandoned" him. If her plan worked, leaving him alone would trigger the alter known as Baby Les. She wasn't certain that her approach was completely ethical, but it was the best way to delve into Lester's childhood, a topic he had resisted discussing with her.

Six minutes passed, and then eight. She heard him pacing in the next room. At ten minutes she heard a pounding on the door, and Lester was calling for help. She unlocked the door and found him sitting on the floor, sobbing.

"Lester, are you all right? I'm sorry it took me longer than I expected."

"I don't know where I am."

"Let's get you sitting back in the chair and see if you can calm down."

He rose unsteadily and collapsed on the sofa. He curled up into a ball, much as he had when she had interviewed him at Bellevue.

"Where am I? Where's Mommy?"

"Mommy went out, Baby Les. There's nothing to worry about."

"She's not here."

"No, she's not."

"Are you babysitting me?"

"Yes, I am. Is that okay?"

"The other babysitter doesn't care about me She leaves me alone. Last week I had a tummy ache and I yelled and yelled for her to come and help me, but she didn't come."

"That must have been awful."

"Do you have friends?"

"What do you mean?"

"The other babysitter has friends. They come over all the time."

"Well, I do have friends, but they won't be coming here. You'll be safe. Do you trust me?"

"No. I don't know who you are."

"Well, I promise you that no one will come over. I can't do any better than that. I hope you'll learn to trust me."

"I don't understand why Mommy always has to go out."

"I don't know either, but it must be important. How does that make you feel?"

"She doesn't love me." Lester was sobbing uncontrollably. "If she loved me, she wouldn't leave me alone all the time."

"I'm sure she loves you, Baby Les. But sometimes grownups have things they need to do."

"Not all the time."

"Why does it bother you so much when the babysitter has friends over?"

"They do bad things."

"What kinds of things?"

"They hurt each other."

"What do you mean? How do they hurt each other?"

"When I had a tummy ache, I woke up and called her. She didn't come in to see me. Then I opened the door and looked in the living room. They were hurting each other."

"What were they doing?"

"They were on the couch. Her friend was laying on top of her. He was hurting her. She was screaming."

"Well, maybe they weren't really hurting each other. Maybe they were doing something else."

"I don't care!" he yelled. "I want Mommy."

"She'll be coming home soon, I promise." She reached out

and pulled his chin in her direction, so he was looking her in the eye. "Did you hear me? I promise."

"I guess so."

"Now Baby Les, I have something to show you. I'm going to get up and get it from the closet. I'm not going to leave, but I need to bring it in here so I can show you. Is that okay?"

He nodded. She walked into the reception area, opened the closet, and grabbed the watercolor Louis Bétancourt had painted. When she sat down across from him, she lifted up the painting so he could see it.

"I wanted to show it to you. Isn't this pretty?"

"I guess."

The switching wasn't immediate this time: it took nearly a full minute of staring at *Dawn at Dieppe* before his eyes glazed over. For Weissberg, it might have been one hour. *God, I hope I haven't screwed up here. I have no idea what I'm doing.* Eventually his expression came into focus and he straightened his body on the sofa.

"My goodness, you've had the painting framed." He regarded her with a pleasant smile. "And they did a very nice job, I must say. It will make a splendid addition to your office."

"Father Humphries?"

"I suppose you can call me Gordon. It appears that our conversations will be ongoing."

"I'm very glad you like the framing job."

"Strangely enough, it's not dissimilar from the frame I chose for the original. It complements the canvas very well."

"Thank you."

"I seem to be a bit disheveled." He looked around him in confusion. "My shirt appears to be wet, and my nose is running. Perhaps I'm coming down with something."

"Well, it's allergy season. Don't forget that."

"Quite true." He chuckled. "I suppose that's the flip side of nature that the Impressionists never told us about."

"You could be right. I don't suppose any of them ever went camping."

"Hah! You have quite a sense of humor."

"That's what they tell me. Do you have any questions for me before we wrap up, or any concerns you want to raise?"

"No, I don't think so. How long have we been conversing? I'm afraid I'm a bit fuzzy on the details."

"Oh, it was mostly small talk. Nothing of importance." She handed him a card. "This is your next appointment. Would you do me a favor and post it in a prominent place when you get home?"

"Goodness, of course I will. I may be old, my dear, but I'm not forgetful."

CHAPTER 15

The two men watched as the refrigerated truck backed up toward the loading dock. A young man wearing a yellow jumpsuit came down from the cab and approached them.

"Afternoon, gentlemen. Which one of you is Jeffrey Horshak?"

"I am," said the Director.

"Sorry, sir, but I have to trouble you for some identification."

"Of course."

Horshak handed over his South Carolina driver's license and watched as the young man inspected the picture.

"Thank you. I'm going to retrieve the painting. We can inspect in for any possible damage in transit, and then I have some paperwork for you to sign."

"Very good."

The driver opened the rear door of the truck, and the two men were hit by a rush of cold air. Horshak and Father Gordon Humphries watched as the driver laid a padded mat on the loading dock. He opened the cardboard box, removed the painting, and carefully dislodged the Styrofoam frame. He then unwound numerous layers of bubble wrap to reveal the canvas underneath.

"Here you go, sir."

Horshak stared at the painting. Just as Humphries had said, it appeared to be a study for Seurat's *Parade de Cirque*, or *Circus Sideshow*, painted between 1887 and 1888. He had seen the original several times at the Metropolitan Museum in New York, and he recognized the three musicians that appear on the left side of the original canvas. They were playing a cornet, tuba, and clarinet, just as they do in the finished work, but the trombone player was missing from the foreground.

"It's beautiful," said the Director.

"I agree—the work of a genius," said the priest. "It has given me many hours of pleasure. On numerous occasions, viewing the paintings in my parents' collection has made me wish I had become an artist myself. Sadly enough, I can't even draw."

Circus Sideshow was Seurat's first attempt to convey a scene occurring at night. Although it was a controversial picture, most critics tended to agree that the canvas was a vindication for his elaborate theories of color. Even in the study there was a masterful use of the white space behind the dots, creating a luminosity of light that was both arresting and striking.

"Take your time, sir," said the delivery man. "As soon as you're satisfied about the condition, you can sign off."

Horshak looked at Humphries, and the Jesuit nodded.

"Go ahead and bring me the paperwork."

The young man stood by patiently while Horshak signed the multiple forms.

"Do you want me to box it up again for you, sir?"

"Thanks, but that won't be necessary. I'll have one of our people transfer it directly into the vault."

They watched the delivery van disappear into the distance.

"We owe you a tremendous debt, Father Humphries," said the Director as they waited for the painting's escort. "I'd have a hard time even beginning to thank you."

"That's quite all right. After all, I do have the satisfaction of knowing the painting is in good hands, and that a large number of visitors will be able to view it."

"With your permission, we'd like to organize a small reception in your honor a few days from now. It won't be elaborate, but there are a number of people who have been active in our local arts scene over the years, and I know they'd like to meet you. I recognize your modesty, even though we haven't spent that much time together, but this small gesture from us will go part of the way toward showing our appreciation."

"That's very kind of you indeed." The priest was beaming. "But I'm afraid I must return to New York in the morning—I have business there. I only wanted to come here to make sure the painting arrived safely."

"Forgive me if I've put you on the spot," said Horshak. "Perhaps we could arrange this for a future time."

"I'd like that very much."

"This is a small community, and the circle of people involved in art is fairly small as well. I know they'd enjoy making your acquaintance. And to be completely frank, some of those folks haven't come close to matching your generosity, even though they're in a position to. You would be a terrific example for them. A role model, so to speak."

"I understand. My plan is to return to Columbia when the second Seurat canvas is delivered. Hopefully we could do it at that time."

"Excellent. I look forward to it."

"And if I may say so, I believe you'll be even more pleased with the other painting."

"Can you give me some details?"

"Certainly. It was painted in 1890, the year before Seurat's death. The title is *Madonna and Heir*. It is a portrait of his mistress Madeleine Knobloch and their infant son, Pierre-Georges. She is reclining on a settee in their Paris apartment, holding the child and regarding him in a loving fashion. Since we know that Pierre-Georges was born in February and Seurat died the following March, the canvas most likely dates to the end of 1890."

"Sounds very exciting, and I can't wait to see it."

"I might be busy over the next several weeks, but I will make some inquiries about shipping. I'll be in touch when I have a time frame for you. And if you'll be gracious enough to give me a rain check, I look forward to your party."

*

Later that day Horshak and Elizabeth Pattinger stood in the vault, admiring the study for *Circus Sideshow*.

"Amazing," she said. "Absolutely remarkable."

"Have you ever seen the original?"

"Many years ago. But in a sense, this is even more interesting, because it gives you an insight into the process of creation, about how these ideas evolve."

"True."

"Did you float the idea of the reception with him?"

"I did, but he has to go back to New York tomorrow. He promised we could do it when he comes back with the second Seurat. That's the one I'm really curious about."

"Well, it would be nice to do something to show our appreciation."

"Yes it would. It would also be nice to get some of these people to reach into their pockets for the new wing. We're still a million and a half short. Maybe the example of Father Humphries would finally motivate them."

"Spoken like a true fundraiser." She smiled. "This is incredibly exciting, Jeff. Whoever would have thought that we'd be in this position?"

"True."

"I assume you're going to get it authenticated before we hang it?"

"I'm going to do another pre-authentication assessment. That may be all we need in this case. There's no doubt in my mind that it's real."

"It certainly looks like Seurat. I'm not worried either. No one else could paint like that."

"It's real, all right. If it's not, I'll eat my hat."

CHAPTER 16

"**G**ood afternoon, Lester. "How are you?"
"I'm okay, thanks."

"Please come in."

Therapist and patient settled down across from each other.

"I see your painting still isn't framed yet."

"Not yet, no. It's almost finished," said Weissberg. "You seem concerned about it."

"I'm not concerned, but the walls do look bare. You could use some art."

"I agree completely. And I should have some by the next time we meet." She smiled. "What I thought we'd do today is talk a little bit about your daily routine. What do you do?"

"What do you mean?"

"I'm wondering what your days are like, how you fill your time. It's something we haven't really talked about yet."

"Why would you want to know that?"

"It's just something that would allow me to get to know you a little better, if that's okay."

"Honestly, it's hard for me to remember. I've been forgetting a lot of things recently. I seem to lose track of time."

"I see. Well, what did you do yesterday?"

"I don't know." He looked puzzled. "I can't recall. But I can tell you that I don't do much with myself. You know, the day just flies by."

"I understand—sometimes I feel the same way myself. I gather that you don't work a regular job?"

"No, I don't have to. My parents weren't wealthy, but they left me in a comfortable position."

"You're very fortunate."

"Yes, I agree. So I'm free to spend my time pursuing things that interest me."

"Let's talk about some of those things. What do you do in the course of any given day?"

"Oh," said Lester, "I keep myself occupied. I go to different museums. Very often I spend whole mornings or afternoons studying one particular painting. And I sketch a great deal. When the weather's nice I go over to Prospect Park. I watch people, and I can sit there and draw."

"I know from our previous conversation that you admire the Impressionists. So I imagine that what you draw is focused on nature, on outdoor scenes?"

"Most of it, yes."

"Do you have a studio at home? I gather from Dr. Hannity's notes that you live in the rent-controlled apartment you inherited from your father. Is there enough space for you to work in?"

"Yes and no. I used to paint in the living room, but recently I've been leasing the space out to one of the local painters. He needed a place to work, so I let him have it for a small monthly fee. The money's not important, but I'm trying to help him out."

"That's very generous of you. Is he a friend of yours?"

"An acquaintance, really. Just someone I admire. His name is Louis Bétancourt, and we share a lot of interests in common. He's also very passionate about the Impressionists. We like a lot of the same painters, people like Signac and Seurat." Lester laughed, a rueful expression on his face. "I have to admit that I wish I had his talent. The guy is truly amazing: you look at one of his canvases, and you really think it was done by a major Impressionist. You can barely tell the difference."

"That's quite a coincidence, because I've met Mr. Bétancourt."

"Really?"

"He came to my office several times before I opened. In fact, I bought a painting from him. It's the one I'm having framed right now."

"Yes, it's a small world. I can't wait to see it. Knowing him, I'm sure it's very impressive."

"How did the two of you get to know each other?"

"When I first moved to the neighborhood, I was excited because I knew it was full of artists. But pretty soon I realized they were mostly frauds. They were people with a lot of pretense and no talent. They hung around in cafes all day talking about art, but none of them created any. And the ones that did focused on modernist crap, abstract paintings with no meaning or emotional impact."

"But you thought Mr. Bétancourt was different?"

"He's one of a kind, the type of painter you almost never see anymore. In addition to his exceptional talent, he has an incredible work ethic. He doesn't care if it takes him years to complete a canvas. But when it's done, it's something that can change your life when you look at it."

"He struck me as a bit of an eccentric."

"Possibly. I see how you might think that. But it all depends on how you define normal, doesn't it?"

"Quite true. So if Mr. Bétancourt is using your living room as his studio, does this make it more difficult for you to get your own work done?"

"Sometimes, sure. But if I'm honest with myself, I have to recognize that he's far more talented than I am. He's the real thing. I believe that he's the guy who will bring the Impressionist style back into fashion. When you look at his paintings, you're hooked—the beauty of nature just overwhelms you."

"I have to agree, based on the one painting I saw. You mentioned Signac and Seurat a few minutes ago. I'm obviously not as well-versed in art as you are, so I'm wondering what it is about those two artists that you find particularly attractive."

"They're both what you would call Neo-Impressionists, although they came directly out of the Impressionist movement. Both of them were friends of Claude Monet. In terms of history, Seurat came first: he was very involved in color theory and developed the Pointillist style. Signac was his disciple and heir. He lived much longer than Seurat, so he was able to take it further."

"I've seen a few Pointillist paintings, and I have to admit they're a bit disorienting at first."

"In the beginning, yes. But when you study those canvases, you see that they're works of genius. They picked up where Impressionism left off. As precise as the images are when you view them from a distance, the play of light on those images is both subtle and intense at the same time."

"That's a good way to put it. Looking back, do you think you got your love of art from your parents?"

"Maybe in some way I'm not aware of. Neither of them were particularly fond of art, as far as I knew, so I have no idea where it came from."

"My parents used to take me to museums when I was younger. I imagine yours did the same."

"Not really. My father was in the army most of his life, so he wasn't artistically inclined. My mother mostly socialized with other wives and played bridge. I'm not sure I remember them taking me anywhere."

"Were you close to them growing up?"

"Here we go." He shook his head. "I told you I wasn't going to rehash my childhood."

"Okay, let's move on. Speaking of memory, you said before that you had trouble remembering things. Has that always been the case, or is it something that started recently?"

"More recently, I think. It seems to have gotten worse over the past five or ten years. There are times when I lose track of a few whole days, sometimes close to an entire week."

"Are you aware that you missed another session last week?"

"No! How could that be?"

"I gather you find that disturbing?"

"It's a little scary, yes."

"I might be able to help you remember some of the things you're losing track of. Would that be all right with you?"

"Sure. I guess so."

"You've seemed a bit more comfortable today. Hopefully that's the way you feel."

"I think so."

"It's true that you didn't have a choice about coming here, and I know it bothered you in the beginning—you mentioned it several times. But if you get to the point where you trust me, we can start to work on some of the issues that brought you here."

"I like you fine. But I don't think I had any problems that were serious enough to put me in a mental hospital."

"Remember, you were arrested. The security guards thought you were going to slash the Rauschenberg with your box cutter."

"I told you I would never harm a painting, even a piece of crap like a Rauschenberg. That should be obvious from everything I've said in here. I told you, I was trying to make a statement."

"What kind of statement?"

"That there should be a limit to profiting from the stupidity of people, to getting rich by capitalizing on their weakness and their desire to be hip and trendy. I realize I shouldn't have brought the box cutter into the museum. But I don't think anyone would have listened to me otherwise."

"Do you think that was an effective way of getting your message across?"

"Probably not. Either way, I'm not sure anyone would have paid attention. They never do." He smiled. "At least you seem to be listening, though, and I appreciate it."

CHAPTER 17

"Thank you so much for seeing me," said Cheryl Weissberg.

"Give me a break, please." Dr. Brillstein's tone was one of tolerant amusement.

"Well, I know how busy you are, and I appreciate it."

"Cheryl, you were one of the most promising graduate students I had in years. I'll always find time for you."

"Thank you."

"And I don't mind supervising you on this case. I know how complex these situations can get. It certainly seems like you've hit the jackpot right out of the gate."

"The patient shows all the signs of DID. It's eerie. I'd feel much better if you would examine him yourself."

"And I probably will at some point, but that's in the future. In the meantime, bring me up to speed."

"He loses track of time, and there are periods of days, maybe as long as a week, when he can't remember where he's been. He keeps missing sessions."

"Don't make a big deal out of that. Mention it, but don't stress it until you've given him the diagnosis."

"Agreed. As I think I told you, there are three recognizable alters. There's the Jesuit priest, who gives the paintings away,

114

and a child alter of the patient named Baby Les. The third alter, Louis Bétancourt, is the actual forger. I haven't been able to get him to emerge thus far, but I've had considerable success with the other two."

"Did the other two alters emerge spontaneously, or did you induce them?"

"A little bit of both. They emerged spontaneously at first, and then I experimented with pushing buttons when I wanted to talk to one of them." She hesitated. "This was one of the things I wanted to discuss with you. During a recent session, I wanted to speak to Baby Les, so I induced his appearance. I still feel somewhat guilty about it."

"How so?"

"I knew that neglect and abandonment figured prominently in Lester's childhood issues. At the beginning of the session, I apologized and told him I was expecting a phone call. I went into the outer office and locked the door. He was pounding on the door after about ten minutes. When I opened it he was on the floor, crying hysterically."

"Sounds good to me."

"So why do I feel so badly about it?"

"Probably because you're identifying too closely with the patient on an emotional level. It sounds like transference in reverse. You need to separate your problems from his."

"Was what I did ethical?"

"Did it work?"

"Yes. Baby Les came out, and I got some useful information."

"Then it's ethical in my book." She removed her glasses and leaned back in her chair. "Do you remember when we were studying Jung?"

"Of course."

"He used some controversial techniques, if you recall. They worked, so he became a hero."

"Well, not to everyone."

"It's not often that you please everyone. If you gave me the choice between being Karen Brillstein or Carl Jung, I'd pick him."

"Okay, I get your point."

"Let's step back a moment. What's your theory of this case?"

"The patient experienced abuse in childhood in the form of extreme neglect. He wasn't harmed physically, but he came away with the feeling that his parents didn't love him because they were never around. He was left in the care of babysitters, who were almost more neglectful than the parents. They ignored him when he needed them, and one of the babysitters frequently invited boyfriends over to have sex with her. Baby Les told me he witnessed this and interpreted it as violence, which obviously made him feel insecure and threatened."

"Sounds charming."

"I don't know this for sure, but the late Dr. Hannity's notes indicate that Lester may have walked in on his father having sex with the babysitter. The patient has exhibited extreme reluctance to discuss childhood issues with me, because those discussions haven't led to any progress in the past."

"Why was that?"

"Either because Dr. Hannity wasn't skilled enough to exploit the material, or because he got himself killed in a rafting accident about six or seven years ago."

"I see."

"So my theory is this. You have the childhood abuse in the form of neglect, which is not insurmountable but certainly damaging—it plants the seed in his mind that nobody loves him. Then he goes to art school and gets ridiculed, despite being incredibly gifted, because he refuses to paint in the style his instructors want. He goes into a serious tailspin after this, and possibly he begins to dissociate, but it's not crippling. The *coup de grâce* is the unexpected death of Dr. Hannity followed by the death of his father, both within a year. That's what puts him over the edge, and the alters start to come out."

"So we have this Bétancourt individual, whom you feel is the forger. Exactly how talented is he?"

"Apparently he's brilliant. I haven't tracked down all the threads yet, and I'm not an expert, but it appears he can paint as well as the Impressionist masters."

"And then we have the Jesuit priest, who gives these paintings away. In memory of the parents, I believe you said."

"Yes."

"So he is the figure who is operating on a transactional level. He glorifies a fictional connection to the parents by donating these paintings in their memory, and he legitimizes the talent of the forger at the same time."

"From what I can tell, that's correct. I haven't contacted the people at the Palmetto State Art Museum yet, in South Carolina, but my understanding is that the canvases were good enough to pass as authentic."

"Fascinating. So what are your concerns at this point?"

"I don't know whether to confront the patient with the diagnosis. Obviously I don't want him going off the deep end and harming himself, or even me."

"It doesn't sound like there's much risk of that. Has there been any display of anger from him or the alters?"

"No."

"From the way you describe it, I would argue for an aggressive approach. You say you're not dealing with exaggerated psychosis caused by extreme childhood trauma. The onset of DID was delayed and gradual, rather than immediate and severe. If it were me, I'd confront the patient. Just remember that you'll meet resistance. He probably won't believe you."

"That wouldn't surprise me. But how do I integrate the alters, in a case like this?"

"You're getting ahead of yourself. But when you do get there, my guess would be that you have to deal with the alter who's pulling the strings. And that sounds like the priest."

"From where I sit, my weak link is that I haven't been able to confront the forger directly. I've dealt with him in real life, as I told you, but I haven't yet seen him emerge during a conversation with the patient."

"He's the key, in one sense, which is why he's being so well guarded. Do you have any ideas on how to bring him out?"

"I do, but I'm hesitant. This goes back to my reservations about what I did to induce Baby Les. I feel like I'm in a grey area, where I'm not sure exactly what's right and what's wrong."

"What's right is what helps the patient. If you have an idea of how to induce the forger to come out and talk to you, my advice is to go ahead and do it."

"So if I induce the alter of the forger, and employ a similar technique to the one I used with Baby Les, you think I'm okay?"

"Here's what I think: a patient is never going to sue you for curing them."

CHAPTER 18

Liz Pattinger poked her head into Jeffrey Horshak's office. "Morning, boss."

Horshak nodded without a word. His lips were pursed together, and his face was contorted into a near-scowl. His appearance was so different from his usual cheerful behavior that Pattinger was alarmed.

"Is everything all right?" She approached the desk with caution. "You look upset."

"Damned right. I'm pissed off, to put it mildly."

"Gracious. Is this anything you can talk about?"

"Have a seat, Liz."

As she settled into a chair across from him, she noticed a baseball cap with the insignia of the Gamecocks, the University of South Carolina football team.

"Planning on taking in a game this weekend?"

"I said I'd eat my hat if the painting wasn't real. I figure a Gamecocks cap might be more palatable. Next time you go out, pick me up some salt and pepper. A nice *béarnaise* sauce would probably help also."

"What on earth are you talking about?"

"Here." He pushed a sheet of paper across the desk. "Read

this. It came this morning."

Dear Mr. Horshak:

Thank you for submitting your recently acquired canvas to Truth in Art for pre-authentication assessment. As always, we appreciate the trust you place in us.

As you noted, the canvas purports to be a study for Circus Sideshow *by Georges Seurat. It depicts the trio of musicians who appear in the background of the left side of the actual painting. In keeping with the tone of the original work, the lighting is hazy and the musicians are playing a cornet, tuba and clarinet.*

An initial examination of the painting points toward authentication. The style and technique appear to be that of Seurat, and the canvas itself is legitimately from the period. However, when we looked closer we found discrepancies in the brushwork. The Pointillist dots created by Seurat were sharp and precise. The dots here seem to be slightly broader and somewhat less focused. Is it possible that the artist did not apply as much effort to this work, given that it was a study?

Knowing Seurat's near-maniacal dedication to his craft, the probable answer is no. We feel that Seurat would have put the same amount of effort into a study, on the theory that the results would be predictive of the final work he was contemplating.

In addition to the brushwork, there are other factors that we find troubling:

1. *This canvas does not appear in the* Catalogue Raisonné *of Seurat's work. The 240 works that are included encompass studies for other major paintings, so why not this one?*

2. *You indicated that this painting was confiscated by the Nazis and purchased after World War II by the donor's father. This is of course a possible scenario, yet Seurat died in 1891 and the full extent of his work was well known for decades prior to Hitler's rise to power.*

3. *There is no certificate from a gallery or museum on the back of canvas, and no indication that such a certificate was removed.*

Given these factors, we advise against proceeding with a full authentication. We do not feel it would be money well spent. As noted, the materials and execution here are close to faultless, so spectroscopic examination would likely not reveal any discrepancies in those areas. If we were to conduct a full battery of tests on this painting, our conclusions would probably be similar to what they are at this moment: while the painting looks real, we could not in good conscience authenticate it. Science can only take you so far, and common sense needs to carry you the rest of the way.

If you choose to exhibit this canvas in your museum, the safest attribution would be something along the lines of "Believed to be a study for Circus Sideshow *by George Seurat, 1887-1888." Such an attribution would release you from any liability, and it would also be an accurate statement of the truth.*

"My God." She placed the letter back on the desk. "I don't know what to say. This can't possibly be right."

"It's pretty concise."

"But they're certainly not saying the painting is a fake. They just can't authenticate it."

"From our perspective, it's the same damn thing. If we hang it, we have to put something on the wall that says maybe it's a Seurat and maybe it's not, but we don't have a clue. That'll do wonders for our reputation. Not to mention how much it will help on the fundraising front."

"I'm sorry, but I really don't understand this. It looks like a Seurat to me. And to them."

"And to me as well. But something's up here." He picked up the baseball cap and turned it over in his hands. "Let's face it, Liz: we've been had. This Father Humphries, or whoever he is, has made jackasses out of us."

"I wouldn't go that far. We don't know that he isn't well-intentioned. The most likely possibility is that his father bought this painting thinking it was real, but he was duped. It's been passed on and become part of the family legend."

"Maybe. The best argument for the fact that it might be real is that no one else could possibly paint that way. And it still might be legitimate—there's a chance. But I doubt very much that Father Humphries' story is for real. Something's up with him."

"Well, you've been suspicious of him for a while."

"It's nothing I could put my finger on, even now. But it wouldn't surprise me if he turned out to be some sort of con artist."

"I'm sorry, but that makes no sense at all." She shook her head. "He's donating these paintings and asking nothing in return. Why would he do that?"

"I don't know, but I intend to find out. I'm going to do some digging on him. At the end of the day, I really don't care what his motivation is—fraud is fraud. But I can't take this any further unless I get some facts."

"Please keep me posted. I have to say this is the strangest thing I've ever heard."

"Here's the strangest thing I've ever heard: there's someone out there who can paint like Georges Seurat, and no one has a clue who he is."

CHAPTER 19

Jeffrey Horshak and Elizabeth Pattinger stood at the Palmetto State Art Museum's loading dock, watching the truck back up toward them. The young man jumped down from the cab and approached.

"Afternoon, sir."

"I'm Jeff Horshak, the Museum Director. Would you like to see some identification?"

"Not necessary—I remember you from last time. Give me a minute and I'll get the painting."

Father Humphries was absent from the scene. He had called the director one week before, explaining that he was unable to leave New York city due to urgent Church business. He would most certainly ship the canvas, as he had promised, and he regretted that he could not be there to welcome it to Columbia. He looked forward to visiting the painting in its new home as soon as possible. It was the first time the priest had telephoned Horshak—all of his previous communication had been via email.

Once again the driver laid down the padded mat, opened the box and carefully extracted the picture. When it was unwrapped, the pair came forward to view it.

It was the canvas Father Humphries claimed to be *Madonna and Heir,* completed in the fall of 1890 in between the birth of Seurat's son and the painter's death the following spring. As Humphries had described, it depicted his mistress Madeleine Knobloch and their infant son. It was painted in the Pointillist style, with a muting of color that emphasized the tenderness of the scene. Madeleine was sitting in a rocking chair, against the familiar backdrop of Seurat's Paris apartment, a setting that had been rendered in previous works. She was holding the infant and regarding him with a loving expression that clashed with the coarseness implied by her size and general appearance. She wore a loosely fitting night shirt, which gave the impression that she was either just starting or had just finished the process of breast feeding.

"Take your time," said the driver. "Make sure that there's no damage of any sort."

"Goodness," said Pattinger. "This is quite amazing."

"I have to agree," said Horshak. "It's beyond what I was expecting." He looked at the delivery man. "You can bring me the paperwork, and I'll sign off and let you go."

"Would you like me to pack it up for you again?" he asked when the Director had autographed the forms.

"No thanks. We're going to take it directly inside."

As they walked down the hallway toward the vault, Horshak stopped and handed her the painting.

"Liz, come into my office for a minute. I want to look at something."

He sat down behind his desk and fiddled with the computer.

"Do me a favor and bring the picture over here, please."

Pattinger walked behind the desk and saw that her boss had pulled up a reproduction of *Jeune Femme se Poudrant* (*Young Woman Powdering Herself*), painted by Seurat between 1889 and 1890. It showed a buxom Madeleine Knobloch sitting at a cosmetic table, applying makeup with a powder puff and glancing into a mirror. Paittinger followed Horshak's eyes as he looked from the computer to the canvas and back again.

"Well? What do you think?"

"It looks like the same woman to me," she said. "And the same color pattern, more or less, except the mother and child canvas isn't quite as vibrant. But given the emotional effect I think he was angling for, it's quite understandable."

"I have to agree. But I also have to tell you that this situation gets more bizarre by the day."

"How so?"

"There are only two possibilities here, Liz: either this guy is a fraud, or we've won the lottery. And I swear, as I look at this painting, I don't have a clue which one it is."

"I know you're skeptical about this man, and I'm not expert, but I don't see how on earth this could be a forgery. I mean, look at it—it's magnificent."

"Yes, it is." Horshak kept alternating his gaze between the painting and the computer. "I have no idea what to think. I really don't. I go back and forth from moment to moment."

"I guess you'll have to let the real experts sort it out."

"Maybe not." He kept staring at the painting. "I have another strategy in mind."

"What's that?"

"Let me ponder it a while longer, and I'll tell you. But I have an idea on how we can get that new wing built."

★

A few days later, the buzzer sounded on Jeffrey Horshak's desk intercom.

"Yes?"

"Chuck Hawkins on the line for you, sir," said his secretary.

"Thank you."

Hawkins was a private investigator hired to look into the mystery of Father Gordon Humphries. After conducting his initial research, he had reported to Horshak that the Jesuits had no record of an ordained priest by that name. In fact, Humphries had no digital trail at all—he did have an email address, but there was no trace of him on the Internet, nor did he surface in any of the telephone databases. Until his recent call to Horshak, he officially did not exist.

"Morning, Chuck. How's my favorite super sleuth today?"

"Outstanding. How's my favorite penny-pinching client?"

"Give me a break. If I had deep pockets, I'd happily share the wealth with you."

"Just busting your chops."

"What's up?"

"I have some information for you. And you'll be pleased to

know that it didn't take a lot of time to round up, so it won't cost you more than a few hours' work."

"Tell me what you've got."

"The phone call from Humphries came from an apartment in Brooklyn, New York."

"Well, I'm not surprised. I knew he lived in the city, but I didn't know where."

"It wasn't his apartment. The lease is in the name of some guy named Lester Gordon."

"Hmm. What's the relationship between the two of them?"

"I don't have a clue. But I can tell you that the apartment was originally rented by Gordon's father about thirty years ago. It's rent controlled—you've probably never lived in New York, but that's an incredibly big deal up there. Once you have one, you don't let it go. It looks like Gordon inherited the lease from his father."

"Very strange."

"His dad was an army guy, retired as a master sergeant, so I assume they moved around a lot. He rented the apartment a few years before he left the service. And it wasn't his primary residence. The family apparently lived in Queens."

"Interesting. Why would he need an apartment in Brooklyn if he lived in Queens?"

"Good question."

"And you say you're not aware of the connection between Gordon and Humphries? Or who this guy Gordon is?"

"Not so far. I wanted to check in with you before I pursued

it. I don't think it'll be too time-consuming to track down, though."

"Go ahead, please. I'd look into the military angle. I know Humphries mentioned to me that his father was in the army. I believe he said he was a general officer when he retired."

"That's a possibility. I'll start by running the standard checks on Gordon."

"I'd be very curious to find out more about him. It might shed some light on Humphries."

"Done," said Hawkins. "But as I told you, be careful. Sometimes these investigations turn out to be like a dog chasing a truck. When the dog finally catches it, what does he do with it?"

CHAPTER 20

"You're back."

"Just out doing some shopping," said Cheryl Weissberg. "I thought I would stop in to say hello."

"You don't look a day older." Bennie grinned. "How's the headshrink business?"

"I'm just getting started, so it's slow going."

"Well, you picked a recession-proof industry. There'll never be a shortage of crazy people."

"This is true. They just have to find me."

"How did things work out with Louis Bétancourt? Did you ever get the painting?"

"Yes, I did—in record time, actually. It turned out it was almost done, so he just had to put some final touches on it. It's absolutely beautiful."

"Really?"

"Way beyond my expectations. The man is incredibly talented. You should feel confident recommending him."

"That's good to know. Was there anything I could help you with today?"

"I need a few more pieces, although I'll have to get them one at a time. Mr. Bétancourt's painting is magnificent, but I think

I'd like to change things up. I was thinking about something modern, maybe from the Cubist period. I don't think I can afford another commissioned piece just yet, though. Could you suggest something?"

"Right this way." Weissberg followed him to the stack of reproductions and watched as he pulled out three or four. "A lot of these are Picasso, and they're fairly recognizable: *Girl Before a Mirror, Three Musicians, Les Demoiselles d'Avignon*. That kind of thing."

"Maybe something a little less familiar."

"Here's one by Picasso that might work. It's called *Le Guitarist*."

The picture was a mass of geometric shapes. Weissberg studied it for a moment, trying in vain to isolate a human figure.

"I think you're on the right track, but the colors seem too muted. There's nothing but drab browns."

"Hang on one minute," said Benny. "I have something already framed that might work."

He disappeared into a back room and returned with a Cubist version of the Mona Lisa. One side of the woman's face was a burnished gold color; the other half was a composite of green and maroon circles, triangles and half-moons. The smile was unmistakable. Against the cobalt blue background, stars swirled in the manner of Van Gogh.

"That's perfect! I love it."

"Hopefully your patients have a sense of humor."

"Actually, I have one in particular who might really appreciate this. How much do I owe you?"

"Oh, I don't know. Can we do $90?"

"Sure. That's much cheaper than what I paid for Bétancourt's painting."

"Remember, it's a poster---the framing costs more than the art itself." He grinned. "There's a huge difference between an original and a copy."

*

Cheryl Weissberg was waiting for Lester Gordon in the reception area of her office.

"Good afternoon, Lester. How are you feeling today?"

"About the same, I guess."

"Please come on in."

He followed her into the consulting room and sat down on the sofa. When he looked up at Weissberg he noticed the painting on the wall above her head. His eyes glazed over, and when they came into focus his face displayed a mixture of arrogance and anger.

"*Sacre bleu!* What is this *merde* on your wall?"

"It's a Cubist rendering of Leonardo da Vinci's *Mona Lisa*. I bought it at a gallery—"

"I know very well what it is." He shook his head violently, scowling as if someone had given him a lemon wedge to suck on. "Where is the painting you commissioned from me?"

"I'm having it framed, Mr. Bétancourt. I told them to take

their time, since I want the best job possible. While I wait, I thought I would change the décor up a bit."

"This is disgraceful. Thank God my great-great-grandfather is not here to see this."

"Oh, it's not that bad." She glanced up at the painting, speaking as pleasantly as possible. "I think it takes a certain sense of humor to appreciate it."

"If this is what passes for humor today, we are truly at the end of civilization."

"Well, explain this to me. After all, you know much more about this than I do. As a painter, what do you find offensive about it?"

"The original Mona Lisa is a monumental canvas. It is a work of great subtlety and depth. This is a cartoon. It is a desecration of a great work of art."

"Obviously, then, you don't think art changes with the times?"

"Everything changes, my dear lady. But not everything changes for the better. Decades and centuries pass, tastes become coarsened. Sometimes it happens so gradually that we barely notice it. But this is where we end up. *Mon Dieu,* what a disgrace."

"Look at it this way. When your great-great-grandfather was painting, art was only for the rich. But today almost everyone can own a work of art—not necessarily an original, such as the one you painted for me, but at least a poster like this."

"As I said, not everything changes for the better." He glanced up again at the painting, scowling. "In my culture, this type of vile affront would not go unaddressed. The so-called artist who created that distasteful work would likely find himself challenged to a duel."

"A duel? You mean, with pistols?"

"That's precisely what I mean. It would be regarded as a matter of honor, to be resolved on the dueling range with the appropriate weaponry."

"Have you ever taken part in a duel, Mr. Bétancourt?"

"Thus far I have not found it necessary, but I assure you I would not shrink from defending both my honor and the reputation of great art. My father was an officer in the French Foreign Legion, and he took me to the firing range many times when I was a boy. As a result, I am a crack shot: I can knock the ear off a rabbit at fifty paces."

"That's good to hear. Unless you're a rabbit, of course."

"I can assure you that this is no laughing matter. My only regret is that such expedient remedies are no longer available."

"Anyway, you'll be pleased to know that everyone who has seen your painting loves it. I've been able to recommend you to a number of people, and hopefully you'll find that helpful."

"You're very kind." He blushed slightly, and red splotches appeared on his pale skin. "I owe you a great debt."

"Not at all. It's the least I can do for a neighborhood artist. I believe your studio is actually very close to here."

"Five or six blocks away, yes. I can walk it easily."

"Hopefully you have a large, comfortable space to work in."

"It's adequate. I'm actually renting the living room of a friend and using it as a studio."

"Really? It's unusual that someone would do that. He must really need the money."

"Not really, no." His right hand went reflexively to his lip to tweak the pencil-thin moustache he had neglected to wear today. "I would say that he's sympathetic to my goals and dreams."

"Is he a painter as well?"

"I wouldn't call him a painter, no, except in his own mind. Some things in life are very sad."

"How so?"

"Many people dream of being artists, of producing work that will live on after them and become their legacy. But not everyone can do this. Some are missing the talent, and others lack the drive."

"What's your friend's name? I might have seen him around the neighborhood."

"His name is Lester Gordon, but I doubt that you have met him. He spends most of his time in Manhattan, visiting the major museums." He laughed. "He seems to think that if he sits long enough in front of great canvases, some of that greatness will rub off."

"My parents used to take me to the museums when I was a child. I was lucky to have developed an appreciation for art early on."

"You seem to have very good taste." He glanced up at the

Mona Lisa. "With some exceptions, of course."

"Tell me a little more about your friend. Is he actively trying to become a painter?"

"He's been at it most of his life, but I'm afraid he doesn't really have the talent. On a basic level, he can copy fairly well. He used to do reproductions of Impressionist works and sell them on the Brooklyn pier, before they demolished it. Some of them were very good. But he's extremely dedicated—he truly believes that if he works and studies hard enough, he'll succeed in the end. If only that were the case."

"I would guess that family background matters as well. Obviously, you came from an environment where great art was respected, so I'm sure it's something that has to be reinforced from an early age."

"*Bien sur.*" He nodded. "Talent and appreciation must be nurtured. Look at your own case—you say your parents sparked an interest in art. I've always thought that was one of Lester's problems. His parents never encouraged him to be a painter, or much of anything else from what I understand. He describes them as aloof, neglectful."

"You're right. That's very sad."

"But enough of the vicissitudes of the soul." He waved the subject away with his hand. "Even though we sit here surrounded by the monstrosities of modern life, let us focus on something finer and grander."

"I agree completely." She rose and removed the Mona Lisa from the wall. "What I'm going to do, Mr. Bétancourt, is place this out of sight. That way we can converse without distractions."

"I am greatly in your debt, and I apologize for inconveniencing you."

"Not at all."

She walked out to the reception area and put the reproduction in the closet, next to Bétancourt's framed rendition of *Dawn at Dieppe*. When she returned, Gordon's eyes were glossy and he seemed to be in a dreamlike state. She sat down and waited patiently.

"What were we talking about?" He focused and looked around. "I seem to have lost track of time."

"Oh, we were just chatting about art. I gather you're still having trouble with your memory?"

"From time to time, sure. It seems to have gotten better, though. For a while it was a little scary."

"How so?"

"I used to lose entire days pretty frequently. Several times, I lost nearly a week."

"Tell me about it."

"One day I was getting ready to go to the Museum of Modern Art. I knew it was important to get there before the doors opened at 10:30 a.m. It was Sunday, and I knew that visitor traffic would be heaviest on that day."

"Go on."

"I woke up before the alarm, put on the *Today* show in the background, and started my morning routine. I was brushing my teeth when I heard the TV commentator announce that the weather for Wednesday was coming up right after the commercial break. I was upset: it was Sunday, so how could they say it was Wednesday? I thought it was a prank of some sort—you know how they're always joking with each other on that show. But then, Al Roker appeared on the screen and the date was displayed underneath. It was Wednesday."

"How did that make you feel?"

"I was really upset. I didn't understand. Where did Sunday, Monday and Tuesday go? And then I looked over at the nightstand, where I had left my sketchbook and other materials the night before. They were exactly where I had left them."

"I can see how that must have been upsetting. What happened next?"

"I went over to the closet to get dressed. I wanted to look neat and presentable, but not too formal. On the right side of the closet, I saw a black suit hanging next to my jackets. It was bright and shiny, and resembled a priest's habit. I had no idea what it was doing there. Was it another of Louis Bétancourt's strange costumes? I moved it to the other side of the closet, near all his other crap: his embroidered vests, his cape and his sashes. I decided to have a talk with him about it. I mean, it's one thing to share the living room with him, but my closet should be off limits."

"What happened then?"

"I'm sorry, I'm rambling on about this. I'll shut up."

"No, please go on. I think this is extremely valuable. I'm proud of you for sharing it with me."

"Well, I looked down and saw an overnight bag next to my shoes. It was a beat-up piece of junk, like something that would be worth about five bucks in a second-hand store. It was open. I felt badly about snooping around in it, but it was my closet, you know what I mean?"

"Yes, I do. What did you see when you looked inside?"

"There were some recent airline boarding passes, a shaving kit, and a map of Columbia, South Carolina. Maybe Louis had taken a trip, and he hadn't had the time to go home and stash his clothes and luggage. I guess that would explain it. But I still don't know how to explain the lost time."

"That sounds like a distressing situation."

"Well, you tell me: what does it mean?"

"You know, Lester, I do have an idea, but I'd like to think it over a little bit. Our time is almost up. If you let me process it until next week, I think I'll have an answer for you. And I'm pretty sure that answer will help you, if you accept it. Is that okay?"

"I guess so."

"Well, thank you for sharing that with me. I really appreciate it. We'll pick this up next week."

CHAPTER 21

To occupy his time while he waited for 2 p.m., Jeffrey Horshak flipped through the file on his desk. It had grown thicker in the past week as he received the reports from Hawkins. There was still no evidence of the connection between Humphries and Lester Gordon. Much as he wanted to take it further, the question of exactly who Humphries was, and what his motivations were, couldn't possibly be resolved within the confines of Horshak's budget.

At exactly two o'clock he dialed the number in Washington, and a secretary answered.

"My name is Jeffrey Horshak. I have an appointment to speak with Kent Blaisedale."

"Yes, he's expecting your call. I'll put you through."

Blaisedale was the head of the FBI's Art Crimes Unit. The Curator had overnighted all the information on the Signac and Seurat donations to him several days before.

"Mr. Horshak?"

"Thanks for speaking with me. I appreciate it."

"Happy to. It looks like you're the guy in charge down there at the Palmetto State Art Museum."

"That's correct."

"And you believe you have a case of forgery on your hands. Seems like an interesting case, too. Very few people would even bother to reproduce paintings of this type. It would be too much work."

"That's what I understand. And to be honest, I'm not 100% certain if they're forgeries. But the circumstances surrounding their acquisition were very suspicious."

"So let's see if I follow this. You received a visit from this Gordon Humphries, who was a Jesuit priest. He told you that he had inherited a large art collection from his parents and wanted to donate most of it to museums before he died."

"He was dressed as a priest and claimed to be one. But I now have proof that was a false identity."

"I see. And he just gave you these canvases—the Signac and the Seurat?"

"Correct."

"And no money changed hands? There was no consideration?"

"None at all. I took him to dinner, but that was about it."

"Well, that's very unusual."

"With all due respect, sir: I know that, or I wouldn't be calling you."

"I'm just trying to ascertain the facts. I gather that neither of these paintings appeared in the catalogs of the artists?"

"That's also true. With the Seurat, he said the work had been confiscated by the Nazis, and purchased after the war by his father, who was a military man stationed in Germany with NATO."

"And have you tried to have these paintings authenticated?"

"I got pre-authentication assessments on both of them. Palmetto State is a regional museum, and our funds are somewhat limited. The reports said that the Signac was probably real, while the Seurat was probably not."

"Have you displayed them in the museum?"

"We've hung the Signac, yes. We held off on the Seurat."

"And apparently there's a second Seurat?"

"Yes, we have it. He claimed the first one was a study for *Circus Sideshow*, while the second is an unknown major canvas titled *Madonna and Heir*. That one doesn't appear in the catalog of Seurat's work either."

"So, Mr. Horshak. How can I help you today?"

"I'm not sure I understand the question. Doesn't this sound like a case of forgery to you?"

"It does sound that way, yes. But I'm not sure I see the evidence to prove that, certainly not with the second painting. If Seurat never created a canvas called *Madonna and Heir,* we could certainly debate whether it's actually a forgery."

"Well, it's a confusing case. I grant you that. But shouldn't someone be prosecuting him? He's a con man."

"Not exactly, no. The problem you have is that he hasn't conned you out of anything."

"I've very surprised to hear you say that. After all, fraud is fraud."

"But my understanding is that you haven't been defrauded of anything. He never asked you for any money, correct?"

"No, but—"

"Frankly, Mr. Horshak, it sounds like his crime was making you look foolish. But that's not fraud. In order for there to be crime, there needs to be a victim. And I don't see a victim here."

"So you're okay with this guy traveling around, pretending to be a priest and giving away artwork that may be phony?"

"If no one gets hurt, the answer is yes. Say that someone gives me a signet ring with a huge emerald and tells me it used to belong to the Queen of Someplace or other. They tell me it's worth a fortune. It becomes a family heirloom, passed down through the generations. And then one day we have it appraised and discover it's a worthless piece of glass. The whole family is angry, of course, because their fantasies have been mocked. But who's to blame? The person who gave it to me, or me, for believing the story?"

"I don't think that's a useful analogy. These were artworks intended to deceive the public."

"But they haven't deceived the public, because you're telling me that you haven't even displayed the one with questionable provenance. Don't get me wrong, Horshak: it's a very strange case, possibly the strangest one I've ever heard. It sounds like you have a forger of unbelievable talent, and another person who gets a charge out of giving these intricate canvases away— unless, of course, they're the same person."

"I don't think so. Humphries told me he couldn't even draw."

"So the forger was obviously someone else. And that brings me back to my analogy of the emerald ring. The reasonable assumption here is that this man's parents purchased forgeries. Either he doesn't know, or he can't bring himself to admit it."

"I see your point."

"Normally, these guys are in it for the money. You have a few famous ones that make millions, but the typical profile is a failed art student who has enough proficiency to make a copy that will fool most people. He copies an Old Master, approaches the victim, says that he found it at a yard sale or secondhand store, and convinces the victim that it's worth millions. But he needs money right away—for a child's operation, or whatever. The mark coughs up five or ten grand, and then the forger disappears. But this case completely breaks the mold."

"So I gather you're not going to pursue it."

"Not as long as I have real criminals to chase, no. But I'd be very curious to know how it turns out. And if you hear that Humphries, or whoever he is, is making money from this elsewhere, please let me know. That changes the situation."

"Well, I appreciate your time, although I'm not thrilled with the results."

"And what about the second Seurat? You say you have it?"

"He shipped it to us, yes."

"Have you had that one authenticated?"

"Not yet. As I told you, we don't exactly have money to burn here in Columbia."

"What's your instinct about it?"

"It definitely looks like a Seurat. The materials are convincing, and the technique borders on genius. I don't know what to make of it."

"Well, what are the odds that there might be a major work of that type that none of the art historians ever heard about?"

"Not very good, I suppose."

"So let me ask you this: under the circumstances, why did you even accept it? You already had doubts about this man."

There was a long pause.

"Okay," said Horshak. "You've made your point: I accepted it on the off chance that it may turn out to be real."

*

"I don't know, Jeff." Elizabeth Pattinger was visibly disturbed. Her lips were pursed in disapproval, and the corners of her mouth were rigidly clamped together. "This sounds like a dangerous game."

"I wouldn't call it dangerous, to tell you the truth," said Horshak. His manner was casual and diffident. "I think we're totally within our rights."

"Father Humphries, or whoever he actually is, gave us that painting in good faith. It was a charitable act, not to mention that he wanted to donate it in memory of his parents. We can't just go ahead and sell it."

"Of course we can. It belongs to us now."

"Maybe you'd be legally justified in doing so, but there are some moral questions here. Humphries wanted the picture to hang in a place where the greatest number of people could see it. If we consign it to an auction house, it would probably be sold to a buyer for private use."

"So be it."

"What about his parents?"

"What about them? We already have the Signac hanging in memory of his parents. Say we go ahead and hang the first Seurat, with the qualifier mentioned in the pre-authentication letter. At that point Humphries is two for three. So he doesn't win the trifecta—most people don't."

"That's awfully callous of you," said Pattinger. "It just doesn't sound like the man I've known for years."

"You won't know me much longer if we don't get that new wing built, because I'll be looking for a job. The Board has made that pretty clear."

"All right, let's look at this from another direction." She took a deep breath. "Hear me out, please."

"I'm listening."

"You have no idea if that painting is real or not. You never had it authenticated."

"Correct. I never had it authenticated precisely because I didn't want to know if it was real or not. Even if I had gotten a pre-authentication on it and they raised some doubts, we wouldn't have been able to sell it."

"So you had this in mind from the time it arrived."

"More or less. Look, Liz, this guy took us on a magic sleigh ride. Forget about the fact that he made us look like jackasses.

We care about this stuff on many levels. When we received those paintings and started looking into them, our emotions went back and forth like a ping pong ball at a Chinese tournament. I seriously doubt that he didn't do it on purpose."

"I really can't believe that. I'm sure his parents purchased forgeries, and he just couldn't face it."

"Whatever. I propose that we make the best of a confusing situation."

"Do you think the second Seurat is real?"

"Here we go again. Yes, it sure looks real. But as the pre-authentication on the first one points out, there were 240 works in the catalog for decades before the Nazis came to power. The Nazis may have confiscated a bunch of art, but they didn't create any additional paintings. Somebody possibly duped his father, or whoever bought it, and then he duped us."

"And now you want to dupe someone else."

"Not exactly, no."

"What's your plan?"

"I'd like to consign it to one of the New York auction houses, warts and all. We tell them the truth: it looks real to us but we don't know, because we haven't had it checked out. They'll have it authenticated for sure. The best-case scenario is that it passes muster, and we win the lottery. But even if they decide it's a fake, they'd probably sell it anyway. Somebody up there will be crazy enough to pay hundreds of thousands for it, maybe more."

"It sounds awfully sleazy to me, Jeff."

"I'd call it turning lemons into lemonade."

"Who are you thinking about? One of the big houses like Sotheby's or Christies?"

"No, a smaller operation would be better for something like this. I was considering Bonham's, but then I found this place." He handed her a glossy magazine, open to a full-page ad. "This outfit is called the Cantwell Gallery. They've been around for a while, but they've really picked up steam in the past five years. They'll be hungrier and more aggressive, more likely to take chances."

"What are you going to tell Father Humphries?"

"Liz, please: *There is no Father Humphries.*"

CHAPTER 22

Carl Renfro, Professor Emeritus of Art History at Columbia University, opened the door to his office. He looked like a professor from Central Casting: a large man with a shaggy grey beard, bow tie and wire-rimmed spectacles.

"Dr. Weissberg? A pleasure to meet you."

"Thank you for seeing me."

"Well, anything for an alumnus. Please, sit." He motioned her to a chair. "How can I help you today?"

"I have certain aspects of a case that I need to discuss with you. I'll fill you in as completely as possible, but I'm sure you realize that I need to maintain confidentiality."

"Of course."

"And I'll tell you right off the bat, Dr. Renfro, that I'm out of my depth here. My parents took me to museums when I was a child, but I'm afraid that's where my lessons in art appreciation stopped."

"It sounds like you had wonderful parents. And to be honest, you're not very different from the majority of the population."

"Probably not." She hesitated. "I'm treating a patient who I suspect may have Dissociative Identity Disorder, or what most of the public would call multiple personality."

"I see."

"He seems to be focused on one particular period of art history—the Impressionist movement."

"Well, I don't blame him."

"If my preliminary diagnosis is correct, he has at least three or four fully functioning alternative identities. I'm still sorting them out. But it appears that one of the identities, or alters as we call it, may be an art forger."

"Aha!" said Renfro. "This is getting interesting."

"As I say, I'm still struggling to understand the broad outlines of this case. But I wanted to talk to you about the type of personality who may be an art forger. I know that you're an authority in your field, and I came to you specifically because of your work on Beltracchi."

"Yes, Wolfgang Beltracchi." He nodded. "Probably the most notorious forger of our time. There have been many others throughout history, of course, some of them even more successful, but he was the best in the modern era."

Along with many other subscribers, Weissberg had read the profile of Beltracchi in *Vanity Fair*. A flashy ex-hippie and self-taught painter, Beltracchi had captivated the art world with his personal charisma and luxurious lifestyle. In 2004, Steve Martin paid $860,000 for one of his forgeries, a fake Heinrich Campendonk; two years later, a French magazine publisher purchased a phony Max Ernst for over $7 million. Beltracchi sold canvases through Sotheby's and Christies, and one of his paintings had been hung in a Max Ernst retrospective at New York's Metropolitan Museum of Art.

"Here's what I think I understand." She paused, visibly searching for the words. "If I have the correct diagnosis, one of the alters is a forger of incredible talent—we're talking about someone who can actually reproduce Impressionist masters so faithfully that experts can't tell the difference. And we seem to have another alter who goes around the country, literally giving those canvases away."

"Hmm. Which Impressionists are we talking about?"

"Specifically, Seurat."

"Well, that would be virtually impossible." Renfro shook his head. "I can't see why anyone would want to attempt to reproduce a work as difficult as that. And even if they wanted to, how could they do it? The technique would be extremely hard to replicate. It would take years to do a single canvas, and on top of that you have the challenge of finding authentic materials."

"As I said, I'm no expert. But it seems that this might have happened."

"I can't see how. And I believe you said that the person was giving these works away? Not selling them?"

"So it appears."

"That would also be highly unusual." He stroked his beard. "You mentioned Beltracchi. He was in it for profit, which of course is the most common scenario. The other situation we see most frequently is the failed art student, someone with a chip on their shoulder. This type of person typically feels that the art establishment is to blame for not recognizing their talent."

"I've heard that theory, yes."

"But you say that someone is creating these enormously complicated works and giving them away?"

"That's what I think."

"Why would they do that?"

"If my suspicions are correct, they'd do it for a number of reasons. Part of it may be what you describe: that they want to prove exactly how talented they are and rub it in the noses of the establishment that rejected them. There's also another factor with patients suffering from DID, or multiple personality. These are usually people who endured significant childhood trauma of some sort. If such a person were to give away a masterpiece in honor of their parents, they would be maintaining a connection with the abuser."

"Well, Dr. Weissberg, I'm out of my depth here as well. I can't honestly say that I follow your reasoning."

"Are you saying that such behavior would be totally out of character for a master forger?"

"Not totally, I suppose."

"Then if my suppositions are correct, what could their motivations possibly be?"

"I'm not sure." Renfro looked out the window, gathering his thoughts. "At this stage of my life, I look upon art forgery in a very different context than I did when I was younger."

"How so?"

"When I was a young man, it seemed open and shut. As I

told you—they were failed art students, or they were doing it for the money. But now I'm starting to perceive things differently."

"Go on."

"Take someone like yourself. You say you don't know much about art. Yet your parents took you to museums as a child, so you acquired a rudimentary grasp of what was supposed to be good. And say that tomorrow you visit a museum again, and you see a famous work by an Old Master or an Impressionist or whoever. You stand in front of it and you have an emotional reaction to it. It moves you in some way. At that moment, does it actually matter if the painting is real or a forgery? What is precisely the difference? Say it's a forgery. If it were real, would your emotional reaction to it be any more intense?"

"Wow."

"Wow indeed. You would not have heard this from me when I was younger. But after a very long time investigating these things, you stumble on a painful truth: that it may not ultimately matter if an art object is real or not. What primarily matters is how it affects people."

"I see your point."

"And these are very complicated issues, Dr. Weissberg. The cynics would have you believe that nearly 40% of the fine art sold each year is fake. But very often throughout history, when a painting achieved great critical or commercial success, dozens or even hundreds of copies flooded the market. In many cases, the painters did duplicate copies of their original canvas. So if you buy a copy executed by the artist himself, is that a forgery?"

"I have no idea."

"Well, neither do many experts."

"So let me ask you this. Let's go back to the theory that the forger is a failed art student. Assume for a moment that he was obsessed with the Impressionists, and he entered art school with the goal of painting in the style of the 19th century French Impressionist masters. How would such a person be received?"

"That's easy. He would be ridiculed, of course."

"Why?"

"Because time marches on, Dr. Weissberg. Are you old enough to remember Nehru jackets?"

"I've seen pictures of them online."

"Good enough." Renfro chuckled. "In the 1970s I owned a number of them. They were very fashionable. Can you imagine what would happen if I started wearing them around campus today? I wouldn't just be ridiculed. I'd probably be accused of suffering from dementia and would be confined to an old age home."

"But even I know that great Impressionist canvases aren't Nehru jackets. Certainly you and others like you are also aware of that."

"Yes, yes." He stroked his beard again. "How can I best explain this to you? Everything is cyclical. In the late 19th century we reach a point where art is calcified, restricted, where it can only mean one thing. And then the Impressionists come along. They take their paints and canvases outside and create a revolution. People are aghast, they think the world is coming to an end. And the Impressionists triumph, they create a different way of looking at the world. But fast forward one century later. That way of viewing things is no longer revolutionary. It is quaint, old-fashioned, archaic. Say you're twenty years old, and you pay a courtesy call on your maiden aunt. She offers you a painting, says it's valuable, she wants you to have it. You look at it and it seems seriously outdated, but you accept it to preserve her feelings. One year later you sell it for $10 at a garage sale. Someone buys it, and it turns out to be a Renoir worth millions. Who's right? Who's wrong? As I sit here today, I'm not sure I could tell you."

"So this type of student would be under considerable pressure to conform, in art school?"

"Certainly. He would be going against the grain of what the entire art world believed. He would probably be regarded in the same light as the way the Impressionists looked at the Old Masters back in the 19th century. Everyone would be telling him to get with the program, to create art that was viewed as compatible with the times. If such a student were extremely talented, he would be in an untenable position. Internally, he would probably think he was a genius, while all the people around him would describe him as someone with no original talent."

"That sounds like a very painful and traumatic position to be in."

"I think it would be awful. If you're Edouard Manet in 1863 and the Salon rejects your painting, maybe it seems initially like the end of the world. But think of it this way: Manet isn't competing with radio, TV or movies. There's no Internet, or technology of any kind. Sooner or later he knows he will have an audience, if only by default. Your art student isn't in the same spot, unfortunately."

"He's competing with reality TV."

"Exactly." He reached back into a bookcase, pulled out a volume and leafed through it. "Here you are: Van Gogh's *Sunflowers.*"

"I believe I've seen it."

"There were many different versions. This one was sold to a Japanese businessman in 1987 for $40 million. What would it be worth today? Half a billion? A billion?"

"Something like that, I imagine."

"And we're talking about a man who was seriously disturbed—not the Japanese businessman, of course, although you might question his sanity as well. Van Gogh had hallucinations, he was institutionalized. If he came to you, you would likely commit him. He ended up killing himself."

Cheryl Weissberg flashed back to dozens of patients who passed through Bellevue during her year there. Many had presented with symptoms that were probably not dissimilar to those of Vincent Van Gogh. A number of them were undoubtedly dead.

"I have one more question, if you don't mind. Can you tell me a little bit about Pointillism? I'd like to understand the technique involved."

"Well, let's see if I can explain this without getting too technical. Please stop me if I get carried away. Basically, as you probably know, you have a painter who uses fields of dots to convey shapes: people, animals, trees, clouds, whatever. These dots seem chaotic and meaningless when you examine the canvas up close, but as you walk away the dots start to come together to form the desired images."

"That's the way I've heard it described."

"And that's what the average person understands, but it's really far more complicated than that. Traditional artists mix pigments on their palettes to achieve a wide range of hues. With Pointillism, the emphasis is on basic colors: blue, red, yellow and black. When dots of these colors are arranged in various patterns, they create contrasts. That's what Seurat was all about. He was deeply involved in color theory. Strangely enough, the idea is similar to the process used by some modern color printers."

"So the Pointillists didn't mix their colors?"

"Sometimes they did, and here's where it gets complicated. If you blend blue, red and yellow, you get a luminous effect that is strangely similar to white light. In the Pointillist paintings, this is accentuated by some of the white canvas showing through the dots."

"That's probably too much information for me. Tell me about the dots. How did they apply them?"

"As I mentioned, it was a very painstaking process. Seurat used something called a Kolinsky sable hair brush. Are you familiar with sable?"

"I've heard of the furs, but that's about it."

"It's similar to a weasel. The Kolinsky is a rare species found in Siberia, so the brushes are hard to find and also very expensive. They say the best ones come from male hair." He threw his head back and laughed. "I guess we males are just exceptionally bristly by nature."

She smiled. "From my experience, that sounds about right."

"Seurat's technique, in particular, was very time-consuming. He would typically apply a few dots, stop and wipe off the brush, then add a few more. Given that the man died at 31 and turned out a large body of work in a short time, he must have been working 24 hours each day."

"Could someone get those brushes today?"

"It would be very difficult. The Kolinsky is now regarded as an endangered species, so shipments have been halted by the U.S. government."

"I see."

"So, Doctor." His expression was genial, almost paternal. "Any other questions? I don't know if I've helped you. I hope I have."

"I think that's about all I can absorb." She stood up. "At the very least, you've given me a lot to think about."

"Good." Renfro smiled. "That's what professors are supposed to do."

CHAPTER 23

Columbia was a small airport, and Jeffrey Horshak was able to park at the curb while he waited for his guests. After a few minutes the two men emerged from the terminal. One was tall and patrician, wearing an elegant blue blazer and white linen slacks—presumably Philip Cantwell. The other man was shorter, bulkier and frumpy in appearance, clad in a tweed sports jacket and jeans. He rose from the car to greet them.

"Mr. Horshak?" The tall man extended his hand. "I'm Phillip Cantwell. This is my friend, Edward Kovacs."

"A pleasure to meet you. Welcome to South Carolina."

He stashed their carry-on bags in the trunk. Cantwell slid into the front passenger seat, with Kovacs in the rear.

"Thank you for coming. I know Columbia isn't an easy place to get to."

"Oh, it was no bother," said Cantwell. "We did have to change planes in Atlanta. But then again, it's not every day that we're contacted about an undiscovered Seurat."

"Would you like to go to your hotel and freshen up?"

"No, I believe we'd like to take a look at the canvas first." He turned to look at Kovacs. "Does that sound good, Eddie?"

"Sure."

"You work for ArtSleuth, Mr. Kovacs?" asked Horshak.

"That's right. Have you dealt with us before?"

"No, I just know the outfit by reputation. I know you're one of the leading authenticators in New York. I've used Truth in Art a few times. They're located in Atlanta."

"I've heard of them. They're supposed to be one of the best regional firms."

"You would be regional as well, wouldn't you?"

"What do you mean?"

Horshak looked at Kovacs in the rear-view mirror. "The Northeast is a region of the country. Just as the South is."

"I suppose you're right. No offense meant. Truth in Art is supposed to be very good."

"None taken."

"As you know," said Kovacs, "it's getting harder and harder to find anyone at all to do authentications. Most of the major committees have been disbanded, because of fear of litigation."

"That's what 've heard. I imagine you have to be very careful."

"We try to be as thorough as we can."

"Well, gentlemen, we have a few minutes' drive to the museum, so I'll lay the situation out for you and answer any preliminary questions you might have. I'm going to be flat-out honest with you, because I have no desire to hide anything."

"We appreciate that," said Cantwell.

"About six months ago, we received a visit from a Jesuit priest. He said his late parents were major art collectors, and he wanted to give away the most important canvases before he died. He donated a watercolor by Signac that he said was a study for one of the larger seascapes."

"Very generous of him," said Cantwell.

"So it seemed. But the painting didn't appear in the catalog of Signac's work, so I had Truth in Art do a pre-authentication assessment. They said it appeared to be real, so we went ahead and hung it on their advice."

"They didn't do any spectroscopy?" asked Kovacs.

"No. To be frank, we don't have money to throw around down here. They said it seemed okay, so we took them at their word. The priest then told me that he was in possession of two paintings by Seurat. One was a study for *Circus Sideshow,* the other was a major canvas. Both of them didn't appear in the catalogs either. He said his father, a retired general, had been stationed in Germany after World War II, and that was where the paintings were purchased. The priest suspected they had been confiscated by the Nazis and sold later on the black market."

"Hmm," murmured Cantwell. "Have you had them looked at?"

"The smaller one, yes. They said it seemed authentic except for the brushwork—it was a little bit too broad for Seurat. But they were troubled by the lack of provenance, as well as the fact that the canvas was unknown. The second one arrived recently, and we haven't done anything with it."

"Not even a pre-authentication assessment?"

"No. that's where you guys come in. If you're interested, you can have it checked out."

"Very intriguing," said Cantwell. "I look forward to seeing it. What do you think, Eddie?"

"You have to admit it's a bizarre story. Then again, I can't imagine anyone in their right mind trying to forge a Seurat."

Horshak pulled his car into the museum garage and led the two men toward the vault, where they were greeted by Elizabeth Pattinger.

"Thank you so much for coming."

"Do you have both of the Seurats here?"

"Yes, they're side by side. Please follow me."

She uncovered the two canvases. Horshak and Pattinger watched their guests carefully and saw that their eyes were immediately drawn to the larger painting. Cantwell let out a soft whistle. The two men studied the painting in silence.

"I'll be damned," said Kovacs finally.

"What do you think?" asked Horshak.

"It looks like a Seurat to me," said the authenticator. "The technique is correct, the colors are correct, and the paint itself looks right. The woman is definitely Madeleine Knobloch. I'm not too sure about the smaller one, but this is incredible."

"He says the title is *Madonna and Heir*," said the Director. "It apparently dates to late 1890, between the birth of Seurat's son and the painter's death the following spring."

Kovacs tore his eyes away from the canvas. "I have to ask you: Why would you want to sell it?"

"Financial reasons, pure and simple. We'd love it keep it, whether it's real or not. But we've been trying to add an additional wing to the museum for at least five years. We just don't have the donor pool here that you have in New York, and we don't see any other way to raise the money."

"And this priest has no documentation at all?" asked Cantwell. "No bill of sale, no trace of the chain of custody?"

"None."

"And I assume there's no gallery sticker on the back."

"Correct."

"What do you think, Eddie?"

"It's definitely worth checking out. We'd have to run the entire battery of spectrographic tests."

"As long as you pay for it," said Horshak.

"Phil?" Kovacs looked at Cantwell.

"Certainly. Let's go ahead."

"Okay," said Kovacs, "the way this works is that you pay for the shipping, and we handle the authentication."

"Sounds good to me. Do you have any recommendations?"

"I'll put you in touch with a shipping company." He extended his hand. "A pleasure to meet you, Mr. Horshak. I'll admit that I thought this would be a wild goose chase, but I'm glad I came. It will be a fascinating experience either way."

*

"Thanks for calling back," said Cheryl Weissberg. "I appreciate it."

"No worries. I assume this has to do with the DID patient, Lester Gordon. What's up?"

"Something really unusual came out in a session the other day. Lester said he was familiar with one of the alters—the forger, Louis Bétancourt."

"Hmm. That's very unusual."

"I thought so. My understanding, at least as I've received it from you, is that the actual person is supposed to be unaware of the alters. The alters usually know each other, but the original personality is generally oblivious to them."

"This is true."

"But Lester started talking about the forger. He told me that he was renting the living room of his apartment to him as a studio. He more or less presented him as a friend, a person that he admired. He described him as a painter of great talent— talent that he, himself, didn't have. He didn't refer to him as a forger, and I'm not sure he perceives him that way. I asked him if Bétancourt's presence in his living room made it difficult for Lester to get on with his own work, and he said he didn't care. It was worth it to him to be nurturing Bétancourt."

"Did he give you any detail of the forger's life and activities?"

"Not really, but we got into a discussion about the blocks of time that he was losing. He said that he had gone into the closet and seen a black suit hanging in the closet, a priest's outfit. This didn't relate to Bétancourt, of course, but to Father Humphries. But he did make a point of saying that he assumed that priest's outfit might be another one of Bétancourt's costumes. Then he said he looked down at the floor and saw a bag filled with souvenirs of the priest's trip to South Carolina. I didn't press it, but I thought it was significant."

"It certainly is. It reinforces what you've told me up to this point: that the patient is very close to these alters, and that their identities are just beneath the surface."

"That was my impression," said Weissberg.

"I think it's all consistent with all the background you've given me. The fact that the onset of DID in this patient occurred in middle age indicates to me that this is a mild case: if not mild, at least easily curable. When I say easily, I mean it might take six or twelve months rather than six or twelve years. You've described the childhood trauma as significant to the patient but not necessarily severe. If we're on the right track, the challenge of integrating the alters into one personality could be easily achieved."

"Do you have any thoughts on integration?"

"Well, you tell me. He's your patient."

"I'm tempted to bring out all the alters at once. Based on what you're saying, I think it might work. Somehow I induce Baby Les, in an environment where I have both the Cubist Mona Lisa and the fake Signac hanging on the wall. Then I could let them slug it out."

"That sounds like the nuclear option to me, way too risky. The patient could freak out."

"Possibly, but I can't say that I see it happening."

"On top of that, you're not likely to get something new and different from Baby Les, at least not something you can use. I believe you told me the dead therapist's session notes revealed that Baby Les had witnessed the babysitter having sex, perhaps even having sex with the father."

"True."

"So there's limited value in having him admit it again. Plus, the Baby Les alter is at an age where he hasn't processed the experience. He might perceive it as trauma, but it doesn't connect in his mind with any resentment of his parents. That would only come with hindsight."

"I'm not sure that he resents his parents. I think he only blames them for the neglect."

Brillstein laughed. "Everyone resents their parents for something, whether real or imagined."

"Well, any suggestions?"

"Have you revealed the diagnosis to him yet?"

"No."

"I'd start with that and see how he reacts. Whether he accepts it or fights against it will be instructive in predicting his future behavior. Have you been recording the sessions?"

"From the beginning, yes."

"Playing some of the tapes for him would be a good place to begin. Based on what you've told me, I don't get the sense that he would resist the diagnosis, particularly if he heard his own voice assuming the alters. This could be much easier than you think."

"That would be nice."

"On the other hand, even if he resists, you're not looking

at a long slog. There are only three alters, and the onset was in middle age with the recollection of mild childhood trauma. You're in very good shape here."

"Thank you."

"So I'd give yourself some leeway—provided, once again, that Lester hasn't displayed any violent or dangerous tendencies."

"Not to me, no. But remember that he presented at Bellevue after being arrested for trying to slice up a valuable painting. If the guards hadn't tackled him, he might have done it. He denies it now, but that's what apparently happened. I've read the reports. What I don't know is how much repressed rage he harbors against his parents, rage that might be simmering just below the surface."

"Do any of the alters seem violent?"

"Not at all. Bétancourt is quite theatrical at times, but that's totally in line with his adopted persona of being an emotional French painter."

"You have to trust your instincts, obviously, but it seems that there isn't much to worry about in the way of overt threat. I think you're correct that the key to his feelings in this area is Baby Les, but you'll probably never find out how much rage is really lurking there."

"Sounds like good advice. My general impression of Lester is if that rage exists, it's been turned inward, resulting in his general feelings of impotence as a human being."

"Well, proceed cautiously. Remember that inward rage can always be turned outward."

CHAPTER 24

It was a bright April day in Manhattan: sunny, crisp and cool. The air was so refreshing that Phillip Cantwell decided to walk over to the West Side offices of ArtSleuth, rather than taking a cab. He emerged from the elevator to find a receptionist smiling at him.

"Good morning, Mr. Cantwell. Mr. Kovacs is expecting you. Please go right in."

He walked down the hallway to Kovacs' office. The authenticator's short, stocky body reclined in a swivel chair, and his feet were propped up on his desk. *Madonna and Heir* hung on the opposite wall. Cantwell sat down in a leather armchair and stared at the painting.

"Well?" he asked. "I assume you have some news for me, although your phone message was somewhat cryptic."

"This is the strangest thing I've ever seen."

"Don't keep me in suspense."

"Everything about this painting checks out. The canvas is right for the period, the pigments are accurate and properly faded. The technique is Seurat, pure and classic. I don't know what the hell to tell you."

"You've put it through all the spectroscopic tests?"

"Yep," said Kovacs. "We did a few of them more than once. This thing passes with flying colors."

"I'll be damned. So what's your conflict here? Why don't you know what to tell me?"

"Because it's a fake." Kovacs sat upright and leaned forward in his chair. "I *know* it's a fake, but I just can't prove it. I feel it in my gut."

"Are you going to authenticate it?"

"I'd rather not be in this position, to tell you the truth. It's a trap. On the basis of the evidence, I can't refuse to authenticate this. But down the road, if it turns out to be a forgery, I'll be screwed. There'll be a torrent of press, people will laugh at us, our reputation will be ruined. And that's the least of it. Just wait until the lawsuits start."

"Aren't you being a bit melodramatic?"

"Not at all. I advise you to stop and think carefully about the implications here. Say you decide to go ahead and put this up for auction. You'll get a lot of coverage, if that's your goal. But your potential liability is greater than ours. Remember what happened with Knoedler."

Knoedler had been the city's oldest art dealership, established in 1846. It closed in 2011 in the midst of a scandal over allegations it had sold dozens of forged paintings. The trial in the winter of 2015 became a focal point of attention for both tabloids and serious art journals alike. Most of the press coverage chortled over the fact that the Chairman of Sotheby's had paid over $8 million for a fake canvas by Mark Rothko, which turned out to have been painted by an immigrant Chinese artist in Queens.

"Eddie, that business went on for decades. It was intentional and prolonged fraud. This is different. If the picture is a forgery, it's apparently so good that no one on earth can tell."

"So that's okay, in your view?"

"In my view, the painting's probably real. There's nothing that tells us otherwise. The machines say it's real. If it makes you feel better, I'll get a half-dozen academic experts to say it's real." He smiled. "And yes, the publicity over this will be overwhelming. It's a great story. Something like this could put us on the map."

"Or it could destroy you."

"Eddie, Eddie." Cantwell exhaled patiently. "Think about all the stranger things that have happened. Think about the paintings that were believed to be fakes and turned out to be real. Think about the priceless canvases that were painted over and uncovered centuries later. The people who bought paintings at a yard sale for a few bucks, and they turned out to be worth millions. Remember that family out on Long Island, who discovered a fortune in art stacked up in their garage?"

"Seems to me you're taking a big chance."

"Life isn't without risk." Cantwell glanced over at the painting. "How come you have it hanging on your wall, rather than in a temperature-controlled vault?"

"Because I've been looking at it for the past week. It's all I've thought about."

"Sounds like you're getting obsessed."

"Without a doubt." Kovacs walked over to the canvas and examined it at close range. "This is beautiful. It's absolutely remarkable."

"I completely agree."

"But I don't believe that bullshit story about how it was confiscated by the Nazis. Seurat died in 1891. The catalog of his work was well known for forty or fifty years before Hitler starting stealing artwork."

"So what's your theory?"

"I have a bunch of theories." Kovacs sat down on the edge of the desk and looked at Cantwell. "The most plausible explanation is that this was done by an expert forger sometime after World War II. When it was pawned off on the priest's father, it came with the Nazi story—the forger used it as an excuse for his lack of documentation. The father passed the painting along to his son, who believes it to be real."

"I suppose that's possible. But there was a second Seurat, a study. If you recall, it was stored right next to this one."

"That's right, a study for *Circus Sideshow.* We didn't look at it closely, because we were too distracted by *Madonna and Heir.* But he mentioned there had been some problem with the brushwork."

"Yes, I remember that."

"So last week I reached out to Horshak and asked him to send me the pre-authentication report on the first Seurat. It basically said that the dots were too broad to be Seurat. It all adds up."

"How so?"

"Here's what I think: both pictures were done by the same person. As you know, Seurat used Kolinsky sable brushes. For the first painting, the study, the forger decided to start small. He got everything else right—canvas, paint, technique—but didn't have the right brushes, so the dots looked too large and coarse. Sometime between finishing the study and starting on the larger canvas, he got his hands on a set of Kolinsky sables. That's why the dots in the second piece look more precise, and totally correct."

"I suppose that's possible."

"Let me ask you this: if the priest actually believes the painting is real, why give it away? It's worth at least ten million, maybe double that. You'd know the exact figure better than I would."

"God, you're cynical. Maybe he's a true priest. Maybe he took a vow of poverty."

"It still doesn't make any sense. Why doesn't he sell it himself? He could donate the money to the Church and give every nun in the world a lifetime supply of rulers to rap kids' knuckles with."

"I have no idea." Cantwell stood up and put his hand on Kovacs' shoulder. "But here's what I think. You're going to authenticate the painting, and we're going to put it up for sale. Mr. Horshak is going to build the new wing for his museum, and the Cantwell Gallery is going to become world-famous."

CHAPTER 25

"Please come in, Lester. Make yourself comfortable."

"Thank you."

He settled down on the sofa across from Cheryl Weissberg.

"How are you getting along? How was your week?"

"Fine, I guess."

"No problems? Any further incidents of lost time?"

"Actually, no."

"Good. Well, what I'd like to do today is share some of my observations about your treatment with you. Is that okay?"

"Sure."

"I realize you've had a lot of therapy, and you've also been in and out of different facilities several times. And along with that, usually, comes a diagnosis. But when I read your history, I was struck by the fact that there were many different diagnoses. They were never the same."

"What do you mean?"

"You were diagnosed with schizophrenia early on in your life." Weissberg flipped through a thick file on her lap. "And since then, different clinicians have felt that you were bipolar, that you suffered from borderline personality disorder, or that you were a victim of PTSD, or posttraumatic stress disorder. No one has ever seemed to agree on what's bothering you."

"I guess that's true."

"How do you feel about that?"

"I don't think it matters. It's not important what anybody says is wrong with me. The only important thing is whether someone can make me feel better, and no one has ever been able to do that."

She nodded. "That's a very important point, and of course you're correct. I guess it wouldn't surprise you if I told you that I had a different theory on what was bothering you."

"Not at all. The only thing that would surprise me is whether you could actually do something about it."

"I think I can. For the record, I believe you're suffering from Dissociative Identity Disorder, or what used to be called multiple personality disorder."

"I don't understand."

"You have a number of different identities that your subconscious mind has created. These personalities come out when they are triggered by something specific, or when they are stimulated by certain types of stress. There appear to be three of them, and two of them are fully functioning identities in their own right."

"I still don't get it. You're saying that I pretend to be someone else?"

"You're not pretending. When you switch into a different identity, you actually become that person. You take on a different but totally consistent pattern of speech, behavior and thought."

"No offense, but this sounds like bullshit. How come I don't remember it?"

"That's the entire point, Lester. You're not doing it consciously or intentionally. That's the reason you don't remember it. Something happens that triggers your subconscious mind, and one of the personalities comes out."

"Can you give me an example?"

"That's what I'd like to do today. Do you remember when we were talking last week about the way you lost track of time? That you frequently lose whole days, and sometimes you can't remember where you were for almost a week?"

"Of course, yes."

"And you told me that at one point, you went to your closet and saw the priest's outfit hanging there. You had no idea how or why it got there, but you assumed it was one of Louis Bétancourt's disguises, so you moved it over to his side of the closet. And then you looked down and you saw the travel bag with the maps and souvenirs from South Carolina."

"Yes, I remember telling you that."

"Well, the priest's outfit belongs to one of your alternate identities, a Jesuit priest named Gordon Humphries. He made several trips to Columbia, South Carolina, and I'm sure the dates of those trips would line up precisely with the time you've lost."

"That doesn't make any sense. Why would I take on the

identity of a priest? I'm not even a Catholic."

"I have no idea, but I don't think it matters very much."

"What was this priest doing in South Carolina?"

"He went there to donate some paintings to the Palmetto State Art Museum in honor of his parents." She stared at Lester. "Impressionist works. One watercolor by Signac and two paintings by Seurat."

"Wow. That's quite a donation. And you say I was pretending to be this priest?"

"Again, you weren't pretending. It was a separate personality, an identity constructed by your subconscious without your knowledge."

"I'm sorry, but this really sounds far-fetched."

"I imagine so." She took the digital voice recorder from her purse. "I'd like to play something for you. It's an excerpt from one of our sessions. Is that all right?"

"Sure."

"Here's what happened immediately before this: you walked in here for the first time, sat down on the sofa, and looked at the painting above my head—the one I told you I'm having framed. Your eyes glazed over, and you switched into the identity of Father Gordon Humphries. Take a listen."

She switched on the recorder.

"Are you familiar with the painting in question?"

"Not really."

"It's a copy of a watercolor by Paul Signac, the famous neo-Impressionist painter. I'm sure you know his work."

"I've heard of him, but that's about it."

"He was one of the founders of the Pointillist style, along with Seurat. This particular canvas was titled Dawn at Dieppe. I believe it was a study for one of his larger seascapes. In any case, I know this work intimately because I used to own the original."

"Really? What an amazing coincidence."

"Indeed it is. So I can assure you that I've spent many happy hours looking at this canvas in the past."

"And where is the painting now?"

"It's hanging in the Palmetto State Art Museum in South Carolina. I donated it to them about six months ago."

"That was extremely generous of you."

"Perhaps so. You see, my parents were formidable art collectors. My father was in the army and retired as a two-star general. As a result of his position he traveled widely, both professionally and for leisure. He had the opportunity to purchase a great deal of art back when prices were far lower than they are today. It was really a question of being in the right places at the right times."

"I see."

"Unfortunately I have a heart condition, and my health has been deteriorating in recent years. This state of affairs forced me to consider what might become of my parents' art collection after I'm gone. I wanted to make sure that the pieces were displayed in venues where they could be appreciated by the greatest number of people."

"I understand. That's very thoughtful."

"I chose Palmetto State precisely because it was a small

regional museum, and my gifts would have greater impact than they would at a larger institution. Had I donated them to the Museum of Modern Art here in the city, for example, they would have rested in some warehouse away from view, only to be brought out every few years as part of a special exhibition. My only condition was that the paintings be identified as having been donated in memory of my parents."

"That's a very touching memorial."

"It was the least I could do, really. I owe a great deal to my parents. My father was a bit taciturn, of course, as you might expect from his choice of profession. But I know he loved me, even though he might not always have been able to show it. My mother, on the other hand, doted on me throughout my childhood. It was very difficult to lose them. Since you're a therapist, I can tell you that I'm still doing my best to deal with it."

"When did they die?"

"My father passed about six years ago. My mother hung on for three years after that."

"Well, the people down in Columbia must have been thrilled by your decision."

"They seemed very pleased. I dealt primarily with a woman named Elizabeth Pattinger, who is the registrar, and Jeffrey Horshak, who does double duty as Curator and Director. In fact, if my unpleasant confinement at Bellevue had continued, I would have insisted that you contact Mr. Horshak as a reference. I'm sure he would have vouched for me."

"Holy shit," said Lester. "That's my voice."

"Yes, it is."

"But it doesn't sound like me. That's not the way I talk."

"Correct. You're talking in another identity, so you sound different."

"Honestly, this sounds worse to me than any of the other diagnoses you mentioned before. This is freaky."

"It's actually not. It's a recognized condition, and it's treatable. Even better, we can treat it without drugs or electric shock or anything like that."

"How, exactly?"

"Partly by doing what we're doing right now: confronting you with the reality that you have these different identities, or what we call alters. At some point we might have to supplement the treatment with hypnosis, but that may not even be necessary. The goal is to reintegrate all of them into the same person. Into you."

"This still doesn't make sense. For what it's worth, my mother never doted on me."

"I know that, because I read Dr. Hannity's notes. But that's one of the payoffs of creating these alternate personalities: you get to reconstruct reality the way you wished it always had been."

"Where did I get these paintings that you say I gave them?"

"I didn't say so, Lester. You said so."

"Whatever. But where did they come from?"

"That's a whole other conversation. What I'm going to suggest is that we stop for the day and give you some time to digest this. Next week, I'll tell you where the paintings came from. Or, if you think things over and decide you want to come in earlier, it's no problem. Just give me a call."

"Okay." He rose and walked to the door, where he stopped and looked at her. "To tell you the truth, my parents didn't give a shit about me. I said I wasn't going to discuss it, and I'm not going into any details, but that's the way it was."

"I doubt very much that was true. I'm sure they loved you, but they either they weren't capable of showing it or didn't know how to show it."

"Maybe both. On top of that, they never seemed to care one way or another."

CHAPTER 26

Lester Gordon was back in Weissberg's office three days later. Despite his initial resistance to the idea of DID, the therapist was relieved to see that he seemed more curious than repulsed by the diagnosis. When he sat down on the sofa, he seemed alert and interested.

"Thanks for seeing me so quickly."

"I told you were welcome to come back early, and I'm glad you called. And I must say you seem very relaxed."

"I did a lot of thinking about what you said the other day, and a number of things fell into place. I guess the main thing was the way I was losing track of time. It was terrifying me, to be honest, although maybe I didn't admit that."

"You didn't, but that would certainly be a normal reaction."

"I guess what hit me is the idea that maybe some of this isn't my fault."

"Lester, *none* of it is your fault. It's a medical condition. If you had an ulcer, or a rash, would you go around blaming yourself?"

"I guess not."

"But you did in this case. Why is that?"

"I don't know, but I've always felt worthless, as if anything I did wouldn't amount to much."

"I know you don't want to talk about it, and so I haven't pressed you, but do you think those feelings go back to the way your parents treated you?"

"That makes sense, I guess. But explain something to me: if I feel that way, why was this priest giving these paintings away in honor of his parents?"

"The neglect you experienced was abuse. And when people carry that into adulthood, they'll do anything to maintain a connection with the abuser. That was your way of doing it, using the identity of the priest."

"I'm not sure I totally get it."

"Typically, patients with Dissociative Identity Disorder experienced severe trauma in childhood. Yours was very painful, but fortunately not severe—I could tell you some real horror stories. If the trauma is severe enough, the patient usually starts dissociating at a very early age. In your case, it didn't begin until six or seven years ago. I think what happened was that the deaths of your father and Dr. Hannity, both of which occurred in a brief period of time, caused you to retreat into a fantasy world. It brought up the feelings of neglect and abandonment you experienced as a child."

"When you first told me about it, it sounded really bizarre. I was afraid I would have to go back into a facility."

"Lester, we all do it. Most of us have our imaginary friends and mythical alter egos. The only difference is that we know those things aren't real. Your defenses were lowered to the point where you created those identities as a coping mechanism. You were only trying to survive."

Lester was crying. Weissberg handed him a tissue and waited for a few minutes until his sobbing stopped.

"Now what I want to do today is discuss one of your other identities. This one is even more important than Father Humphries—he's crucial, in fact. You may not like what you hear at first, but if you listen to me carefully you can make some real progress toward healing. Do you want to go ahead?"

"Yes."

"The other identity is the painter, Louis Bétancourt. You told me you were leasing out your living room for him to use as a studio."

"That's right."

"When you talked about him, you were very complimentary. In fact, you really admired him. You said he had incredible talent and an amazing work ethic. You felt that you had a lot in common with him, since you both love the Impressionists. But you also thought that he was far more talented than you were, and that you could never produce paintings as beautiful as his. Is that accurate?'

"More or less."

"Well, here's what I want you to understand: there is no such person as Louis Bétancourt."

"That's nonsense."

"I'm afraid not. He doesn't exist, Lester. He is an identity projected by your subconscious."

"Look, I like you. And I do trust you. But you're way off base here. Louis has been painting in my living room for nearly a year."

"Then let me ask you this: has he ever been in the house at the same time as you? Have the two of you ever actually had a conversation?"

Lester didn't answer.

"You say you lost track of entire days sometimes. I'll bet those are the days when Louis is working in his studio, aren't they? And I'll also bet it happens constantly."

The was a long pause, during which Weissberg watched confusion, anger and panic flash across his face.

"Lester?" she asked finally.

"I know he's real. He has to be. I couldn't have made him up."

"You did. He's another aspect of your personality. I think he's the person you wish you could be."

"This is ridiculous. I can't paint anywhere nearly as well as he can. He's a genius. He's gifted."

"That's exactly what I mean. Your self-esteem is so low that you can't accept the fact that you're as good as you are, so you had to create him to paint masterpieces for you."

"I don't believe it."

"Here's what I'm going to do. I'm going to play an excerpt from a session when the Louis Bétancourt personality came out. I want you to hear the part where he's talking about you. I think it will be difficult, but you need to hear it. Is that okay?"

"Go ahead."

She switched on the recorder.

"I believe your studio is actually very close to here."

"Five or six blocks away, yes. I can walk it easily."

"Hopefully you have a large, comfortable space to work in."

"It's adequate. I'm actually renting the living room of a friend and using it as a studio."

"Really? It's unusual that someone would do that. He must really need the money."

"Not really, no. I would say that he's sympathetic to my goals and dreams."

"Is he a painter as well?"

"I wouldn't call him a painter, no, except in his own mind. Some things in life are very sad."

"How so?"

"Many people dream of being artists, of producing work that will live on after them and become their legacy. But not everyone can do this. Some are missing the talent, and others lack the drive."

"What's your friend's name? I might have seen him around the neighborhood."

"His name is Lester Gordon, but I doubt that you have met him. He spends most of his time in Manhattan, visiting the major museums. He seems to think that if he sits long enough in front of great canvases, some of that greatness will rub off."

"My parents used to take me to the museums when I was a child.

I was lucky to have developed an appreciation for art early on."

"You seem to have very good taste. With some exceptions, of course."

"Tell me a little more about your friend. Is he actively trying to become a painter?"

"He's been at it most of his life, but I'm afraid he doesn't really have the talent. On a basic level, he can copy fairly well. He used to do reproductions of Impressionist works and sell them on the Brooklyn pier, before they demolished it. Some of them were very good. But he's extremely dedicated—he truly believes that if he works and studies hard enough, he'll succeed in the end. If only that were the case."

"I would guess that family background matters as well. Obviously you came from an environment where great art was respected, so I'm sure it's something that has to be reinforced from an early age."

"Bien sur. Talent and appreciation must be nurtured. Look at your own case---you say your parents sparked an interest in art. I've always thought that was one of Lester's problems. His parents never encouraged him to be a painter, or much of anything else from what I understand. He describes them as aloof, neglectful."

"You're right. That's very sad."

"Son of a bitch!" said Lester. He seemed agitated and angry.
"What is it?"

"He's supposed to be my friend. And then he sits right here, running me down to you."

"Lester, Louis Bétancourt doesn't exist. That's you, talking about yourself. It's you, reflecting back your lack of self-worth because you didn't feel your parents loved you. It's you. There is no Louis Bétancourt."

He started sobbing again, more softly this time.

"Lester, listen to me. Remember the paintings that Father Humphries donated to the museum in South Carolina? The Signac and the two Seurats?"

He nodded, wiping his eyes with the tissue.

"Those were paintings of incomparable technique and beauty. They fooled everyone, including the experts. Everyone thought they were real Impressionist canvases. And you were convinced that they were painted by Louis, in your living room and his rented studio?"

"Yes."

"Those pictures were painted by you, Lester. Louis doesn't exist. You're the genius, the gifted one. You're as good as any of the Impressionists."

"It's not possible."

"It doesn't fit into your concept of yourself as a worthless human being, but it's true. You're one of the most talented painters of this generation. And when we integrate Louis with you, you'll be able to paint like that all the time if you want to."

He stood up and walked toward the door.

"Where are you going?"

"I have to take a break and see if I can process this. I'll be back."

"Anytime you want to come back, just pick up the phone."

"Thanks. You'll be the first to know."

*

The phone rang in the reception area just as the therapist was preparing to leave for the night.

"Hello?"

"Is this Dr. Cheryl Weissberg?"

"That's me. Who's calling, please?"

"My name is Jeffrey Horshak. I'm the Director and Curator of the Palmetto State Art Museum in South Carolina."

"Ah, yes. How are you, Mr. Horshak?"

"I gather you're familiar with me?"

"I've seen your name. I did some preliminary research into your museum and was actually considering contacting you at one point."

"But you didn't do that. May I ask why?"

"I thought you might have some information or insights that could be helpful in treating a patient under my care. As time went on, it became unnecessary."

"I see. Can I assume the patient was Lester Gordon?"

"I'm sure you realize that I can't discuss the details of Mr. Gordon's treatment with you, or even reveal if he is in fact a patient. I need to make that clear at the outset."

"Of course I realize that." There was a pause. "But I already know he's a patient of yours. I did some research of my own. I've read the police report on the incident at the Museum of Modern Art. I know that you were one of the physicians who took care of him at Bellevue. And I also know that he goes to your office very Wednesday at 3 p.m."

"How on earth do you know all that?"

"Because I hired a private investigator to find out. With all due respect, doctor, I think we should stop playing footsy. I already know a lot about him, and obviously I understand you can't reveal anything that goes on in therapy. But you could help me cut through a mystery if you so choose."

"If I can help you, I will. But why would you go to the trouble and expense of hiring a private investigator to track Mr. Gordon? Is he a friend of yours?"

"Please, doctor." Horshak laughed. "I may be a country bumpkin, but I'm not stupid. I've never met Mr. Gordon, no. Or I'm not sure I have."

"Then why—"

"Let me run this down for you, in the interests of time. Some time back we received a visit from a Jesuit priest named Gordon Humphries. He said he was in possession of a large art collection bequeathed to him by his parents. The priest was in failing health, and he wanted to donate some of the more important canvases to museums before he died, so that the greatest number of people would be able to see them. His only condition was that the paintings be donated in memory of his parents."

"Go on."

"He gave us three pieces of art. The first was a watercolor by Paul Signac, the Impressionist. The other two are supposed to be works by Georges Seurat. But you probably know all of this, I'm sure."

"So why were you interested in Lester Gordon?"

"I was always suspicious of the priest. I mean, he was nice enough, and the paintings looked real to me, but there was something about the situation that didn't add up. He had no documentation on any of the canvases, and we couldn't authenticate one of them. I'm not sure how familiar you are with the art world, but obviously these things are very important."

"I'm not terribly familiar with it, no."

"In any case, all my communication with Father Humphries was via email. Then one day, he happened to call me. I had the investigator trace the call, and discovered it came from Lester Gordon's apartment in Brooklyn. That's why I started looking into him. I even had the investigator take a candid picture of him. And do you know what?"

"What's that, Mr. Horshak?"

"When I look at this picture, I'll be damned if it doesn't look like Father Humphries."

"I see."

"So here's what I think. I believe that Lester Gordon is an art forger, and that he somehow painted the pictures that Humphries donated to us. Don't ask me how, because it would seem to be impossible. He'd have to be incredibly talented, and painting those pictures would have taken a very long period of time. But somehow he did it, and then he masqueraded as

Humphries to give us the canvases. What I can't figure out is why."

"I can't help you there."

"Normally, there are two scenarios with forgers. Either they're in it for the money, or they're failed artists who want to prove their value. Mr. Gordon appears to fall into the second category. What I don't get is why he would give the paintings away, and why he would pretend to be a Jesuit priest in order to do so."

"Well, I believe I can tell you one thing without breaking confidentiality. I can assure you that Lester wasn't pretending to be the Father Humphries who came to see you."

"There's nothing wrong with my eyes, Dr. Weissberg. From the picture, he certainly looks like the same guy."

"I'm afraid that's as far as I can go, given that I don't believe Lester is a danger to himself or others. I couldn't break confidentiality without a court order, and you have no basis to get one."

"I'm just curious, more than anything else. To be honest, this whole episode drove me up the wall."

"I can understand that. I wish I could help you further."

"Have you ever been to Columbia?"

"No, I'm afraid not. I've been pretty busy lately and haven't had much time for travel."

"If you ever visit our fair city, make sure you come to the museum and look me up. I'd like you to see the paintings in question, or at least the ones we have displayed."

"In a sense, I already have. I have a copy of Signac's *Dawn at Dieppe* hanging in my office."

"Really? That's quite a coincidence."

"I'm very taken with it. I think it's a beautiful picture."

"You're more of an art lover than you think."

Weissberg smiled. "I suppose I'm getting there."

CHAPTER 27

"Good afternoon, Lester. Please come in."

"Thank you."

"How are you feeling today?"

"Much better, thanks."

He sat down on the sofa, folded his hands and smiled at her. Weissberg noticed that he seemed more relaxed than she had ever seen him.

"You certainly look happy."

"I feel different. The last two sessions really hit me, and it took a while for me to make sense of the whole thing. I still have a lot of questions, and I've had a bunch of feelings over the past three or four days."

"Tell me about it."

"One of the first things I did was go online and visit the website for the Palmetto State Art Museum. I wanted to see the pictures. I found the watercolor, *Dawn at Dieppe.* They have it listed as an original painting by Paul Signac. I guess that's when I realized that you were right, that I was much more talented than I ever really thought."

"You should be very proud of yourself."

"I am. I mean, I painted it, and no one can even tell that it's not a real Signac. I can't explain how that made me feel, but it's very powerful."

"I would imagine so."

"They also have the second painting listed as part of the collection. I gather it was a study for Seurat's *Circus Sideshow*, and I guess they're not completely sure if that one's real or not—it's listed as 'believed to be' Seurat. I couldn't find the third painting, which I thought was strange, so maybe they're having it appraised or authenticated."

"Very possibly."

"Both of them are listed as donations in memory of Theodore and Lillian Humphries, who of course never existed." He laughed. "I thought back to the session where you played the tape of Father Humphries. He actually promoted my father from master sergeant to two-star general. Nice work if you can get it."

"I'm glad to see you can laugh at it."

"The only thing that bothers me is I can't see the third painting. I looked over some of the sketches that Louis left in the living room, and it looks like a major piece. There's a woman who looks like Madeleine Knobloch, holding a baby. I assume the baby was Seurat's infant son."

"I'm sorry, who was Madeleine Knobloch?"

"Seurat's mistress. They lived together in Paris before he died. I'd really like to see that painting. And I can't figure out why it's not displayed in the museum."

"In time, I imagine it will be."

"Anyway, I went through the closet and threw out a bunch of stuff. I got rid of the priest's outfit, along with the costumes Louis used to wear—the embroidered vests, the berets and the sashes. I even found the fake moustache in a shaving kit."

"Wow. You're definitely making some significant progress."

"I want to put all of that behind me, and I don't want any reminders around that might tempt me to lapse back into those people. I want to go forward. I've started doing some sketches for new work. I'd like to start painting some Impressionist renderings of New York street scenes."

"Good for you. It sounds like things are really changing for you."

"In some ways, they are. But it's strange: the more progress I make, the angrier I seem to get at my parents. I feel like I lost so much time. I really should have been at this point twenty or thirty years ago, except I never thought I had any talent. And I know I can't blame it all on them, but they never spent any time with me or encouraged me." He shook his head. "They just didn't care."

"I'm sure they cared, but it doesn't sound like they were able to show it."

"Don't make excuses for them." He was glaring at her. "Try growing up in a household where nobody gives a shit about you and see how you feel."

"I wasn't making excuses. There are many, many people who are incapable of showing love."

"I know. I've had a lot of therapy, remember? I've been

listening to that crap for years and years. But the fact is, my mother didn't care. She cared about her bridge game, about going to the hairdresser and talking on the phone with her friends, but she didn't care about me. And my father was never around."

"You seem very angry."

"Wouldn't you be?"

"Probably. But I think it's important not to let it overshadow the real progress you're making." Weissberg shifted in her chair, uncertain how to proceed. "Up to this point you haven't shown any desire to talk about them at all. I think that's significant in itself. What do you think you're most angry about: that they didn't seem to love you, or that they never encouraged you as a painter?"

"Both. I don't think it mattered to my mother what I did. As far as my father goes, I think he took it as a personal affront that I wanted to be an artist. To him, real men weren't artists. Real men were like him—they stayed out all night and only came home when they wanted to screw the babysitter."

"Lester." She leaned forward and spoke to him gently. "The important thing for you is to start the process of letting all this go. That's the work you have to do now. Because if you can't do that, you'll be fuming over your parents for the rest of your life."

"I have a right to fume if I want to."

"Of course you do. But focusing on it won't just hold you back from doing what you want to do in life. The angrier you get, the more you let your parents control you. And they can't really control you anymore. You shouldn't let them."

"It's easy for you to say."

"Not really, because I feel the pain you're going through. But you have to let this go, and I think the best way to do that is to focus on the new life you're building for yourself. It's important to vent your anger, certainly. But if you get stuck in it, you continue to give them control. I'd like to see you continue to take charge of your own life."

"How do you suggest I do that?"

"One way would be to socialize, to get out and make friends. There are a lot of artists in this neighborhood, as you've observed."

"True. And most of them think that modern art is the only art worth creating."

"When you described your experiences with them, remember that you were interacting as the old Lester Gordon. You're feeling differently now. You know how talented you are, and you know you don't have to prove anything to your fellow artists. It wouldn't hurt to have some people you could talk to."

"I suppose."

"Have you met anyone you might be interested in dating?"

"Not really. Every time I try to be friendly and strike up a conversation with a woman, she threatens to call the police. This is New York City, remember."

"Well, I know there are singles groups out there, people who get together and socialize. I'll try to put get a list of suggestions for you. If you put yourself in that kind of situation, at least you know that everyone else is there for the same reasons."

"Thanks. I wouldn't know where to start."

"I also want you to remember that you're making terrific progress, but you may not be completely cured. It's entirely possible, maybe even expected, that you'll lapse at some point, and one of the alters will reemerge. If that happens, I'd like you to contact me as soon as you come back to yourself and realize that you've lost time once again. Will you do that?"

"Sure. But it's weird, because when you suggest I go out and make friends, I realize that I already have some."

"Really? Who?"

"The other identities, of course. I may not pretend to be Louis Bétancourt or Gordon Humphries anymore, but they're still friends of mine. I think about them a lot. And often, I'll be in situations where certain things happen, and I'll be reminded of how those two would react. It's funny sometimes."

"Well, you did spend a lot of time as both of them, particularly as Louis. But you do understand that they're not real people, even though they might seem real to you?"

"Of course. But they're still my friends. They looked out for me for years, when I couldn't do it for myself, and now I feel I should watch out for them. Louis in particular—I never would have understood how talented I was if it were it not for him. I owe him a lot."

"I see how you feel, but I have to warn you that identifying too strongly with them could be a bit dangerous."

"How so?"

"Because, as I said, they're imaginary. And thinking about them too much might trigger a situation where you lapse back into pretending to be them."

"Oh, I don't think that's going to happen."

"Anyway, I still believe it would be good for you to get out and make new friends." She looked at the clock. "I'm afraid it's time to stop. I'll have some suggestions on social groups for you the next time we meet. And if you have problems, please pick up the phone."

He walked to the door, then stopped and looked back. "Dr. Weissberg?"

"Yes?"

"Thank you. I really appreciate it."

*

"How are things coming along?" asked Karen Brillstein. "How's patient Lester doing?"

"Really well," said Cheryl Weissberg. "His progress is far more rapid that I ever thought it would be."

Since Lester's therapy had intensified, the two women made a habit of speaking by phone at least once each week.

"Last time we talked, you had played the tape of Father Humphries for him. You said he was beginning the accept the diagnosis of DID, although he was still skeptical. You also said he seemed to harbor a lot of resentment against his parents."

"All true, yes. And I believe I called you a day or two after the session. The day after that, he was back in the office.

Apparently, listening to the recording of Father Humphries had a deep effect on him. It made him realize the DID diagnosis was correct and real. At that point, I told him that Louis Bétancourt was another one of his alters. He was resistant at first, but I made him understand that Louis was fictional and that he, Lester, had actually created those paintings. I reinforced the idea of what it meant: that he was really an incredibly talented artist, on a par with the real Impressionists."

"And how did he react to that?"

"He was in tears. It really hit him. After being told for most of his life that he was worthless, he was suddenly validated on a very deep level."

"How did the session end up?"

"He said he needed to think about everything and digest it. Basically the same way he reacted the first time."

"So that was an extra session. I gather you've had another one since."

"Yes, and it was probably the most successful one thus far. He came in very confident and relaxed, which is unusual for him. He said he had been on the Palmetto State Art Museum website and had seen the paintings—or the first two, anyway— and he was amazed at how good they were. It seemed that the realization had sunk in gradually."

"Didn't he see the third painting? I thought you said that was the most important of the three."

"It definitely was, but I'm not sure what happened to it. I gather it's not displayed in the museum yet. And to digress, I also received a call one day from Jeffrey Horshak, who's the Curator and Director down there at Palmetto State."

"Weren't you intending to call him?"

"I was going to, but then I thought better of it. It would have been difficult to speak with him without revealing too many confidential details about Lester. And I'm glad I didn't."

"What did he want?"

"To him, the whole episode is still a mystery. Father Humphries shipped him the third painting but never came back, and it drove him nuts. He actually hired a private investigator to track him down and discovered that the priest didn't exist. Then Humphries called Horshak for the first time, and the investigator tracked the call to Lester's apartment. I gather that he also dug up the background on Lester and found out I had treated him at Bellevue and that the treatment was ongoing. He was grilling me on the connection between Lester and Father Humphries, and of course I told him I couldn't talk about it."

"And you didn't ask him what happened to the third painting?"

"No." said Weissberg. "I didn't want to discuss the whole subject with him in too much detail. Anyway, to get back to the most recent session: Lester seemed vastly improved. Realizing how talented he was totally changed his outlook. He said he went through the closet and threw out the costumes and personal effects of both Louis and Father Humphries."

"That definitely sounds like progress."

"He's almost a different person, to tell you the truth. Now that he has confidence in himself as an artist, he's starting to paint in his own identity. I encouraged him to get out and socialize more, to try and make some friends. At that point he said something that was a little disturbing. He said he regards the alters as his friends, particularly Louis, since Louis was the one that allowed him to realize how talented he was."

"Hmm. That sounds like a potential danger for regression."

"That's what I thought. I tried to reason with him about it, but he wouldn't budge. I also have to tell you that his anger and resentment against his parents hasn't receded. He talks about it a lot."

"How do you intend to deal with that?"

"I'm pretty well convinced that exploring the Baby Les alter is the key to unlocking it. If I read the deceased therapist's notes correctly, Lester walked in on his father having sex with the babysitter at the age of seven. That's why he projects himself back to that point. But thus far, I haven't been able to engage him on it."

"I suggest playing the tape of the Baby Les alter coming out in therapy. That might get him going."

"I'll definitely try it."

"And if that doesn't work, hypnosis might be the best course."

"I can't hypnotize him," said Weissberg. "I'm not qualified."

"Then that would probably be the point for me to step in. I've been trying to let you handle this on your own, but I could always hypnotize him if he's willing."

"I'll broach the subject with him and see what he says."

"Let me know. And remember that since the progress seems to be accelerated, there's a chance he might relapse at some point."

"I've warned him about that, so he's ready for it if it happens."

"Are *you* ready for it?"

"I agree that things are moving along quickly, possibly too quickly. But you've observed all along that the onset of DID occurred in recent adulthood, and that the alters seemed very close to the surface, so the chances of resolving this quickly were better than average."

"That's all correct, but I caution you to remember that he's a gifted person. And you may well succeed in uniting all his alters and healing him, but that won't necessarily mean that he'll be a successful artist. From everything you've said, he's still out of step with the times."

"In other words—"

"You may end up with a cured patient who can paint as well as an Impressionist. But that won't make him an Impressionist."

CHAPTER 28

"Good afternoon, Lester. How are you doing today?"
"Great, thanks."

"Please come in."

As he sat down, Weissberg was relieved to see that her patient still seemed cheerful and calm.

"How did your week go?"

"Fine. No problems that I can remember."

"No incidents of losing time?"

"No, fortunately not. I think I may have that licked."

"That's great to hear. Just remember, that if you do suffer a lapse at some point, it's not the end of the world. Your situation is similar in some ways to a person trying to stop smoking. A few stumbles along the way aren't unusual."

"I'll remember that, thanks."

"How's the painting going?"

"Pretty well. I told you that I wanted to do a series of canvases in the Impressionist style, focusing on local scenes here in the city. I've done the sketches for the first one, which will be set in Washington Square Park, and should be able to start on it soon."

"That sounds great. Congratulations." She handed him a

sheet of paper. "Here's a short list of social groups that might interest you. Most of them are local, although the focus of each one is slightly different. Hopefully it will help you get out and meet people, make some new friends."

"Thank you."

"There are a few things I wanted to focus on today. I'd like to start by going back to something you said at the end of last week's session. You were talking about the alters, and you made the observation that you still felt very close to them. While you may not be taking on their identities anymore, you said you regarded them as friends."

"Absolutely. Close friends, I'd say. I think I mentioned Louis in particular. I really feel indebted to him, because without him I never would have realized how talented I am. There's no way I ever would have attempted a piece of work that was as large and complex as that third canvas." He blushed. "At least, that's what I assume. I still haven't seen it."

"On one level, what you're saying is perfectly understandable." She spoke slowly, trying to choose the right words. "But I am a little afraid that your feelings of gratitude toward the alters, and your closeness to them, might stand in the way of becoming a fully integrated person. Because the goal here is for you to become Lester Gordon, and no one else but Lester Gordon."

"I realize that, of course. And I appreciate the fact that you think I've made progress. But I wouldn't have been able to make that progress if Louis hadn't blazed the trail for me. He showed me the way by doing those paintings."

"But you were the one who did the paintings, Lester. Louis was just a projection from your subconscious. He had to do them for you, because you didn't think you were talented enough to do them yourself."

"That's exactly my point."

"Okay, let's shift the subject a bit. Why do you think you are more focused on Louis than you are on Father Humphries? I don't hear you talking about him."

"I'm not sure. I guess Louis is more similar to me in a lot of ways."

"You mean, less socialized?"

"Yes." He smiled. "I suppose you could say that. And he was a painter, which Father Humphries wasn't. He just gave the canvases away."

"Why do you suppose he did that, when he could have sold them and probably made a fortune?"

"It wasn't about the money. The whole point of the Signac and the two Seurats was to prove to the world that Louis—actually, me—was just as talented as the real Impressionists."

"Agreed. But why do you think he wanted to donate the paintings to the museum in memory of his parents? He was incredibly focused on that."

"I'm not sure. I guess when I look at it, I realize that when he described his parents, he was really talking about the parents I wish I had. I guess that's it."

"So in your fantasies, you imagined your mother to be very doting and loving. And you envisioned your father as being a bit reserved and taciturn, but still very devoted to you?"

"Yes, that would have been nice. Much nicer than what I ended up with, that is."

"Given that your actual parents behaved very differently from Father Humphries', why do you think it was so important to him—to you, in fact—to honor his parents?"

"I don't know, beyond what I told you. I just wish I could have had parents like that."

"You're aware that there was a third alter, Baby Les. We really haven't talked much about him."

"I guess I don't know too much about him."

"He wasn't a baby, even though that was his nickname. He was actually seven years old. Why do you think you projected an identity of someone that age?"

"I have no idea."

"Did anything particularly traumatic happen to you when you were seven?"

"Sorry, I can't remember."

"Here's what I'd like to do. Baby Les came out in one of our sessions. I'd like to play part of that session for you and see if it jogs your memory. Are you okay with that?"

"Yes, that's fine."

"Let me set the scene for you. This occurred at the beginning of the session. I had to leave the room because I was expecting an urgent phone call, and I was out for about ten minutes. I gather the situation reminded you of being abandoned as a child. You became very anxious, and the Baby Les alter came out."

She switched on the recorder.

"Where am I? Where's Mommy?"

"Mommy went out, Baby Les. There's nothing to worry about."

"She's not here."

"No, she's not."

"Are you babysitting me?"

"Yes, I am. Is that okay?"

"The other babysitter doesn't care about me She leaves me alone. Last week I had a tummy ache and I yelled and yelled for her to come and help me, but she didn't come."

"That must have been awful."

"Do you have friends?"

"What do you mean?"

"The other babysitter has friends. They come over all the time."

"Well, I do have friends, but they won't be coming here. You'll be safe. Do you trust me?"

"No. I don't know who you are."

"Well, I promise you that no one will come over. I can't do any better than that. I hope you'll learn to trust me."

"I don't understand why Mommy always has to go out."

"I don't know either, but it must be important. How does that make you feel?"

"She doesn't love me. If she loved me, she wouldn't leave me alone all the time."

"I'm sure she loves you, Baby Les. But sometimes grownups have things they need to do."

"Not all the time."

"*Why does it bother you so much when the babysitter has friends over?*"

"*They do bad things.*"

"*What kinds of things?*"

"*They hurt each other.*"

"*What do you mean? How do they hurt each other?*"

"*When I had a tummy ache, I woke up and called her. She didn't come in to see me. Then I opened the door and looked in the living room. They were hurting each other.*"

"*What were they doing?*"

"*They were on the couch. Her friend was laying on top of her. He was hurting her. She was screaming.*"

"*Well, maybe they weren't really hurting each other. Maybe they were doing something else.*"

"*I don't care! I want Mommy.*"

"*She'll be coming home soon, I promise. Did you hear me? I promise.*"

"*I guess so.*"

"Wow." He shook his head. "That's pretty intense."

"There's a lot of pain there. Where do you think it came from?"

"I really don't know. I'd like to help, but it was so long ago."

"Obviously there's some significance to the fact that Baby Les is seven years old. Something traumatic must have happened to you at that age. Any ideas of what it might have been?"

"I'm sorry, Dr. Weissberg. I just don't know."

"When I reviewed Dr. Hannity's notes on his sessions with

you, I believe he thought that you witnessed your father having sex with the babysitter when you were seven years old. Does that sound about right?"

"I don't want to talk about it."

"Because you don't remember, or because it's too painful?"

"It doesn't matter. I just don't want to talk about it."

"You don't have to," she said gently. "But sooner or later, I think you'll need to confront those memories. There's no point in carrying all that pain around with you as an adult."

"I'm sorry to disappoint you, but I'm not going to discuss it. At least not today."

"Well, I have a suggestion for you. I work with another therapist named Dr. Brillstein. She was one of my professors in school, and she's supervising some of my cases. She happens to be an expert on Dissociative Identity Disorder, the condition you were suffering from. If you don't mind, I'd like her to come to one of our sessions and have you speak with her. How does that sound?"

"Okay, I guess."

"I'd really like to have Dr. Brillstein hypnotize you. I think that would allow us to get to the root of what's bothering you, and we could do it without you being consciously aware of it. That way, you wouldn't have to directly talk about what happened."

"I don't know about that. It sounds scary to me."

"How so?"

"I don't know much about it, other than what I've seen in

the movies. But I don't like the idea of not being responsible for what I'm saying or doing."

"You would be responsible. You're just in a different state of consciousness. You wouldn't say anything under hypnosis that you don't actually feel or believe."

"But it would be a different state, as you say. It wouldn't be the real me."

"Look at it this way, Lester: when you projected the alters, you were also in a different state. It wasn't your whole or complete personality, but rather a projection of part of it. Sometimes it was wish fulfillment. But now you say that you regard the alters as friends, and what happened during those projections was very valuable for you."

"I just don't know."

"Would you try it once? If you don't like it, you don't have to do it again. But I think it might really help you."

"All right. I'll give it a shot."

CHAPTER 29

In early July, the team at ArtSleuth carefully packed *Madonna and Heir* for transport. A pair of security guards picked up the precious cargo on a Sunday morning and guided it though the near-deserted streets of Manhattan to the Cantwell Gallery on the Upper East Side. Phillip Cantwell and George Portius were waiting for them. On arrival the painting was transferred to a secure, air-conditioned room on the third floor of the townhouse, where it was unpacked and inspected for damage. As Portius saw it for the first time, his eyes widened.

"My God." He stared at the canvas, transfixed. "It's everything you said it was."

"Indeed." Cantwell beamed. "It's a beauty."

"Any ideas of where we'll start the reserve?"

"We'll have to think about it carefully," said Cantwell. "Obviously it should be an eight-figure number, but I'm leaning toward the low eight figures---twelve million, possibly as low as ten. It's a tricky business. We have no idea of how high it can go, and the odds are it will approach the record, but we don't want to price too many bidders out of the market right off the bat."

"We're getting a lot of calls on this," said Portius. "Rumors are spreading about an undiscovered, major canvas. There's a huge amount of interest, and people don't even know what it is yet."

"Let them stew. It's all part of building up the suspense."

"Speaking of which, I'm surprised you passed up the opportunity for publicity today. We could have gotten some coverage on this, if it hadn't happened on a Sunday morning. I assume you didn't want to take any more risks with the painting than you had to."

"No, I did that on purpose," said Cantwell. "The publicity will be carefully planned and calibrated. I don't want to turn this into a circus. The type of person who will buy this canvas won't be reading the *Daily News* or the *Post.*"

"True."

"I've engaged a high-powered PR firm to handle it. They'll set up all the publicity beforehand, and co-ordinate it for a few months after the sale. We want to see this in *Forbes, Barron's,* the *Times* Sunday magazine, places like that."

"That couldn't have been cheap."

"Eighty thousand for four months." He smiled. "But it should be worth it, because this has to be handled in the right way. We can't be perceived as pandering for publicity. The media outlets that pick it up need to be upscale because that's where our customers are, and that type of coverage also creates the perception that this is an extraordinary event for people of exceptional taste. That way, the painting doesn't end up in the hands of some rapper or basketball superstar."

"I couldn't agree more. Have you given any thought to how to handle the actual sale?"

"It has to be exclusive, obviously," said Cantwell. "There will be a lot of buzz by the time the day rolls around, and people will be clamoring to get in. The auction room only holds a little more than hundred, and we'll have to block off some space for the press. I'm leaning toward selling tickets and making the price fairly stiff, something in the range of a thousand dollars per head."

"Do you think that's wise? It might strike potential bidders as a bit cheesy."

"The goal is to limit the gawkers and keep the riffraff out. I don't think there will be too many bids coming from the people in the room anyway. Most of the action will be online or by phone, so we'll probably want to increase the number of staffers we have on hand to track those bids. The people who show up in person will be curiosity seekers, so let's make them pay for their curiosity."

"I like it," said Portius. "It's a gutsy strategy."

"You said you're getting calls on this. Any pattern to them?"

"Some local collectors, with a sprinkling of interest from Asia. I assume you've heard from Charles Wong?"

"Not yet," said Cantwell, "but I'm sure I will. I'm not going to encourage him too much this time around, though. For one thing, I'd like to see the painting not leave the country. I think it's much better for our reputation if it stays here. Then too, I'm not looking forward to rebating the buyer's premium to him on this one."

"Well, we're going to need him going forward, so we can't discourage him from bidding on this."

"Agreed. If push comes to shove, I'm sure I can negotiate with him. Charles is a businessman. He'll realize that we're not in a position to hand over 15% of a $20 million sale. He's greedy, but he'll be reasonable."

"There should be very intense competition for this."

"Absolutely," said Cantwell. "For the person who ends up buying this painting, bragging rights will be far more important than money."

CHAPTER 30

"Good afternoon, Lester. Please come in."

The two women rose from the couch in Weissberg's consulting room, and Karen Brillstein extended her hand.

"This is my colleague, Dr. Brillstein."

"Nice to meet you, Lester."

"Same here. I gather you're the hypnotist."

"Well, I'm a clinical psychologist, but I'm also trained as a hypnotist. I've been using it as a tool to treat patients for many years." She gestured to the sofa. "Please, have a seat."

Weissberg sat down behind her desk, and Brillstein pulled up a chair to face Lester Gordon on the sofa.

"To start with, I'd like to explore any concerns you might have about hypnosis. Are you familiar with the process?"

"Not really—just what I've seen on TV and in the movies."

"That's the case with most people, as far as I can tell. There are a lot of misconceptions about it."

Weissberg watched her mentor carefully. Despite extensive study with her in graduate school, she had never actually seen Brillstein treat a patient. Her manner was impressive: friendly and open, empathetic yet businesslike.

"The main thing you have to understand, Lester, is that

I can't make you do anything under hypnosis that you don't want to do. You're not going to suddenly think you can fly or start barking like a dog if I ask you to—unless, of course, that's one of your hidden desires." She chuckled along with the patient, putting him at ease. "You'll have just as much control of yourself in the hypnotic state as you have in real life. The main difference is that you'll be far more relaxed, and certain thoughts and feelings are likely to be closer to the surface."

"I understand."

"This is assuming, of course, that you actually go into a hypnotic state. Many people don't. The main thing is not to put expectations on yourself. Just go with the flow, and we'll both see where it takes you. How does that sound?"

"It's okay, I guess. I'm willing to give it a try."

"Very good. What I want you to do, Lester, is to lay down on the couch on your back, in whatever way you're most comfortable." She waited while the patient arranged himself in a prone position. "How does that feel?"

"Fine, thank you."

"I'm going to ask that you put your hands out at your sides, rather than keeping them folded over your chest."

"Okay."

"How do you feel now? Is this a relaxed position for you?"

"Sure. This is similar to the way I go to sleep at night."

"Well, we'll try to avoid having you fall asleep here, but I want you to be as comfortable as possible."

"I think this is it."

"Very good. Now what I want you to do, Lester, is close your eyes and start taking a series of very deep breaths. When you inhale, I want you to take as much air into your lungs as you can. When you get to that point, hold the air in for a moment, then start to exhale. When you've exhaled all the air, hold that position for another moment and inhale again. I want you to do that over and over. How does that sound?"

"Fine."

"Go ahead and try it." She observed the patient's breathing. "Very deep breaths, Lester. Take in the greatest possible amount of air, hold it for a second, exhale completely, hold for a second again, and then repeat."

"How am I doing?"

"Very well, but I'm going to ask you to keep your eyes closed and not speak for a while." Brillstein paused. "Deep breaths, Lester. Inhale deeply, hold it, exhale completely, hold it, then repeat."

Several minutes passed.

"How's this?"

"Fine, Lester, but try not to distract yourself by talking. Just continue to breathe, as steadily as possible."

Weissberg watched as Lester's breathing became slow and rhythmic.

"Very good, Lester," said Brillstein. "Now I don't want you to answer me verbally, but if you're feeling completely relaxed, please move one of the fingers on your right hand."

The two therapists watched as Lester's right pinkie twitched.

"Excellent. Just keep breathing deeply. Inhale, hold, exhale, hold, slowly, slowly." Brillstein looked at her watch. "Now if you can, I'd like you to focus on a moment in your childhood when you felt particularly peaceful and happy. It could be anything: a birthday party, a new puppy, anything that brought you a feeling of joy. When you have a memory like that, please move your finger again."

After a moment, Lester's right pinky twitched slightly.

"Very good. Where are you, Lester?"

"At the beach."

"Sounds great. So again, without speaking, I want you to focus on that memory. Please continue breathing in and out, slowly and completely. Allow yourself to feel the joy you felt that day at the beach. Maybe you were building a sandcastle, or playing in the waves, or just feeling the sun on your face. Whatever it was, just experience it. Breathe in, breathe out, and feel that joy."

Brillstein again allowed several minutes to pass.

"Now, Lester, we're going to go back to a time when you were seven years old. You would have been in the second grade. You may have some unpleasant memories associated with that time, but I don't want you to focus on those. Just place yourself back in that moment and continue to breathe in and out. Breathe in deeply, hold it, exhale and hold it. Slow, deep breaths. When you're back at age seven, I'd like you to move the finger on your right hand once again."

Lester's fingers twitched, and his breathing became shallower.

"Keep breathing, Baby Les. Take as much air into your lungs as you can, hold it for a second, then force it all out and start over again. Breathe in, exhale out. Don't focus on all the bad things, because things weren't all bad. Remember how happy you were at the beach."

Brillstein looked at Weissberg and raised her right thumb.

"How do you feel, Baby Les?"

"I'm scared."

"Why are you frightened?"

"I'm all alone. Mommy's not here."

"Well, I'm sure she'll be back soon."

"She's been gone almost all day."

"I don't want you to think about that. Just remember how happy you were at the beach. Do you remember that?"

"Yes."

"Just focus on that and keep breathing. Deep breaths in, exhale completely out. In and out. Slow and steady.

"Now," said Brillstein, a minute later, "I'm going to take you forward in time. I'm going to take you to a time when you were seventeen years old, and you were getting ready to graduate from high school. You won't be Baby Les anymore. You're going to be seventeen. All right, Lester?"

The patient didn't answer.

"Lester, can you hear me?"

"Yes."

"How old are you?"

"Seventeen. I'll be eighteen in May."

"Excellent. And how are you doing?"

"I'm excited. I'll be studying at the Art Students' League next year."

"You must be very happy about that."

"I'm looking forward to learning more about the Impressionists and sharpening my technique."

"How do your parents feel about that? Are they excited too?"

"They don't care. My mother doesn't pay any attention to me, and my father thinks I'm a sissy because I want to be a painter."

"That must be difficult for you."

"It doesn't matter, because I'm going to be a world-famous painter someday. And then they'll be proud of me. They'll have to be—they won't have any choice."

"That sounds like a very good plan. You're a smart boy."

Weissberg tapped Brillstein on the shoulder and motioned her toward the opposite corner of the room.

"Just keep breathing, Lester. Try to focus on inhaling and exhaling. Remember what is was like to be seventeen and feel that excitement about going to art school."

*

"What is it?" whispered Brillstein.

"I thought you were going to probe deeper on his feelings as

Baby Les," said Weissberg. "That's where most of his unresolved conflict seems to be."

"He's not in a position to resolve any of those feelings at the age of seven. We have to bring him forward to a point where he's able to deal with it. And more importantly, all the alters won't be united until Baby Les is integrated into his adult personality."

"Well, if you think so—"

"I know so," said Brillstein. Her manner was sympathetic but firm. "I'll ask you to trust me on this. We have a chance of sending him out of here as a complete person, or at least as complete as he's ever going to be. There aren't too many cases where you can do that."

"You're the boss."

The two therapists walked back to the sofa.

"How are you doing, Lester?"

"Fine."

"Good. Now what we're going to do is bring you forward in time to seven years ago. Dr. Hannity has been killed in the rafting accident, and your father has just died. I want you to come with me and be in that space, to experience that again. You're not seventeen anymore. You're forty-five, and both of those things have just happened to you."

Lester's body began to shift and stretch on the couch.

"Please try to remain relaxed, Lester. Breathe in and breathe out, slowly and steadily. Take as much air into your lungs as you can, hold it for a moment, then exhale as completely as you can." Brillstein watched as Lester seemed to relax. "That's very good. Breathe in, breathe out. Tell me how you're feeling."

"Awful. I'm all alone. Nobody loves me."

"Does it feel the way it did when you were seven?"

"Maybe. Maybe worse. Everybody has abandoned me. Nobody cares about me one way or another."

"Your mother is still alive, isn't she?"

"It doesn't matter. She doesn't care about me—she never did. But Dr. Hannity really tried to help me."

"What about your father? Do you think he cared about you?"

"In his own way, I guess so. He always wanted me to be somebody else. He wanted me to be anybody else other than who I really am. But he showed some interest, at least."

"I know you're upset, and you have a right to be. You've had a terrible experience. What I'm concerned about is how you're going to deal with it."

"I don't know."

"What do you think? What comes to mind?"

"If my father always wanted me to be someone else, then I can be someone else. I can try." Tears were rolling down the patient's cheeks. "Maybe if I'm someone else, I can be the person he wanted me to be."

"I don't think you'll ever know that for sure, Lester. But I think the important thing is that you continue to be yourself. That's the best you can do."

"But I'm a failure. No one thinks I'm a good painter, and no one buys my work. All they do is make fun of me. I'd be better off as someone else, someone completely different."

"I don't think so, Lester."

"Why not?"

"Because when it comes to your talent as a painter, you're probably right and everyone else is probably wrong. You have tremendous talent, or you couldn't have created all the work you've accomplished."

"You think so?"

"Absolutely. That's a lonely and sad place to be at times, but it could be worse—everyone else could be right. You have to remember that they're probably jealous of you. As much as they criticize you for wanting to paint like an Impressionist, it's something they would never be able to do. You could definitely paint the way they do if you wanted to, but they'd be lost if they tried to imitate you."

Lester lay motionless on the sofa, breathing silently. Weissberg watched the slow rising and falling of his chest.

"Lester?"

"Yes?"

"How are you feeling?"

"Better, I guess. I'm just letting everything sink in."

"You're a tremendously intelligent, creative and brave person," said Brillstein. "Your problem is that you don't conform to the way people think right now. You'll have some difficult moments. At times people will attack you out of jealousy and envy, but what they're really saying is they wish they could paint as well as you. And there will be times when it will seem that no one cares about you, but you know that isn't true. Do you realize that?"

"I guess so."

"When you wake up, and when you resume living your life, I want you to remember that. I want you to always remember that you, Lester Gordon, are a creative and worthwhile person with a wonderful contribution to make. People may not always like you, and you don't have to like them in return. But you don't gain anything by pretending to be Louis Bétancourt or Father Gordon Humphries. Whatever you gain is outweighed by the loss of something precious— you. Do you agree?"

"Yes."

"When you're tempted to slip into those identities, to deny your own self-worth by pretending to be someone else, I want you to remember that there's no one more valuable in this world than Lester Gordon. Do you believe that?"

"Yes, I do. Thank you."

"You don't have to thank me. All I'm doing is pointing out something that is very obvious. You can always come back to this space, and you can be as happy and joyful now as you were when you were a child at the beach. And you and I will come back to this space every so often, just so you do remember."

"Okay. That sounds nice."

"I want you to keep breathing, Lester, and in just a few minutes you'll open your eyes. And when you do, you'll see a world in which Lester Gordon is just as important as Louis Bétancourt or Father Gordon Humphries. You'll be in a world where you are yourself, for better or for worse, no matter what happens."

CHAPTER 31

L ike many other citizens who began their day by surfing the web, Cheryl Weissberg was aware that bad news travels fast. Since taking on Lester Gordon as a patient, she had subscribed to the feeds of the major Internet art sites, to try to stay current on the latest developments in the field. On this particular morning she was greeted by the following story:

Discovery of Major Seurat Canvas Electrifies Auction Circuit
Artnet.com, July 22:

The art world was rocked last week by an announcement from Manhattan's Cantwell Gallery, stating that they were in possession of a previously unknown painting by the Neo-Impressionist master Georges Seurat (1859-1891).

"The discovery of this major work by Seurat will prove to be one of the most significant developments of this generation," said owner Phillip Cantwell. "We are grateful and delighted to be entrusted with the task of selling it."

Improbable? Impossible? The lottery? No one knows for sure, but Cantwell appears to be quite serious about the legitimacy of the undiscovered canvas.

The work is titled Madonna and Heir *and is believed to have been painted during the interval between the birth of Seurat's son in February 1890 and the painter's death in March 1891. It is said to depict Seurat's mistress, Madeleine Knobloch, tenderly holding the infant Pierre-Georges. The painting is set in Seurat's Paris apartment, a venue familiar to art lovers as the scene of* Jeune Femme se Poudrant (Woman Powdering Herself), *painted between 1888 and 1890.*

Seurat has long been regarded as the most important artist of the Neo-Impressionist school and the originator of the Pointillist technique. Art historians have always maintained that the catalog of his work consisted of 240 paintings and drawings executed during his short life and career. The existence of another major canvas, hidden from public view for more than a century, has set off a frenzy of excitement and speculation.

According to sources, the painting was part of a private collection purchased in the years following World War II. It was given by an anonymous donor to the Palmetto State Art Museum in South Carolina, which in turn has offered it for public sale. The work has been authenticated by ArtSleuth in New York City, who subjected it to extensive spectroscopic examination, and their authentication was confirmed by leading members of the academic community.

No one knows for sure how much Madonna and Heir may realize at auction. Seurat's drawings have fetched between three and four million dollars, and comparatively minor paintings are conservatively worth twice that amount. In 1999, Island of the Grand Jatte (1884), a final study for his masterpiece A Sunday Afternoon on the Island of Grand Jatte, sold for $35.2 million including commissions. While most experts don't expect the same result in this case, the auction process can be quirky and unpredictable—particularly when bidding wars erupt between prospective buyers.

The key question being debated by members of the art world, or course, is whether Madonna and Heir is a legitimate work by Seurat.

"To be honest, I was skeptical until I saw it," said Carl Renfro, Professor Emeritus of Art History at Columbia. Renfro was one of a battery of experts called in to pass judgement on the authenticity of the canvas.

"There's no doubt in my mind that Seurat created this canvas. By the time I inspected it, tests had already confirmed that the materials dated from the 19th *century, so I was primarily focused on technique. The painting is a marvelous example of Seurat at the height of his powers. The colors are subtle and poignant, and the rendering of his mistress and infant son shows us a personal side of the painter that never surfaced in his other works."*

Despite the support of heavyweights such as Renfro, some historians are skeptical. They point to the complete absence of a bill of sale, gallery sticker or other evidence to suggest that that the work passed through the normal chain of custody. However, those who have seen it seem to have little doubt that it was created by Georges Seurat. Much of the speculation has been fueled by the anonymity of the donor, and centers on questions about why he or she would simply give away a work of such exceptional value.

"People do things for a wide variety of reasons," observed Mr. Cantwell, "and strange as it may seem, not everyone is motivated by money. My understanding is that it was an act of altruism, and that the donor wanted the painting to have the greatest possible impact on the art world. Since the sale will enable the Palmetto State Art Museum to finally construct a long-planned and long-awaited additional wing, I'd say that the donor's goal will certainly be achieved."

Founded more than twenty years ago, the Cantwell Gallery first achieved prominence during the dot-com boom of the 1990s. The gallery's public profile has increased greatly in the past five years largely due to the efforts of Mr. Cantwell, who has traveled widely to aggressively source paintings and other fine art objects. The Seurat will be their first sale of a major canvas by a leading artist and will likely be the highlight of the New York auction season.

It is expected to be offered in early September, at which time all eyes will be on the Cantwell Gallery.

*

Elizabeth Pattinger walked into her boss's office on a sunny June morning.

"Do you have a moment, sir?"

"Liz. How the hell are you?"

"I've been better. I just got off the phone with Father Humphries."

"No kidding. He actually called you?"

"He foamed at the mouth for about twenty minutes. Seems that he saw the story on *artnet.com* about the sale of the Seurat. He's extremely upset."

"What's his problem?"

"Come on, Jeff. He donated that painting to us with the sole request that it be noted as honoring the memory of his parents. Then he turns on his computer one day and sees that we're selling it. He knows full well that the painting will end up in a private gallery in a billionaire's mansion. The man is furious. He's coming unglued."

"Well, I can deal with him." Horshak chuckled. "I went to parochial school. I'm used to priests coming unglued."

"This isn't funny. The man is angry, and I think he has a right to be. He feels like he's been betrayed."

"I don't agree that he has a right to be angry." He typed something into his computer screen, and Pattinger assumed he was pulling up the story from *artnet.com.* "And I also don't happen to believe he was betrayed. He gave us the painting, Liz. Once it became our property, we had a right to do whatever we wanted with it. It will probably turn out—hopefully, at least—that his gift of the painting will fund our new wing, and he'll have the satisfaction of bringing art to a wide swath of Columbia's citizens. When you look at all the possible outcomes, I don't see how he can bitch about that."

"It wasn't what he wanted. He gave us the painting with the understanding that it would be displayed here, in memory of his parents."

"We don't always get what we want, Liz." Horshak stared at the computer screen. "The *artnet* story looks pretty flattering to me, actually."

"He's particularly frosted by the fact that he's referred to an anonymous donor. If we had at least mentioned his parents in the press materials, it might have pacified him."

"Liz, it was a *gift.* And once you give someone a gift, you give up control over it." He looked up at his assistant. "What does he want?"

"He'll tell you himself. He's going to call you."

"I assume you blamed it on me."

"Basically, yes. I told him it wasn't my decision, and it wasn't. If you recall, I opposed it strenuously at the time."

"Sure you did. I have no problem with you blaming it on me. It was my idea. And I don't mind discussing it with him. When should I expect the call from God's representative on earth?"

"Sometime this afternoon, I believe. He said he had some errands to run, and he would call you later."

"Sounds good to me." He smiled. "Don't worry about a thing. I'll handle this."

Shortly before 5 p.m., Horshak's secretary buzzed him on the intercom.

"Yes?"

"There's a Mr. Lester Gordon on the phone for you, sir."

"Very interesting indeed. Put him through."

There was a pause, and a voice that sounded similar to Father Humphries came on the line.

"Mr. Horshak?"

"Speaking."

"I'm calling on behalf of Father Humphries. My name is Lester Gordon."

"What's your relationship to Father Humphries, Mr. Gordon?"

"He's a friend and associate of mine. He asked me to call

and speak with you. He felt that he was too upset to be able to communicate with you properly."

"You know, it's strange, but your voice sounds exactly like his."

"A number of people have said that. I guess there's a resemblance."

"I'm happy to discuss it with you. How can I help you?"

"I happened to talk to Father Humphries today, and I noticed that he didn't seem like his usual self. He was quite agitated. I asked him what was bothering him, and he finally told me about the business with the painting. He's really devastated that you've decided to go ahead and sell it."

"I'm very sorry to hear that."

"As you know, he donated that painting on the condition that it be displayed in memory of his parents. It never occurred to him that you would turn around and put it up for sale. I can't imagine what your motivations were."

"They were quite simple, Mr. Gordon. For a number of years, the Palmetto State Art Museum has been trying to raise money for the construction of a new wing, and we haven't been able to meet our fundraising goals. Selling the painting will enable us to do that."

"But even so—"

"We have dozens of artworks in storage that we can't display, because we don't have the space. When the new wing is constructed, we'll be able to give the entire community access to that art. I think that's a noble goal. As far as Father Humphries' parents are concerned, I'd have no problem naming the entire wing after them. That should make him happy."

"Well, that sounds quite generous of you, and I'll make sure he knows that. I just think your decision to sell the painting took him by surprise. I don't want to offend you, but I believe he saw it as dishonest."

"I don't know you, Mr. Gordon, and I don't want to offend you either. But since you raise the issue of dishonesty, I'll tell you this: I did some research on your friend, and as far as I can tell he isn't a priest at all. He's someone else who's playing a role of a priest, for some reason. I have no idea what that reason might be, but maybe you would know."

"I'm not going to speak for him, sir. All I can tell you, looking at it from the outside, is that he has been extremely generous with you. I don't think you can deny that."

"Of course not. But put yourself in my position for a moment. Someone masquerading as a priest appears on my doorstep with priceless paintings under his arm and wants to give them to the museum. And it turns at that some of them, at least, are of questionable provenance. If you didn't know anything about the situation, wouldn't that seem fishy to you?"

"We both read the story online. *Madonna and Heir* has been officially authenticated, and many art historians believe that it's real."

"And I also believe that, or I wouldn't have offered it for sale. It would have been unethical, even criminal, to consign that canvas if I had any suspicions about its authenticity. I just don't believe that Father Humphries is a priest, and of course I wonder about his motivations. And now I find myself talking to someone who sounds exactly like him. By any chance, you wouldn't be Father Humphries, would you?"

"I'm not even going to answer that, Mr. Horshak. I understand that you're suspicious, but remember what they say about looking a gift horse in the mouth. It sounds like you're going to get exactly what you wanted out of this."

"Quite true, and I'm grateful for that. I've stopped looking into Father Humphries' background, and I no longer even wonder about this particular mystery. I'm only discussing it with you because you called and raised the issue. I hope I've reassured you about the situation, and I sincerely hope he'll be satisfied with the outcome. On the subject of gift horses, though, I'd appreciate it if you would convey a message to him."

"What's that?"

"If he really is a man of God, I would remind him of 2 Corinthians 9: 'Each one must give as he has decided in his heart, not reluctantly or under compulsion, for God loves a cheerful giver.' And if that's not enough, there's Matthew 6: 'Beware of practicing your righteousness before other people in order to be seen by them, for then you will have no reward from your Father who is in heaven.'"

CHAPTER 32

"How are you, Lester?"

"Okay, I guess."

Weissberg studied her patient carefully as he sat down facing her on the sofa. He looked tense, and his breathing was erratic.

"How did your week go?"

"Fine."

"I get the sense that something is bothering you."

"I hate to say it, but I did have a relapse. I slipped into one of the alternate personalities."

"Which one?"

"Father Humphries."

"Well, that's not the end of the world. I believe I told you that occasional lapses were normal and expected. And you're aware of it, which is certainly a step in the right direction."

"You did say to expect it, yes."

"So please tell me what happened?"

"I went into the Gordon Humphries identity and called the Palmetto State Art Museum. I wanted to talk to them about their decision to sell the second Seurat."

"Hmm. And why did you do that?"

"Because it wasn't fair. In fact, it was outrageous. Louis spent

238

a huge amount of time on that painting, and he was proud of it. And then Father Humphries gave it to the museum, asking that it be displayed in honor of his parents. He only wanted it to be seen by as many people as possible."

"I understand that you're upset about this, and I understand why. But as disturbed as you are, you still realize that you were the one who painted that canvas, don't you? It wasn't Louis."

"Of course I do. But either way, it was proof that Louis—or me—was just as talented as the real Impressionists."

"But selling the painting doesn't change that. If anything, it validates your talent. Someone will probably pay a huge amount of money for it. I know the money isn't important to you, but it's an indicator of the value of the painting."

"They went back on their word. It was an insult to Louis, to Father Humphries, and to me."

"Okay. I follow why you're so angry about the insult to both Louis and yourself. But what about Father Humphries? The parents he wanted to dedicate the painting to weren't your parents. And as you know, they weren't even real."

"Look, I get all of this on a logical level. I know that it was a fantasy, that his parents were everything I wanted my own to be. But emotionally, it's still an outrage. They had no right to do that."

"What started all of this?"

"There was a story online a few days ago about the upcoming sale of the painting. When I read it, I was infuriated."

"You're referring to the story on *artnet.com*?"

He looked surprised. "I didn't think you followed the art news."

"Since I've been treating you, I've been trying to keep up with it. It gives me more insight into your world."

"If you read the piece, you know that they didn't even mention Father Humphries by name. They kept calling him an anonymous donor. It was almost like he didn't exist."

"Well, he didn't really exist, did he?"

"For God's sake, I know that." Lester was exasperated, and Weissberg realized she needed to dial back her confrontation level. "That's not the point. Those people down in Columbia made a deal with him, and then they went back on it. It's bad enough that they did that, but they didn't even have the courtesy to call him by name."

"I gather from your point of view, they disrespected him twice. First they went back on their agreement to display the painting, and then they pretended he didn't exist. In a manner of speaking, they denied the value of two of your creations— the painting and Father Humphries."

"Exactly." He smiled and seemed to relax. "I didn't think of it exactly that way, but that's a very good way of putting it."

"The whole point, though, is that they think it's a real Seurat. That should be incredibly flattering, and not something to criticize them for."

"I guess you're right."

"Tell me about the conversation. What happened when you called?"

"I actually called twice. The first time I was Father Humphries. Horshak wasn't there, or at least they said he wasn't there, so I spoke to Elizabeth Pattinger."

"What did you say? Do you remember how the conversation went?"

"Not really. I know I was very angry, but I don't think my end of it could have been too bad. After all, Father Humphries is a very genteel and refined individual."

"At least you remember that you had the conversation. That's a very positive sign."

"I called back later in the afternoon and spoke with Horshak. That time I called as Lester Gordon. I figured there was no point in not being myself, and I wasn't going to consciously pretend to be one of the other personalities."

"Excellent. How did that go?"

"It went pretty well, to tell you the truth. I had calmed down by then, so it was a civilized conversation. I told him how I felt about his decision to sell the painting, and he defended it. He said the sale would allow them to put a new wing on the museum. In fact, he even said he would name the wing after Father Humphries' parents."

"That must have made you feel good."

"It was more than I could have hoped for, provided he's telling the truth."

"All in all, this sounds very positive. As I said, you may have been upset enough to slip back into one of the alters, but the fact that you're aware of it is very significant. It sounds like you're on the right track."

"Thank you."

"I have to tell you, though, that I'm still bothered by your close relationship with the alters. I'm not sure that it's useful to continue to regard them as friends of yours."

"But they *are* friends of mine. We've been through a lot together over the past six or seven years. And they've always been there for me."

"If they were real people, Lester, that would be great to hear." She shifted in her chair. "How are you coming along with socializing? Have you attended any of the groups on the list I gave you?"

"Not really, no."

"How come?"

"I don't know. I've been busy, I guess. I've been working on my painting."

"I still think it would be healthy for you to get out and socialize more. If you made some new friends, you'd be less dependent on the alters. You wouldn't think about them as much."

"That may be true, but I'm not going to abandon them. They're the only true friends I have."

*

"You sound disappointed."

Karen Brillstein made the observation during her weekly phone call with Cheryl Weissberg. Ever since the hypnosis session, she seemed more keenly interested in Lester's case.

"I wouldn't say disappointed. Frustrated, probably."

"How so?"

"I thought he was making real progress. And I suppose he *is* making progress. I guess what I'm saying is I thought he was cured."

"Cured is a relative term, not an absolute state of being. I suspect he's as cured as he's going to get. The fact that he slipped back into the Father Humphries alter is just part of the journey. Ask anyone who stops smoking how many times they've had a cigarette."

"I know that, and I've told him that. But he's still very close to the alters. He thinks they're his friends. He won't go out and make any real friends."

"He didn't come into therapy because he was having trouble making friends. He was dissociating. Technically he's been cured, because for the most part he's not dissociating anymore. The guy is a painter, remember? He probably lives in a fantasy world, and probably always will. You're acting like you want him to behave like an insurance salesman."

"I had the illusion that he was going to come out of this completely cured."

"And basically, he is. He now knows that he's Lester Gordon, warts and all, rather than the other identities he constructed for himself. He's rational, self-sufficient, and united in his own personality 99% of the time, at least as far as we know. That's not bad. I think we need to have a few more follow-up hypnosis sessions."

"It wouldn't hurt. I thought he had really made some progress, but he seems just as confused as ever."

"With some patients, the process takes a while. You have to keep giving them reinforcement."

"I guess you're right. But I swear, sometimes I think he was better off when his personality was fragmented and he was dissociating all the time. Now that he's more or less healed and aware of the alters, he seems more conflicted than ever."

"You're just starting out, and I know you want to be perfect. But just be a clinician—don't try to be God, or Joan of Arc. If you want to be God, focus on transmuting base metals into gold."

"All right, I get your point."

"The real issue here is this: how angry was he, and how likely is he to act out on that anger?"

"He admitted that he was angry when he called the museum, but he's always been very mild-mannered with me. I've never seen anything that resembled a potential for violence."

"You've said that a few times, and I believe you. But you don't think he'll try to make a scene at the auction itself?"

"Oh, he might protest outside. He's done that kind of thing before. But I don't believe he'd create any real trouble, even if he wanted to. I hear they're going to be selling tickets to get in. There are rumors the tickets could cost as much as a thousand bucks apiece. He doesn't have that kind of money."

"Where did you hear this?"

"I read it online. I've subscribed to the major art blogs and news feeds, just to keep up with what's going on."

"I have to take you at your word, because obviously you know him better than I do. But I'll tell you this: I did read the police report on the incident at MOMA. Witnesses said he was waving the box cutter around and screaming before the guards tackled him. It sounded like there was a basis to believe he might have been violent."

"I imagine he was screaming, or at least yelling, because nobody would listen to him."

"Of course not. People don't go to exhibition openings to hear some lunatic tell them that the art displayed there is garbage. And if he wasn't planning on attacking one of the paintings, or some other person, I don't understand why he brought the weapon with him."

"All I can tell you is that type of rage has never come out in therapy."

"Well, watch him closely. As the auction approaches, he's likely to become more agitated. If you see any signs of trouble, let me know."

CHAPTER 33

The story ran on a Sunday during the last long stretch of summer leading up to Labor Day, and it appeared that Phillip Cantwell's investment in PR was well spent:

A Forgotten Piece of Art History Surfaces on the East Side

Amid Multiple Controversies, the Art World Prepares to Turn Curiosity into Gold

Special to The New York Times Arts and Leisure Section

Georges Seurat was a study in contrasts. He was a person of refined and sensitive taste, yet also capable of analytical precision in his analysis of color. He came from a wealthy family but opted for the Bohemian life of an artist. In his art he was a rebel against the established order, yet he also became famous for formulating extremely detailed theories about the way colors interacted with each other to create—and exclude—light.

Seurat died at the age of 31. In his short life, he achieved renown as the painter who inherited the mantle of Impressionism and took the movement one step further. Today he is best known to us as the founder of the Pointillist school. His canvases exemplify the contradictions of the man himself. Seen up close, they appear to be nothing more than a jumble of dots. The further you retreat from a Pointillist painting, however, the more the world seems to come into sharp focus.

For well over a century, art historians have agreed that the Seurat oeuvre consisted of 240 masterfully executed paintings and drawings. Collectors have fought over them with a ferocity that pushed prices upward toward the stratosphere. In no small part, the price tags for his work—between $3-4 million for his remarkable drawings, and more than double that amount for the paintings—have been based on the scarcity of those efforts. Dead men, as we know, paint no more, and death is one of the most valuable currencies in the world of art.

Now another Seurat canvas has surfaced, and it appears to be legitimate. Number 241 is a major painting created toward the end of the artist's life. It is titled Madonna and Heir, *and it depicts Madeleine Knobloch, the artist's mistress, cradling their infant son in the familiar confines of their Paris apartment. Because of the subject matter, experts assume that the work was created between the birth of Seurat's son in February 1890 and the artist's death the following March. It has passed a battery of spectroscopic tests and has been authenticated by numerous experts in the field, all of whom have marveled at its beauty and technique.*

What no one seems to be able to explain is where it came from.

Origins of The Mystery

Slightly over one year ago, a Jesuit priest stepped into the Palmetto State Art Museum in Columbia, South Carolina. His name was Gordon Humphries. The frail, aging cleric met with the museum's directors and told a compelling story.

Father Humphries said that his parents had amassed a significant collection of Impressionist and post-Impressionist paintings. He told Museum officials that he was in ill health and wanted to disburse the major pieces in that collection prior to his death. His goal was to place the paintings in settings where the greatest number of people could view them.

The priest donated a watercolor titled Dawn at Dieppe, *by Paul Signac. It was authenticated and hung in the gallery near the museum's other Impressionist masterwork, a Monet. Humphries then told the museum that he was in possession of two paintings by Seurat: a study for* Circus Sideshow, *and a previously unknown work titled* Madonna and Heir. *The study for* Circus Sideshow *was ultimately displayed in the Museum, with a disclaimer: it was believed to be a work by Seurat, but its legitimacy could not be verified.*

Several months later, Madonna and Heir *arrived in Columbia. Museum officials and everyone else who saw it were dazzled by its beauty, yet no attempt was made to authenticate the painting.*

And this is where the story becomes interesting.

Gateway to the New and Old South

Columbia, South Carolina is a city of 130,000 people, located at the confluence of the Saluda and Broad Rivers. Founded in 1786, it is home to the University of South Carolina. Observers would be justified in viewing Columbia as a community in the vanguard of the region's renaissance. Yet, like other places in the New South, the city is schizophrenic in many ways. A renewed and bustling downtown is surrounded by pockets of rural poverty that have not changed greatly in more than a century.

The Palmetto State Art Museum is similar to many other regional institutions of its type, although it is not—as its name implies—a state-supported institution. It is a thriving local hub of art and culture, kept alive by a small group of dedicated donors. The permanent collection consists of a core of significant canvases, along with a bevy of minor works by major artists. There is an active schedule of exhibitions that serves as a drawing card for the area's cultural elite. For nearly a decade, the museum's dream has been the creation of a new wing, a venue that would help house their burgeoning collection and someday serve as the home base for an Impressionist gallery.

All that suddenly seemed possible last year, when Father Humphries walked through the door.

The Mysterious Benefactor

Jeffrey Horshak, museum director at Palmetto State, submitted Dawn at Dieppe *to the Atlanta-based company, Truth in Art. He obtained a pre-authentication assessment on the painting that indicated it was likely real, and he decided to take Truth in Art at their word. The priest's only stipulation was that the painting be noted as having been donated in honor of his late parents.*

Shortly after the Signac watercolor was hung at Palmetto State, Father Humphries made another visit to the museum. This time he had an interesting and compelling story. His parents' art collection contained two works by Seurat: a study for Circus Sideshow, *and a previously unknown major canvas titled Madonna and Heir. He offered both canvases to the museum and was on hand when the study for* Circus Sideshow *arrived.*

Once again Mr. Horshak submitted it to Truth in Art for a pre-authentication assessment, but this time the verdict was mixed. The painting appeared to be real, but there were inconsistencies in the brushwork. Truth in Art advised against a full authentication. Horshak hung the painting with the qualification that it was "believed to be" a Seurat.

Then, Madonna and Heir arrived in Columbia. Once again, everyone who saw it was captivated by it. They were also giddy with the thought that the painting was a previously undiscovered masterpiece by Georges Seurat. This time, however, Jeffrey Horshak did not submit the canvas for authentication, nor did he display it in the museum. What he decided to do was put it up for sale.

Enter the White Knight

Phillip Cantwell is known in the art world as a comer. After learning the auction trade at several of New York's biggest houses, he assembled a group of investors and branched out on his own, establishing his small but toney operation in a townhouse on the East Side.

Cantwell was not content with eking out a living

by selling antique teacups and Victorian armchairs. From the beginning, he wanted to bag big game. To be competitive in his situation, he understood he would have to take risks, and had no problem doing so. He traveled the world seeking out priceless and unique art objects, and he scoured Asia courting a series of wealthy collectors. The incentives he gave to those collectors helped establish the Cantwell Gallery as an essential stop on the Manhattan fine art trail. High-rolling bidders soon realized that attendance at auctions sponsored by Sotheby's, Christies or Bonham's might be de rigueur, but an afternoon at Cantwell's was likely to provide pure thrills. Last year, the gallery sold a Seurat drawing for $2.8 million to an online bidder from Singapore, nearly breaking the auction record.

It wasn't enough. Within the superheated world of the Manhattan art scene, it was widely known that Phillip Cantwell was hunting for a major canvas by a leading artist. Such paintings are not easy to find: most of them are either hanging in museums or on the walls of mansions. Cantwell was understandably elated when, several months ago, he received a call from Jeffrey Horshak offering him the opportunity to auction off one of the art world's biggest prizes.

For many months, since the day the first Seurat was delivered to Columbia, nothing had been heard from

Father Humphries. Mr. Horshak had made extensive efforts to locate him, but the priest seemed to have vanished without a trace. Following a recent article on artnet.com that revealed the museum's intention to sell Madonna and Heir, *the priest broke his silence with a phone call to Palmetto State. During that conversation, he revealed his distress at the institution's determination to sell the canvas at auction.*

Horshak has since decided to name the new wing in honor of Humphries' parents, which he feels is the fairest solution. However, he has come to believe that the person who identified himself as Humphries was actually an actor playing the role of a priest at the request of the real donor. But who could that person possibly be? Who would drop a priceless work of art on the doorstep of a regional museum and then completely disappear?

Real or Fake?
Beyond the mystery of the donor's identity is the very real question of the painting's authenticity.

ArtSleuth, the leading authenticator in New York City, conducted extensive spectroscopic tests on Madonna and Heir *and bestowed their seal of approval on the painting. A battery of academic experts also gave it their blessing. To both the trained and untrained eye, it represents the artistry and talent of Georges Seurat at his peak. Despite the small mountain of expert evidence, though, some observers remain unconvinced.*

For his part, Cantwell is ebullient. The gallery owner is just as confident that Madonna and Heir *will set a new auction record for a work by Seurat as he is convinced that the painting is authentic.*

"The sale of Madonna and Heir *will break new ground in many ways," he remarked recently. "When outsiders look at the art world, they frequently criticize it for being too focused on money. In a sense, they are correct: the huge sums being paid for famous paintings is something that the original artists never intended and couldn't have visualized. But money is merely a symbolic currency to judge the importance of a work of art. Just as important are the many ways in which a work expands the perceptions of the people who view it. This discovery of this particular painting is revolutionary, and its sale will make history."*

On September 22, when Cantwell picks up the hammer and points to Madonna and Heir, *the world will determine whether or not he is correct.*

CHAPTER 34

As Lester Gordon sat down in Weissberg's consulting room, the therapist once again noticed that her patient seemed agitated.

"How's everything, Lester? How did your week go?"

"Okay, I guess."

"You seem upset today."

"I'm still infuriated over this whole business about the painting," he said. "I'm flabbergasted at the coverage—the press seems to be in a feeding frenzy over it. It's so amazing that some days I don't even have the time to be angry."

"What in particular is bothering you?"

"You said you've been following the art world recently. I assume you saw the piece in the *Times* on Sunday?"

"Yes, I did." She smiled. "You're becoming quite a celebrity."

"The story didn't mention me at all, so I'm not a celebrity. And there's no reason why I should be. I didn't paint *Madonna and Heir*: Louis did. It took him over a year. According to the newspaper, he didn't exist."

"But we've talked about this before. The whole idea was that the painting would be perceived as a real Seurat. If people knew Louis had painted it, they might not be interested in it. At the very least, the Cantwell Gallery wouldn't be featuring it in a high-profile auction."

"I understand all of that. But all they talked about was Father Humphries, and they made him out to be either a con man or a freak. You read it yourself."

"I didn't read anything about him being a freak. They simply couldn't understand why he would give away a painting that valuable. And as far as him being a con man, I think most people would tend to view his actions with suspicion." She leaned forward to emphasize her point. "These people are in the business of selling newspapers, Lester. It's their job to create and exploit drama. You shouldn't take it so personally."

"How can I not take it personally!" He rose from the sofa and paced back and forth in the consulting room. Weissberg had never seen him this disturbed. "I'm the one they're talking about, directly or indirectly, so of course I take it personally."

"But—"

"Okay, they're getting mileage out of the news. I understand that. But what I don't understand are people like Horshak. Someone gives him a gift in good faith, and he turns around and sells it. And this Cantwell guy is the scum of the earth. All he cares about is making money and promoting his gallery."

"As far as I know, that's the way the art world works." Her voice was calm and soothing. "Please sit down, Lester. I can't talk to you if you're pacing back and forth, and it's only going to get you more upset."

"Sorry." He collapsed back onto the sofa. "This whole thing

really frosts me. This isn't the way people are supposed to act. Particularly art lovers."

"Once a work of art leaves the painter's hands, he has no control over what happens to it or how people view it. I'm sure you know that. The Impressionists didn't have that control either."

"I guess not."

"How do you plan on channeling your anger over this?"

"What do you mean?"

"I would imagine you might have fantasies about getting back at them. If you did, that would be normal."

"What I'd like to do is reveal the fact that the canvas was painted by Louis. As you know, I'm not going to profit from the sale, and I've already proved my point. I've demonstrated that no one can tell the difference between my work and the great Impressionists. If I could prove that Louis actually painted it, that would fix all of them—especially Horshak and Cantwell. Their multi-million-dollar payoff would go up in smoke."

"Do you plan on doing that?"

"There's no point, because no one would believe me. I've got the sketches and studies to prove that *Madonna and Heir* was painted in my living room. But if I tried to convince people of that, they'd make me out to be a raving lunatic. It would be worse than art school."

"I think you've already accomplished your goal. You had Louis paint the picture because your self-esteem was too low to do it yourself. Now you know you're capable of something like that. The only important thing is that you know it, not that others realize it."

"You could be right."

"Remember that this is all part of the healing process, which can be painful. You created the alters as a survival mechanism, a way to avoid feeling that pain."

"What do you mean?"

"Well, you might say that Louis represented the ambitious, aggressive artist you wanted to be. And Father Humphries, I imagine, embodied your gentler and more altruistic side. All your resentment toward your parents was channeled into the identity of Baby Les. Now that you've become a single, whole person, there are bound to be some rough edges."

"The rough edges are coming out because scumbags like Horshak and Cantwell want to take Louis's painting, ignore Father Humphries' wishes, and pocket twenty or thirty million dollars. This has to do with their actions, not my problems."

"Still, here's your challenge: now that you're a unified personality, you have to find a way to deal with those actions that will allow you to remain at peace with yourself."

"I'm working on it, but it doesn't seem like I'm making much progress."

"What are your plans for the day of the sale? Are you going to stage a protest?"

"I'll be there, and I'll do something. I'm just not sure what."

"Can I trust you not to create another situation similar to the one at the Museum of Modern Art?"

"Absolutely. That wasn't very effective either, when I look back on it."

"In a sense it was. It brought you to Bellevue, which in turn brought you into therapy. And you've made very significant progress."

"I know, and I appreciate it."

"You don't have to thank me, I just want you to reflect on how far you've come, and I wouldn't want you to jeopardize that."

"I won't. I'm not sure exactly what I'll do the day of the sale, but I'll come up with something that will make people understand the truth."

CHAPTER 35

Three weeks remained before the auction for *Madonna and Heir*. When Phillip Cantwell returned from lunch one day, his secretary handed him the usual stack of phone messages.

"Anything urgent?"

"No, sir, but there's another message from Dr. Cheryl Weissberg. She says it's important to speak with you."

"Have George call her back and see what she wants."

"Sorry, but she insists on only talking to you."

"All right." He looked at his watch. "I have about fifteen minutes before my next appointment, so let's get this over with. Please get her on the phone."

Weissberg picked up on the first ring.

"Dr. Weissberg?"

"Yes?"

"Please hold the line for Phillip Cantwell."

In a moment, she heard the gallery owner's voice on the other end: elegant and restrained, with a touch of an English accent.

"Thanks so much for calling, sir."

"I apologize for not being in touch sooner. I'm aware you've called a few times, but this has been a hectic period for me."

"I imagine so, and I appreciate it."

"What can I do for you, doctor?"

"This is a difficult subject, so please bear with me while I sketch it out for you. I'm a psychologist, and I'm bound by a code of ethics that forces me to respect the confidentiality of my patients, so I have to be careful what I say. But I can tell you that I've come into possession of some information about the painting you're planning to auction off."

"I presume you're referring to *Madonna and Heir*, by Georges Seurat?"

"That's the one, yes."

"And what is this information you'd like to share with me?"

"I don't know quite how to say this, but the painting is a forgery. I know it for a fact."

In the interval that followed, Cantwell's explosive laughter was at odds with the gallery owner's patrician manner.

"Do tell? And may I ask how you know this for a fact, as you say?"

"I'm afraid I can't tell you that, because I'm bound by confidentiality. All I can tell you is that I know it was painted by someone else."

"One of your patients, I assume?"

"I can't tell you that either, sir."

"Well, that's very informative. I thank you."

"I hope you believe me."

"The painting has been authenticated by ArtSleuth, the leading firm in the city, and their assessment has been verified by any number of academic experts. To be honest, I'm inclined to believe them rather than you."

"I understand that this phone call would strike you as very unusual."

"To the contrary, doctor. This is actually the third call I've had about this in the past week. The person before you claimed the canvas had been created by their great-uncle, who was an itinerant painter in the Warsaw Ghetto immediately prior to World War II. The person before that said that they purchased it at a yard sale in New Jersey, and it was later stolen out of their garage. It doesn't strike me as unusual in the least."

"I knew I was taking a risk by calling you, but my conscience motivated me to do it."

"I assume you're representing the person who painted the canvas? And I assume that this individual is seeking compensation of some sort?"

"Not at all. The person who painted it doesn't care about money. If he was motivated by financial gain, he would have consigned the painting to you himself."

"Well, that's quite refreshing. The previous two callers were gracious enough to offer to share the proceeds with me on a fifty-fifty basis. If you read *The New York Times*, doctor, you're probably aware that the painting was donated to the Palmetto State Art Museum in South Carolina, and that the museum contacted me to arrange the sale."

"I really wish I could share the details with you, sir, but it's much more complicated than that."

"And what would you have me do with the painting?"

"Return it to the museum, Mr. Cantwell, and allow them to exhibit it."

"I'm afraid that's not going to happen." He cleared his throat. "Here's the dilemma with this conversation, Dr. Weissberg: I have no idea who you are. You say you're a psychologist. Perhaps you are, and perhaps you're not."

"You can check me out. I'm in private practice in Brooklyn."

"I'm really quite busy, and I don't have the time or inclination for that. And on top of the question of your identity, you haven't exactly presented a compelling case. You say the painting is a forgery, yet you can't tell me who painted it or why."

"I'm just asking you to believe me. Among other things, I'm hoping to save you some embarrassment."

"Let me ask you this: did you actually observe this person in the act of forging the painting?"

"No."

"Do you have any concrete evidence of any sort to prove that the painting is a fake—not opinion or hearsay, but firsthand evidence?"

"No, but—"

"In that case, doctor, I'll be content with leaving my reputation in my own capable hands. But if you ever do come across real evidence or hard facts about this, please contact me again."

"Thanks for your time."

Cantwell hung up and buzzed his secretary.

"Yes, sir?"

"Kindly do me a favor. If this Dr. Weissberg calls again, please tell her I'm not here."

CHAPTER 36

"This is CNN breaking news. In just a moment we'll be taking you to Manhattan's Cantwell Gallery for an update on a story we've been following for several weeks now: the controversial sale of a previously unknown masterpiece by one of France's greatest painters. The work is reputed to have been created by Georges Seurat, a leading figure in the Impressionist movement of the 19th century. The painting has attracted a good deal of controversy because it was totally unknown to art experts prior to several months ago, and it is expected to fetch a huge sum on the auction block today.

"Let's go to our reporter on the scene, Chuck Gallagher. Chuck, can you hear me?"

"Indeed I can, John."

Gallagher's figure came into focus against the backdrop of the auction room.

"What's the mood there today, Chuck? Give us a sense of what's going on."

"As you can see, John, prospective bidders are just beginning to file into the room. This has been one of the most anticipated sales of the generation. The face value of tickets was one thousand dollars apiece, and we've heard reports of scalpers selling them for two to three times that amount."

"And that's just to get into the hall and have a chance to bid, correct?" asked the anchor.

"Correct. You asked about the mood here, John. I would describe the atmosphere as a cross between a country club locker room and an African safari. New York's Upper East Side, where the Cantwell Gallery is located, is one of the most exclusive zip codes in America, on a par with Beverly Hills or Palm Beach. The crowd here today is likely to be made up of extraordinarily wealthy people, most of whom know each other. But from what I've heard, I can assure you that their familiarity will not obscure the competition to snag one of art's biggest prizes."

"Chuck, describe the layout of the room, for viewers who have never attended an art auction."

"We're on the third floor of the Cantwell Gallery, and as you can see the sales room is fairly small. I'd say the maximum capacity is around one hundred. Directly behind me you see the podium, which is where Phillip Cantwell will stand an hour or so from now, when he bangs the gavel to signal the start of the auction. Behind that is a dais where perhaps one dozen agents will be sitting with laptops and cell phones, waiting for bids to come in from overseas. Insiders tell me, John, that despite all the wealth that will be represented in this room today, the winning bid is likely to come from one of those computers."

"Tell us about the Cantwell Gallery. How did they come to be in a position to conduct this sale? Why wouldn't an event of this importance have been held at one of the famous auction houses such as Sotheby's or Christies?"

"To put it simply, John, they're like Avis: they try harder. Phillip Cantwell worked at some of the large auction houses before striking out on his own. His rise has been meteoric, largely because he has been aggressive in soliciting both important canvases and major bidders. In this case, though, he was lucky. Rumor has it that Cantwell was contacted about six months ago by the Palmetto State Art Museum in South Carolina, who had received the painting from an anonymous donor. The folks at Columbia asked him if he wanted to handle the sale, and the answer of course was yes."

"For viewers who are not art connoisseurs, Chuck, can you give us an idea of the importance of this event?"

"It's huge, John. The Impressionist painters are universally credited with creating the modern art movement. Their canvases are priceless, and there is intense competition for them among collectors. On top of that, Seurat died very young, at the age of 31, and his work was limited. The discovery of a previously unknown major canvas rocked the culture of the art world. It wouldn't surprise anyone today if this painting sold for somewhere between twenty and thirty million dollars."

"There's been some controversy about the painting, hasn't there? I believe that not all the experts have concurred on whether or not it's legitimate. What can you tell us about that?"

"Hopefully, John, Mr. Cantwell can fill us in on that. He did agree to a brief interview." The reporter looked around the room. "And I hope we can locate him soon, because our camera crew will have to leave shortly, before the room fills up and the auction starts. But yes, I can verify that there has been some disagreement over this painting. That's probably to be expected, given that its existence was totally unknown prior to about six months ago."

"What—"

"Hold on, John, there he is. Mr. Cantwell, come on over." Phillip Cantwell appeared in the picture, wearing a dark blue Brioni suit, purple tie and matching pocket handkerchief. "Mr. Cantwell, thanks for your time today. I know you must be extremely busy, and I imagine you're also excited."

"I think everyone is excited here today, Chuck. We're about to make art history, and that doesn't happen very often."

"I was just telling our audience, sir, that there has been a bit of controversy regarding the authenticity of this painting. What can you tell us about that?"

"There's been a certain amount of sniping from the competition, which of course is normal. I would characterize it as sour grapes." Cantwell's manner was genial and confident. "The fact of the matter is that the authenticity of this canvas was verified by experts in the field, and some of the world's leading art historians agreed with them."

"Sir, why do you think the Palmetto State Art Museum asked you to handle the sale, rather than contacting some of your larger and better-known competitors?"

"Because we have a reputation of creating excitement in the

art world, Chuck. We make things happen. For that reason, the most important collectors have been gravitating to us over the past several years. Simply put, people want to be where the action is."

"We don't have too much time left, sir, before your security people ask us to leave, but I was wondering if you had any expectations or preference as to where this painting will end up. As you know, there's a significant divide in fine art between museums and collectors. The public would generally prefer to have great works of art on display where everyone can see them. When a collector purchases a painting, though, it's likely to disappear into his residence, where it will only be viewed by a small circle of friends. What are your feelings about that?"

"That's a great question, Chuck. I think almost anyone would prefer to have this work in a museum and available for public view. At the same time, it wouldn't surprise me if it ended up in the hands of a collector. As much as everyone hates to admit it, the world of art—along with many other realms of human endeavor—is closely connected with money."

"Why do you think that is? Why do you think the sums paid for famous paintings have escalated so sharply over the past few decades?"

"That's simple: excellence and success in one field inevitably attracts excellence and success elsewhere. But it's very important to remember that most collectors who own famous canvases lend them out periodically for museum exhibitions, so it's not fair to say that those paintings disappear. It's really the best of both worlds, when you think about it."

"Speaking of disappearance, sir, it's almost time for us to vacate the premises. One final question: any nervousness on your part? Do you anticipate some butterflies when you take the podium?"

"There's always a sense of anticipation, of course. I would say the main feeling will probably be excitement, coupled with a sincere desire to discharge our responsibility today as best we can."

"Thank you for your time, and we're grateful that you allowed us to broadcast from here prior to the sale."

"My pleasure."

"Phillip Cantwell, owner of the Cantwell Gallery, where the auction of Seurat's *Madonna and Heir* will commence shortly." The reporter turned to face the camera. "That's all for now, John. We're not being thrown out, of course, but we do want to honor our time commitments."

"Thanks for your report, Chuck. We look forward to talking with you after the auction and finding out who the lucky bidder turned out to be."

*

Lester Gordon sat in a café across the street from the Cantwell Gallery, sipping a cappuccino. He kept a close watch on the CNN trucks double-parked outside and waited for the camera crews to exit the building.

Lester wore a blue blazer, gray slacks and a powder-blue shirt. He wanted to fit in with the crowd and had purchased the outfit the week before from a discount men's store on Upper Broadway. The only other option in his closet was the black suit he had worn to his father's funeral seven years earlier, and he was afraid it would make him look like a limo driver. In place of a necktie he wore a brightly colored silk scarf, folded to resemble an old-fashioned cravat, an intentional homage to Louis Bétancourt.

Thirty minutes before the auction was scheduled to begin, he saw the TV crew walk down the steps of the townhouse. He crossed the street, approached the entrance, and handed his ticket to the security guard. He rode alone in the elevator to the third floor.

The auction room was half full, and people were congregating in clumps. Near the front, to the left of the podium, *Madonna and Heir* was displayed on a gold-tinted easel. A small throng of well-dressed people surrounded the painting. Lester took a seat on the inside aisle, roughly in the center of the room. Phillip Cantwell was circulating among the crowd, shaking hands and smiling.

A few minutes before the start of the auction, the crowd around the painting thinned out as people took their seats. Cantwell stood between the picture and the podium, chatting. Louis rose and approached him. He took a cursory look at *Madonna and Heir* while he waited to speak with Cantwell. It was similar to being in a reception line at a wedding, patiently biding your time and waiting for the chance to hug the bride.

"Mr. Cantwell, I presume?" asked Louis as he stepped in front of the gallery owner.

Cantwell smiled and extended his hand. Louis raised his hand, but instead of shaking Cantwell's he reached into the left breast pocket of his blue blazer. He pulled out a revolver, leveled it at the man's chest, and quickly shot him twice. Blood spurted from Cantwell's chest and splattered on the gold frame of *Madonna and Heir*. The last thing Lester remembered was laying at the bottom of a pile of people, listening to high-pitched screams.

CHAPTER 37

Larry Westerfeld was not so much tired as weary. He was also disgusted, having seen three murders in the past month. This was not unusual: Westerfeld was a homicide detective in New York City, and death was his business. Lately, however, he had begun to be repulsed by the senselessness of many of the cases he was assigned to work. "Whatever happened to the good old-fashioned motives like money and sex?" he had recently complained to his Lieutenant. "Give me at least one guy who kills his wife to avoid paying alimony, rather than an endless string of bozos who go around plugging strangers for shits and giggles."

"The press is clamoring for a statement," said Assistant District Attorney Sherri Brancacci, as she stared at Lester Gordon through the two-way mirror. "We can't hold them off all night."

"Fuck the press," said Westerfeld. "If they start missing deadlines, maybe they'll leave us alone."

"I have no clue what to tell them. This guy's story makes no sense whatsoever."

"Since when do these things make sense? Let's assume he woke up this morning and decided to kill a gallery owner for some reason. The man is dead, so it really doesn't matter much what the reason was. Let's send this guy to Riker's and start the legal process of frying him."

"I think we need you working in our office." Brancacci smiled. "We'd clear our calendar a lot faster."

"He was arrested with the gun in his hand, for shit's sake. If the camera crew hadn't been asked to leave before the auction started, we'd have the whole thing on tape. It shouldn't take much effort to convict him."

A uniformed cop stuck his head in the door.

"Excuse me, but we have Dr. Cheryl Weissberg here."

"Who might that be?" asked Brancacci.

"The shooter's shrink."

"Send her in."

Weissberg seemed to tiptoe into the interview room. She was dressed in a pair of khaki slacks and a polo shirt, and had obviously gotten dressed hastily. She looked upset.

"Dr. Weissberg? I'm Assistant District Attorney Sherri Brancacci, and this is Detective Larry Westerfeld."

"Nice to meet you. I wish it could be under happier circumstances."

"You're his psychiatrist?" asked Westerfeld.

"Clinical psychologist. Lester has been seeing me on and off for about a year."

"Well, you did a hell of a job." The detective yawned and glanced at Brancacci. "I love it when the shrink shows up before the lawyer. Tells you exactly where you're heading."

"Lester has been extremely mild-mannered throughout therapy." Weissberg perched on the edge of a chair, trying to avoid looking at the detective. She was afraid she would stare at his shirt cuffs, which were fraying. "At no time did he seem to present any danger to anyone."

"So you believe he just snapped?" asked Brancacci.

"It looks that way. Could you fill me in on the details of what happened?" asked Weissberg. "I rushed over here as soon as I heard the news, but I can't say that I'm up to speed."

"There was supposed to be an auction of a famous painting at the Cantwell Gallery today," said Westerfeld. "I'm sure you heard about it. It apparently was a hot ticket, a thousand bucks per head. What happened was that your boy here walked up to Phillip Cantwell right before the auction was supposed to start and shot him twice at close range."

"He actually had a ticket to the auction?"

"Why are you surprised?" asked the detective.

"I know they were expensive, and I didn't think he could afford it. But didn't they have a metal detector at the auction?"

Westerfeld ran his fingers through his hair. "Does it sound like it?"

"Larry," said Brancacci.

"I'm just trying to understand what happened," said Weissberg.

"He used an old army service revolver," said Westerfeld. "1960s issue. Any idea where he might have gotten that from?"

"His father was a retired master sergeant. He died about

six or seven years ago, and Lester inherited his rent-controlled apartment."

"Ah," said Westerfeld. "Okay."

"Can you tell us what he was doing in therapy?" asked Brancacci. "Since he's murdered someone, the confidentiality rules are out the window."

"Lester was in and out of therapy for most of his life, and he was institutionalized several times. I started treating him after he was committed to Bellevue following an incident at the Museum of Modern Art---I was finishing my residency at the time. I diagnosed him as having Dissociative Identity Disorder, or DID. It's what used to be called multiple personality disorder."

"Like Sybil?" asked Brancacci.

"More or less, yes."

"What was the incident at the museum?" asked the ADA.

"He was at an opening reception for an exhibit of Neo-Dada works. It's a type of art he really hates. He had been protesting the exhibit for some time, calling the museum, circulating petitions, that type of thing. He took out a box cutter and approached one of the paintings in an agitated state. The security guards thought he was going to slash the painting, so they tackled him. The police referred him to Bellevue."

"Let me get this straight," said Westerfeld. "This guy goes to a reception at MOMA, waves a box cutter around and gets himself arrested. But to you, he's harmless?"

"Lester is really a very gentle person. And he's an artist himself. He wouldn't have harmed a painting, no matter how much he hated it."

"No offense, doctor, but you sound a little naïve."

"I'd prefer to think of myself as idealistic."

"So what was he doing at the Cantwell Gallery?" asked Brancacci. "Why was he upset?"

"He was actually the one who painted the canvas they were auctioning off."

"I thought the painting was supposed to be some undiscovered French masterpiece," said Westerfeld.

"It was supposed to be, yes. But it was actually painted by one of Lester's alters, a man named Louis Bétancourt. Another alter, a Jesuit priest named Gordon Humphries, donated it to the Palmetto State Art Museum in honor of his parents. I was working in therapy to reunite Lester's personality, and I thought we had reached the point where he was a whole person. But apparently the decision to sell the painting reopened some very painful childhood trauma for him."

"So he shoots the gallery owner?" asked Brancacci. "That doesn't make much sense."

"She's right," said the detective. "And if he was pissed off at his parents, why would he want to donate the painting in their memory? And why would he care if it were sold?"

"That type of behavior is typical. It allows the patient to maintain a connection to the abuser."

"Well, you lost me," said Westerfeld. "To be honest, I don't care why he shot Cantwell. Motive is only useful to me before the crime is solved."

"And you never had any inkling that this man might be dangerous?" asked Brancacci.

"Not at all. If I had the slightest suspicion, I would have reported it immediately."

"He never threatened anyone, or talked about committing violence?"

"Never." She paused. "There was one occasion when the Louis Bétancourt alter was very upset about a painting he didn't like. He said that in the old days, he would have been obligated to challenge the artist to a duel."

"A duel?" asked Westerfeld. "You mean, with pistols?"

"Yes. Part of Louis's persona was that he was French, descended from a famous Impressionist painter. He wore ridiculous costumes—embroidered vests, sashes, berets, that kind of thing. He said he was an expert marksman. It was all play acting, so of course I didn't take the talk of a duel very seriously."

"Well," he said, "it doesn't take much skill with firearms to shoot someone from two feet away, so that sounds about right."

"What we don't know, detective, is who actually pulled the trigger in this situation. It could have been Lester, although that wouldn't be my guess. I think it's more likely to have been Bétancourt, who actually painted the canvas, or Father Humphries, who was outraged because he donated the picture in memory of his parents."

"Here we go," said Westerfeld. "I feel an insanity defense coming around the bend."

"I'm not an attorney, sir. I just feel badly for Lester."

"If you want to feel badly for someone," said the detective, "try Phillip Cantwell's wife and children."

"Larry, please," said Brancacci. "This isn't useful."

"You're right. The fact that he was neglected as a child gives him the right to murder people in cold blood." He stood up. "If you ladies will excuse me, I have bullshit coming out of my ears. I need to go rinse them out."

"What's going to happen?" asked Weissberg after Westerfeld left the room.

"We're going to charge him with premeditated murder," said the ADA. "His attorney can sort out whether to use an insanity defense. I imagine he'll have the best lawyer money can buy."

"I doubt it. Lester is a person of limited means. I'm sure he'll need the public defender."

"Well, he could afford a thousand dollars for a ticket to the Cantwell auction, as you pointed out. But if he needs an attorney, one will certainly be provided for him."

"May I speak with him?"

"Unfortunately, no. As you say, you're not a lawyer. He'll be arraigned, and you can visit with him after that."

"Lester really is a very gentle person. I can't imagine that he was the one who consciously pulled the trigger."

"Sorry, doctor. I don't make the law---I just enforce it." Brancacci stared at the therapist, not without sympathy. They were around the same age, at the beginning stages of establishing their careers. "I know this is difficult for you, and I'm sorry. I'll make sure he gets a commitment for psychiatric evaluation, which will at least make the early stages of incarceration easier on him."

"Thank you."

"I'll admit that I'm curious about one thing, though. You say he actually painted the canvas that was up for sale at the Cantwell Gallery."

"That's my understanding, yes."

"And as far as anyone knew, that picture was an undiscovered work by Seurat. So Lester must be an incredibly gifted painter."

"I can't say. I'm not an art expert."

"Why would someone like that create forgeries? If he had that much talent, wouldn't he want to be recognized as a genius in his own right?"

"God, I don't know." Weissberg shook her head, as tears fought their way to her eyes. "I guess there wasn't any current market for what he wanted to do. A hundred years ago, I'm sure he would have been famous. Today, it's like he's just wearing his grandfather's shoes."

CHAPTER 38

Cheryl Weissberg sat across from Karen Brillstein, sobbing uncontrollably. After pushing a box of tissues across the table toward her protégé, Brillstein watched her impassively for several minutes.

"Cheryl?" Her voice was low-pitched yet firm. "You'll have to get control of yourself."

"I'm sorry," Weissberg said between convulsive sobs. "I just feel so awful."

"Obviously so."

"This is all my fault."

"That's about the fourth time you've said that. It's normal to feel that way, but it's certainly not true."

"It's true. I should have seen this coming."

"You told me several times that the patient never exhibited any signs of potential violence. You described him as mild-mannered and docile. Isn't that so?"

Weissberg nodded.

"Then what makes you think you should have seen it, if there was nothing to see?"

"I don't know." She dried her eyes and looked at Brillstein. "Maybe I should have thought about it more carefully. Maybe

I ignored something. But I was so focused on becoming successful and making a name for myself with this case, that my ego got in the way of everything else."

"Desire for success isn't a crime, unless it obscures your ability to view the case impartially. From everything you've said, that didn't happen."

"I was in over my head from the beginning. I had no idea what I was doing."

"That's why I was supervising you. Let me ask you this: if I had thought this man was dangerous, don't you think I would have pointed it out to you?"

"Sure."

"But I didn't, because on the basis of your session notes, along with everything you told me, he posed no danger to anyone. He seemed harmless."

"Well he wasn't, after all. And now this gallery owner is dead, and his wife and children are devastated."

"The only display of ego that I see here was your desire to be perfect. You're a therapist, not Wonder Woman. Not everyone can be cured, and not all cases turn out well."

There was a long silence, during which Weissberg's breathing returned to normal. Brillstein waited, allowing her student to process what she perceived to be the facts of the situation.

"Have you seen him yet?" asked Brillstein.

"No. I tried to meet with him the night I went to the police station, but they wouldn't let me talk to him."

"Do you plan on seeing him?"

"Yes, of course. But I'll need to drive out to Riker's Island, so I'm trying to coordinate their visiting hours with my free time."

"I suspect he needs you more than ever at this point."

"You know what gets me?" Weissberg asked. "You know what I think is the ultimate irony of this case?"

"What's that?"

"I *did* cure him. As a clinician, I did everything that was required according to our understanding of the disorder. I gave him the diagnosis and made him aware of the existence of the alters. I reunited two of the alters, Father Humphries and Louis Bétancourt, back into Lester's personality. With your help, we also brought Baby Les back into his psyche."

"I'm not sure where you're going with this."

"When he was suffering from DID, Lester was completely harmless. He never would have hurt anyone. It was only after I cured him, and all the alternate identities were merged into his original self, that he became violent. So I really am responsible for this."

"Cheryl, that's nonsense."

"I wish it was. By curing him, I reunited all the spiteful and potentially dangerous aspects of his personality. That's when he shot Phillip Cantwell."

"Okay, let's reason this out. What's your theory? Why did he shoot Cantwell?"

"I don't have a theory. All I know is the guy was harmless when I got my hands on him, and now he's up for murder. Maybe the cause was repressed rage from the way he was treated as a child. We never quite got to the root of that with Baby Les, so in retrospect I guess it was unresolved. Maybe it was the way Louis felt he was treated by the Palmetto State Art Museum and the Cantwell Gallery. His talent was never really acknowledged, and he never received the credit he deserved as an artist."

"But I thought that was his motivation in the first place: to do the painting anonymously and have everyone mistake it for a Seurat. In order to achieve his goal, he couldn't be recognized as the painter."

"I have no idea. Maybe he started out wanting to be anonymous, then felt differently when he read all the press coverage and realized he wasn't getting credit as the genius who actually painted the canvas."

"Again, I think this is understandable up to a point, but you'll need to let it go. And if you're called to testify at his trial, I strongly advise against saying that you were responsible for the crime because you cured him."

"What if it's true?"

"If it's true, it's an irony you'll have to live with. But don't expect the public, or the legal system, to grasp the complexities of all this. The last thing you want is to end up with is sanctions, or even facing charges yourself—particularly as I don't believe there's any basis for the guilt you seem to be experiencing."

"I don't know." Weissberg shook her head. "As I told you, I don't really have a theory. But when I step back and look at this case, I have the uncomfortable feeling that I created a monster."

*

On the following Sunday, Weissberg drove out to Riker's Island to visit Lester Gordon. He had been incarcerated in protective custody for eight days following the shooting of Phillip Cantwell. The therapist did her best to look cheerful as Lester was led into the room. He was handcuffed, and he seemed smaller in his gray jumpsuit.

"How are you, Lester?"

"Not too bad. I'm OK, actually."

"I apologize for not coming sooner, but my schedule had me tied up. I did go down to the police station the night you were arrested, but they wouldn't let me speak to you."

"There's no need to apologize. I appreciate the fact that you came."

"Let's start by addressing the elephant in the room. I have to ask you: why did you do this?"

"Of all people, you should know the answer. I was angry because of the way they treated both Father Humphries and Louis. They gave them no respect at all, and even gloated over all the money they were going to make by selling the painting."

"When you say 'they,' who are you referring to?"

"Horshak. Pattinger. Cantwell. All of them, the whole art establishment."

"Does this have something to do with the way you were treated in art school?"

"No, it has to do with the way these people behaved. They

have no respect for art. To them, artists are just pawns they can use to buy yachts or build new wings on their museum."

"But why Cantwell? What did he do to you?"

"He was a greedy scumbag. And he didn't do much to me, but he completely disrespected Louis. I know we talked about this."

Weissberg rubbed her eyes, trying to hide her exasperation. "Please tell me you had slipped into one of the alters when you shot him."

"I've already been asked that a number of times, and the answer is no. When I shot him, I was myself. I was avenging Louis's honor and defending the importance of art. He deserved it."

"Lester, please. Do you have any idea what will happen to you in prison?"

He shrugged. "I've been persecuted all my life. But don't expect me to try and get out of this because I'm a crazy person. This is the sanest thing I ever did."

"God almighty." She stared at him for nearly a full minute. "I don't think you're crazy, and I won't try to convince anyone else that you are. But I'm going to do everything I can for you."

"Thank you. I know you mean well."

"I think if we could convince people that you really painted that canvas, it might go a long way toward mitigating your situation. Did you keep all the sketches and studies you did for it?"

"Louis kept them. They're in the living room of the

apartment, right where he left them. I wouldn't have messed with them."

"I'm going to look into it. It might help your defense, and it would finally give you the recognition you deserve as a painter."

"I appreciate that."

"I'll probably speak to your attorney. Are you happy with him?"

"He seems smart enough."

"What's his name?"

"Hoffman. Paul Hoffman."

The guard opened the door and took several steps into the room.

"Just a few minutes left, ma'am."

"Okay, thanks." She looked at Lester. "I wasn't aware that you knew how to handle a gun."

"My father taught me. He used to take me to the firing range. This was early on, before he became convinced that I was a hopeless sissy." He smiled. "I owe it all to him."

CHAPTER 39

Two days later, Cheryl Weissberg took the subway to the City Hall station and walked over to the Public Defender's office at 225 Broadway, where she knocked on Paul Hoffman's door.

"Come in!"

Hoffman was seated at his desk with a telephone to his ear. He motioned Weissberg to the chair directly across from him.

"No, that's not good enough," he said into the receiver. "I don't care how many eyewitnesses you have, the DNA says he didn't do it. No, you're not getting another lineup." He grinned and winked at his guest. "Yeah. Merry Christmas to you too."

He placed the phone in its console and rose to shake hands with her.

"Sorry about that."

"No problem," said Weissberg. "I know you're busy. Thanks for seeing me."

He picked up a file on his desk and started flipping through it. "Let's see. Lester Gordon, Murder One. Unusual case. He doesn't look like the type to go around shooting people." He put down the file and looked at her. "But you're his shrink, so

I imagine you're going to tell me he wasn't in his right mind."

"I don't know what to tell you, but I thought I'd give you some background."

"Go ahead."

"Lester has Dissociative Identity Disorder, or what most people still think of as multiple personality. In his case, he had three functioning identities—what we call alters."

"Yes, all of that is in his file. I assume you can testify that one of the other personalities was in control at the time of the shooting."

"I wasn't there, so I don't know who was in control. But obviously he wasn't in his right mind."

"Maybe not. But here's the problem, doctor: insanity defenses don't work. They're used very infrequently, less than 1% of the time, and they're usually not successful."

"I thought it was more common than that."

"If you watch a lot of TV, that's what you might think. And in this case, we've got further problems."

"What might those be?"

"As bad as the success rate is for insanity defenses, this DID business is even worse. The track record is lousy. It started out with an Ohio case in 1978, where a man was acquitted of kidnapping and raping three women because he had something like two dozen different personalities, and the defense was able to prove that one of the alters was in control during the commission of the crimes. The public outcry was humongous—people were really outraged at the verdict. Things went downhill after that. Ever since, juries in different states have rejected DID as a defense."

"I wasn't aware of that. But I assume you've met with Lester?"

"Several times."

"Then you know how soft-spoken and docile his is. No one would assume that someone like that was capable of violence."

Hoffman smiled. "I'm afraid you're wrong again, doctor. Almost half of male DID cases take part in some sort of criminal activity, and nearly 20% commit murder. I can't comment on the validity of the disorder, but I can tell you that this line of defense doesn't have much promise. And in any event, he won't let me use insanity. He claims he was in full possession of his faculties at the time he committed the crime. I'm afraid we've hit the jackpot here."

"What's going to happen to him?"

"He's charged with Murder One, which is premeditation. And in all fairness, he did go the gallery with a loaded gun and the intention of killing Phillip Cantwell. And he did shoot him twice in the chest at close range, so it's hard to see how he doesn't get convicted. I mean, I hate to sound negative, but he was literally arrested with the gun in his hand. I'm trying to come up with something, but I'm not having much luck. He's not being very cooperative, either."

"Mr. Hoffman, I'll be honest with you: I seriously doubt that Lester is going to survive prison. You've seen him, so you understand what I mean."

"True, and I'm going to do my best."

"I assume you have some experience defending murder cases?"

"Yes, and things could be worse. As long as we're being honest, I have to tell you we're lucky New York no longer has the death penalty."

"There must be some way his mental condition can be taken into account. I'm willing to testify, if you think that will help."

"It might."

"I can line up other testimony as well. I studied at Columbia with Dr. Karen Brillstein, who's the recognized authority in the field on DID. She can testify also."

"I don't think that would be a very good idea."

"What do you mean?"

Hoffman picked up a rubber band and played with it. "No offense, Dr. Weissberg, but someone like Brillstein would probably backfire with a jury. She's probably very knowledgeable, and she may be an expert, but she has attracted a lot of controversy to herself by appearing on tabloid TV shows like Geraldo and Nancy Grace. Maybe you remember some of them."

Weissberg reddened at the reference. She did remember the Geraldo episode, which she had stayed up late to watch and which had turned into a circus between Brillstein and the victims of Arthur Burmeister. Burmeister was a brilliant and charismatic accountant who had suffered from DID. His primary alter was a con man who had engineered a massive

Ponzi scheme, fleecing investors out of nearly $200 million. Many of the victims had been entertained at parties on Burmeister's lavish yacht, which had sailed up and down the Hudson River laden with caviar, Champagne, recreational drugs and hookers. Now sober, the investors regaled the TV audience with tales of ruined legacies, foreclosed mortgages and broken marriages. Brillstein's attempts to present the disease in compassionate terms infuriated the victims, some of whom had to be restrained from physically attacking her.

"All right, forget about Dr. Brillstein. Some of this may have been my fault. I've just started private practice, and Lester was my first DID case. I never picked up on any danger that he might turn violent, and I may well have missed something. It never occurred to me that he'd be capable of something like this."

"Don't beat yourself up over it. He seems perfectly calm and harmless to me, so obviously he just snapped. I still don't get why he shot Cantwell, though, and it would be valuable if we could at least present some motivation for the crime that tied into his illness."

"It's a complicated situation. To the outside world, Lester was a failed art student. Everyone thought he was a loser. He loved the Impressionists and was committed to painting in that style. One of his alters painted the canvas that the Cantwell Gallery was auctioning off as a Seurat. Another alter had donated it to the Palmetto State Art Museum."

"You're kidding me: he actually painted that picture?"

"It sounds incredible, but he did."

"That painting was expected to sell in the vicinity of $20 million, maybe more. How come he didn't consign it himself?"

"He wasn't a typical art forger. It wasn't about the money with him. Most of it was getting the world to realize how talented he was."

"Jesus." Hoffman looked out the window, shaking his head. "Just when you think you've seen it all. Can you prove he painted it?"

"It took over a year to produce. There are numerous studies in his apartment. I think he sourced most of the materials from a local art store, so you could always subpoena them."

"Hmm. We may be on to something there. Let me think about it."

"All I'm asking is that he doesn't wind up in prison in general population. You know what will happen to him."

"Well, I have to tell you that a mental institution might not be much better in some ways."

"You don't have to tell me. I did a residency at Bellevue."

"Then you know the story."

"But maybe there's some alternative path for him. Let me look into it. And in the meantime, I'd appreciate anything you could do."

"I'll sleep on it." He rose and shook her hand. "Anything for art."

CHAPTER 40

October 9: Special to The New York Times

A Case of Blurred Identity
*In what might be the most bizarre twist in a very
strange case, the alleged killer of East Side Gallery
owner Phillip Cantwell now claims to be history's most
accomplished art forger.*

*Lester Gordon, 53, of Brooklyn, is currently being
held without bail at Riker's Island. He is charged with
the murder of Mr. Cantwell on September 22, the day
his gallery was scheduled to auction off a previously
unknown canvas by Georges Seurat titled* Madonna
and Heir. *According to eyewitnesses, Gordon
approached Cantwell shortly before the sale was about
to begin and shot him several times at close range. He
was arrested at the scene.*

The discovery of Madonna and Heir *had electrified
the art world over the past few months. Georges
Seurat was a giant of the Impressionist school and is
considered to be one of the most important painters of*

the 19th century. He invented the technique known as Pointillism and became famous for canvases such as A Sunday Afternoon on the Island of Grand Jatte. *Ever since the painter's death in 1891, art historians have believed that his work consisted of 240 paintings and drawings.* Madonna and Heir *would have been the 241st.*

Lester Gordon, by contrast, was a failed art student who dreamed of painting in the Impressionist style. He also suffered from a mental condition known as DID, or Dissociative Personality Disorder, commonly known to the public as multiple personality. The condition became famous as a result of the 1976 film Sybil. *Hollywood aside, DID is a controversial diagnosis in the psychological world. After suffering childhood abuse at the hands of their parents, patients are believed to construct a number of fully functioning alternative identities. Cases are both rare and difficult to treat.*

Mr. Gordon now claims that Madonna and Heir *was painted by one of those identities, an individual named Louis Bétancourt. The work occurred prior to the point that psychotherapy "cured" Gordon, reuniting his alternative personalities into one person. Gordon maintains that when he pulled the trigger on Mr. Cantwell, he was avenging the shoddy treatment that Louis Bétancourt had received from the art world.*

Exactly how good a forgery is Madonna and Heir? *Good enough that ArtSleuth, the city's leading authenticator, subjected it to an extensive battery of tests and proclaimed in to be real. It was also good enough to fool a number of leading academic authorities.*

"I swore it was the real thing," admitted Dr. Carl Renfro, Professor Emeritus of Art History at Columbia University. "It was an incredibly faithful reproduction of Seurat's technique, and all the materials seemed historically accurate. It never occurred to me that a forger could be that skilled."

Brooklyn psychologist Dr. Cheryl Weissberg treated Gordon during a stay at Bellevue last year and continued to see him in private practice. She is known to be a disciple of Columbia's Dr. Karen Brillstein, regarded as the foremost authority on DID. Dr. Weissberg has refused to comment on the case, citing confidentiality concerns. It is unclear whether both she and Dr. Brillstein will be called to testify at Gordon's trial, if the case eventually comes to trial. According to sources, Mr. Gordon has thus far refused to agree with his attorney's advice to employ an insanity defense. He maintains that he was in full control of his faculties when he shot Cantwell, and in any event legal analysts point out that an insanity defense would be unlikely to work in these circumstances.

There are similarities between Gordon's case and Sybil's. Both individuals were painters, and both suffered childhood abuse, although Gordon's is reported to have been mild. There are differences as well. Sybil had 17 fully functioning personalities, while Gordon had three. And the most important distinction is that Sybil was not a violent person, while Gordon is currently charged with murder.

Gordon's attorney, public defender Paul Hoffman, claims to have assembled a mountain of evidence that points to the likelihood that his client was the painter of Madonna and Heir. *Hoffman obtained a court order to remove art materials from Mr. Gordon's Brooklyn apartment, which has been sealed by police as a potential crime scene since Cantwell's murder. According to Hoffman, he is in possession of numerous sketches and studies that prove Gordon was the true creator of the Seurat masterpiece during the time when he was under the sway of the Louis Bétancourt personality.*

At this point, it's unclear how effective that evidence will be on Mr. Gordon's behalf. Nor is anyone certain what will happen with Madonna and Heir. It may yet end up on the auction block, since notoriety frequently trumps authenticity in the minds of some collectors. If so, it is likely to fetch a large sum, although nothing close to the $20+ million it was originally expected to sell for. It may also be returned to Columbia for display or sale. That determination will be made by Director Horshak.

While he ponders his decision, Lester Gordon sits at Riker's in protective custody. If he does not resort to an insanity defense, he is likely to be convicted of first degree murder, and his fate at that point is equally uncertain. Although New York is no longer a death penalty state, he would probably be facing life in prison without the possibility of parole. If a plea is negotiated in this case, which increasingly seems to be the likely outcome, Mr. Gordon's mental state would almost certainly be taken into account.

CHAPTER 41

"This is horrendous," said Jeffrey Horshak. "It just gets worse and worse. First Mr. Cantwell, and now this."

"On your end, it's not all bad news," said George Portius, Director of Operations for the late Phillip Cantwell. "I need to bring you up to speed."

This was the second conversation between the two men. The first had occurred the day after the shooting, when Horshak had phoned to offer his condolences. Now, slightly more than one week had passed since the *Times* story revealed Lester Gordon as the forger, and Portius had initiated the call this time.

"I met with Gordon's attorney yesterday," said Portius. "He let me examine the evidence found in his client's apartment."

"I'm surprised he allowed that. Did you also have to get a court order to see it?"

"Not at all. The more people they can convince that he was the forger, the better the case looks for them, or so the lawyer thinks. Anyway, he has a whole series of sketches and studies for *Madonna and Heir*. When you examine them in order, there's not much doubt."

"You're telling me this guy actually painted the picture?"

"It sure seems that way."

"But that's impossible. How could he have fooled everybody?"

"I don't know, and I don't think it matters much at this point. Looking foolish is better than being dead. But the reason I called is to tell you the good news. We have an offer on the painting."

"You're kidding me."

"Several offers, actually. A collector in California offered one million eight, and someone from Asia countered at two million. It's not over yet. My sense is that it could go as high as three." There was an audible chuckle on his end of the line. "You may get your new wing after all."

"Why the hell would someone give you three million for a forgery? Why would they even pay five cents for it?"

"It happens frequently, and this painting appears to be particularly in demand. It's received a tremendous amount of publicity—ironically, most of it was paid for by Phillip. But it's not an unusual situation. People paid large sums of money for some of Wolfgang Beltracchi's forgeries, even after they knew they were fake. You'll eventually have to decide whether or not to take the best offer, so I wanted you to start thinking about it."

"That's a lot of money for a fake."

"Yes and no. It's all relative. For some of these guys, it's chump change. They get to hang it on their wall and tell people a fantastic story. The Asian bidder specifically requested that we not clean the blood spatter from the painting. I assume he wanted to regale his guests with tales of the gun-slinging

American art culture."

"Jesus, I don't know. You guys have been through the wringer on this. I'll do whatever makes it easiest for you."

"At this point, I'd be relieved to get this painting out of the building. But it goes beyond that: we'll have to liquidate assets to take care of Phillip's widow. Hopefully there'll be enough left over to keep this place going."

"Why would you have to do that? I had the impression the gallery was doing very well."

"Oh, we were making a splash. But Phillip was overextended. He has always out on the edges, playing the margins. He was convinced it would pay off eventually. It probably would have, if he had lived."

"I don't know what to say. The last thing I want to do I be insensitive to your situation. I'd rather—"

"Mr. Horshak, my advice is to take the money and run. Let's close out this whole business and try to go forward."

"Damn." There was a pause, while the museum director tried to process the information. "I'm really sorry."

"There's no need. It certainly wasn't your fault. I'll keep you posted on the offers."

"What do you think you'll do?"

"Me personally? I haven't given it much thought. My primary focus is settling things here. After that, I suppose I'll have to look for a job if the gallery doesn't survive. I doubt that it will: Phillip was really a one-man show."

"That really sucks."

"Yes and no. It may turn out to be the best thing that ever happened to me. I've given some thought over the past few weeks to getting out of this racket entirely, but I probably won't. The irony is that this whole business will probably make me a sought-after commodity in the industry."

"How so?"

"Nothing sells like notoriety, and everyone is always searching for the next undiscovered masterpiece."

*

"I'd like to help you, Dr. Weissberg," said Assistant District Attorney Sherri Brancacci, as she closed the door to her office. "But I have to tell you it would be a lot easier if this case weren't being tried in the press."

"I don't know anything about the press," said Weissberg. "Like you, I just read the papers. I haven't spoken to a reporter about this case, and it would be against my code of ethics to do so."

"I believe you." Brancacci stared at the thick file on her desk and let out a deep sigh. "But someone is talking to them. I assume it's Hoffman."

"That may well be."

"They're eating it up, and I can hardly blame them. It's a great story: the undiscovered genius who can paint as well as the Impressionists. Deep down, we all think we're Michelangelo."

"I gather you're not impressed."

"This guy shot Phillip Cantwell twice, in the center of his

chest," said Brancacci. "He severed the aorta. Do you know what that looks like?"

"No."

"The amount of blood is staggering. It's like opening a fire hydrant, or a geyser erupting."

"I'm glad I wasn't there. But you've spoken with him. Does he appear to be in his right mind?"

"I think he's crazy as a loon, but here's the problem: he refuses to plead insanity. He won't listen to his attorney. I assume you've raised the option with him also."

"I have, and he won't hear of it. But we can't send him to prison. He won't last ten minutes."

"If he won't help himself, there's not a whole lot I can do. Even if someone convinced him to plead insanity, I don't know if it would hold up at trial."

"Why does the case have to go to trial?" asked Weissberg. "Can't we work out some arrangement for him?"

"Such as what? Do you have any ideas?"

"Give me some time. Let me ask around. I think I might have some possibilities."

"I can't give you a whole lot of time. Judges read the papers too. It seems like almost every week, I pick up the *Times* and see some story about how he's God's gift to the art world."

"Well, he's very talented. You'd have to admit that."

"Tell that to Phillip Cantwell's family. The wife is distraught—she calls me all the time to find out how the case is going. She says her kids are behaving erratically, acting out, getting suspended from school. It's a mess."

"Can I talk to you off the record?"

"Sure."

"I screwed up here. I had just completed my residency, I didn't have enough experience treating patients, and this case was very complex. Yes, I was being supervised, but I made a bunch of mistakes. You and I are around the same age. I'm sure you understand what I'm talking about."

Brancacci rose suddenly and walked to the window. She spent a moment staring down at Hogan Place, then walked back to her desk. She looked like she was about to cry.

"My first year here, I thought I was a hotshot. I was always the brightest student in the room in law school, passed the bar on my first try. Really full of myself. This black kid was arrested for the rape of a young girl in his neighborhood. The kid seemed like a straight arrow—good student, no record, decent family—but we had two or three witnesses who said it was him. I really leaned on him, got him remanded as a predator. Everybody told me to wait for the DNA, but I wouldn't stop. He hung himself at Riker's."

"That's awful."

"It wasn't him, of course. After he died the DNA didn't match, and the witnesses recanted their identifications. I'll spend the rest of my life trying to make up for it. That's not to say I go easy on the bad guys, but you're correct: this is a complicated case. And from what I can tell, your guy is as whacked as you say he is."

"Give me a few weeks, and I'll figure something out. I understand he can't go back out on the street, but there has to be some solution."

"You'll have to find it, not me. I'll have him examined by one of our psychiatrists, which might help. I suggest you write a detailed report on his condition. Throw in the kitchen sink, make it as clinical as possible, so I can use it for ammo. According to Hoffman, he has all the sketches from Lester's apartment, and he really did paint that picture. Hopefully we can work something out. But if we can, it'll be up to you to convince him to go along with the program."

"That would be great. It would mean a lot to me."

"Don't misunderstand me. He's not getting out. I don't want you harboring any illusions that this guy will be paroled some day and end up teaching at Pratt."

"I'd just like to help him. That's what I was supposed to do in the first place."

CHAPTER 42

Joel Needleman walked into the interview room at Riker's, took a look at Lester Gordon, and walked back to the door.

"Do me a favor," he told the guard. "Remove his handcuffs, please."

"That's not recommended. This guy is up for murder."

"I was in the Marines. I think I can handle myself."

The guard shrugged and unlocked the cuffs. Needleman extended his hand.

"I'm Dr. Needleman, Lester. Nice to meet you."

"I appreciate it, thank you." He rubbed his wrists as the doctor sat down opposite him. "You're a shrink?"

"A psychiatrist. As you probably know, I'm here to do a court-ordered evaluation on you."

"Yes, they told me."

"I'm sure you're no stranger to this process. I imagine you've had a lot of therapy over the years."

"More than I can remember."

"I read your file, and that's what I figured. I think we can skip a number of the preliminaries and get right to the heart of the matter."

"Sure. Go ahead."

"Do you know why you're here?"

"Of course. I shot Phillip Cantwell."

"Why did you do that?"

"Because he made a living exploiting art. He was a bottom feeder. And on the day I shot him, he was getting ready to exploit art that was created by a good friend of mine."

"And who was that?"

"His name is Louis Bétancourt. He's an incredibly talented painter—so talented, actually, that everyone believed his painting was done by Georges Seurat."

"I was under the impression that you were the one who did the painting."

"Well, it's complicated. According to Dr. Weissberg, I have something called DID."

"Dissociative Identity Disorder?"

"I guess that's right. I have these other identities, and when I slip into them I lose track of time."

Needleman was taking notes on a steno pad as the pair conversed. "So why would you say that Louis Bétancourt was the one who painted the picture, if you're aware that you actually did it yourself?"

"Because I painted that picture when I was Louis. It took him over a year. It was an incredible amount of work, and when it was finished it was an amazing achievement. As I said, it was impossible to tell it apart from a Seurat. But people like Cantwell didn't care about that. He totally disrespected Louis. He had no regard for his talent."

"According to Dr. Weissberg's notes, you've been unified with your three alters. She now believes that you are a whole person. So why would you remain so attached to Louis?"

"Because people like Louis and Father Humphries became my friends, and I should look out for my friends. I had to defend Louis. He needed someone to speak for him, and that person had to be me."

"Father Humphries was another one of your alternate identities?"

"Yes."

"The way you say Louis was treated by Phillip Cantwell—does it remind you of the way you were treated at some point in your life?"

"Of course. Try many points in my life."

"Then you really felt you were defending yourself?"

"Sure. I guess so."

"But you continue to insist that you were standing up for Louis, even though you're aware that Louis didn't exist."

"Well, I told you it was complicated. Maybe he doesn't exist as a separate person anymore. But he *did* exist at one time, and he painted *Madonna and Heir*. All the shrinks and all the gallery owners in the world can't deny that or take it away from him. I may no longer be him, but he deserves some respect. And as his friend, it's my responsibility to see that he gets it."

"Here's what I don't understand, Lester. Let's agree for a moment that it was greedy and exploitive of Cantwell to sell your friend's painting. But by believing it to be a Seurat and selling it as a Seurat, wasn't he really giving Louis all the respect in the world? In effect, he was saying that Louis was just as talented as a great Impressionist."

"No offense, but that's a cop-out. Cantwell was doing nothing of the sort. All he was interested in was lining his pockets at the expense of other people's talent."

"I'm not sure I'm clear on that, but let's move on. Do you believe that shooting Phillip Cantwell was wrong?"

"I don't see how right and wrong have anything to do with it. He was a greedy scumbag who was disrespecting a great talent, so I shot him."

"I know you're aware that every major religion would say it's wrong. Obviously the law thinks so, or you wouldn't be here. But you don't agree?"

"I told you: I think right or wrong is beside the point."

"Do you regret it?"

"Not at all."

"Then I gather you'd do it again if you had the chance?"

"Sure I would, except I'm not going to get that chance."

"Before you said that the way Louis was treated by Cantwell reminded you of the way you were treated many times in your life. When you shot him, did you feel that you were getting even for all those episodes of abuse and mistreatment?"

"I don't know. I'd have to think about that."

"Do you remember how you felt that day when you pulled the trigger?"

"Sure." Lester smiled. "I felt that everything was finally right."

"What do you mean?"

"For most of my life, nothing made sense to me. The world seemed crazy, along with almost everybody in it. When I shot Cantwell, things finally made sense. Everything sort of fell into place. It wasn't revenge so much as relief."

"I see. Well, your perspective is interesting." He looked up from his steno pad. "Is there anything else you want to tell me? Anything you feel might be important?"

"I want you to know that I really appreciate all the effort Dr. Weissberg made. I know she truly cares about me, and that means a lot, because very few people ever have. And I'm sorry if I disappointed her or let her down. This whole business was just far more complicated than she realized."

"Do you believe you were sick?"

"Of course, and I know Dr. Weissberg was trying to help. But as you say, I've had a lot of therapy, and I know that therapists have their own agenda."

*

"You've got a real winner on your hands," said Joel Needleman later that afternoon, as he sat in Sherri Brancacci's office.

"Care to be more specific?"

"From what I can tell, he's a sociopath. He has no firm concept of right and wrong, and he doesn't regret shooting Cantwell. He'd do it again if he had the opportunity."

"Terrific. Do you think he's capable of standing trial?"

"I don't know what he's capable of doing, to tell you the truth. If you put him on trial, he'd just convict himself with one irrational statement after another. On top of that, it would be a three-ring circus. The press would eat it up. I'm thinking O.J. revisited."

"Should he be committed?"

"He sure as hell should never be out on the street again," said Needleman. "Let's start with that."

"Nobody disputes it. Weissberg is concerned that he wouldn't survive prison, and she's obviously right. I'm not clear on how much better a state mental facility would be."

"Depends on where. The worst-case scenario wouldn't be much better than prison. In most situations, he'd simply be medicated into oblivion and warehoused. Even if you could get him into a sweetheart facility, I'm not sure how responsive he'd be to therapy. This guy has had a lot of therapy, and all he's learned is how to game the system."

"Weissberg seems to be angling for continued therapy."

"She's a very inexperienced clinician."

"She admits that herself."

"I can tell you that her proclamation that she cured this man is wishful thinking. It's a complete fiction. He still thinks his alters are his best buddies. He stands ready to defend them against all enemies, foreign and domestic."

"Then what's your recommendation?"

"Put him somewhere and get this behind you. Take the

control of the situation out of the hands of *The New York Times*."

"You don't sound happy with that as a solution."

"I'm far from thrilled, but this is one of those cases where there's no good solution. If you go the compassion route, the Cantwell family will be outraged. But he can't go to prison, because he'll die there and you'll be accused of killing the greatest painter since Leonardo da Vinci. Let's all put our heads together and figure something out."

CHAPTER 43

"Thanks for your time today. I really appreciate it."

Cheryl Weissberg sat down facing Dr. Peter Jensen, Supervising Resident at Bellevue and her former mentor.

"My pleasure, really. I wasn't sure I would see you again."

She laughed. "To be honest, I wasn't sure you wanted to. I know I was a real pain in the ass when I was here."

"Not really. I actually admired your dedication and idealism, believe it or not."

"There were times when it didn't seem that way."

"Oh, you got on my nerves every once in a while, but it was fine. You reminded me a lot of my oldest daughter. She was also committed to saving the world at one point. In college, she was quite the political activist."

"What's she doing now?"

"Working on Wall Street." There was a pause, and they both exploded with laughter. "My younger daughter, on the other hand, has remained fairly idealistic. She's working for the Sierra Club—or International Treehuggers, as I like to call them."

"I guess a lot of kids go through that phase."

"Yes, and fortunately for society it's not always a phase. As annoying as you might have been at times, I have to admit that we need more people like you. You're a true believer."

"Thank you."

"You're blushing."

"Well, I wasn't expecting compliments. It's very gracious."

"You and I see things differently, that's all. As a clinician, I think you picture yourself as someone who repairs fine Swiss watches: people bring you these intricate pieces of machinery and you work on them until they function as beautifully as they were intended to. I see myself as the proprietor of a pawn shop. Someone brings me a broken Swiss watch, I patch it up and resell it. Sooner or later, I'm aware the watch will break again and I'll get it back."

"That must be frustrating."

"It's realistic. This is a job for me, not a sacred calling. I do the best I can. And if all goes well, within ten years I'll be fishing in Florida. It's just a different in vision and approach."

"I understand."

"And speaking of frustration, it looks like you've had quite a year." He looked at her with unexpected sympathy. "I've been reading the papers."

"It's a mess. It has really cause me to reexamine myself and my purpose in life."

"Sometimes that's a good thing. Have you come to any conclusions?"

"For one thing, I have to keep going and not get discouraged. For another, the human psyche is more complicated than they teach you in school—far more moving parts than a Swiss watch."

"This is true. Well, it hardly seems like a year has gone by since Mr. Gordon appeared on our doorstep."

She nodded. "A lot happened."

"Do you think the case will go to trial?"

"That's what I'm working on now. I'm trying to find some way to get him the ongoing care that he needs, rather than have him sent to prison. He won't survive."

"Are you making any headway?"

"My thoughts are that if I can somehow communicate the complexity of his condition to the authorities, there might be some way to institutionalize him. Are you aware that he actually painted the picture that was going to be auctioned off?"

"I think I just read a newspaper story about that, yes. How did he accomplish that? Was he a savant?"

"He's unbelievably talented, obviously, but his low self-esteem never allowed him to realize it. The painting was done by one of his alters."

"I gather your friend Dr. Brillstein played a role in this?"

"She supervised me on the case. I'm aware you don't like her."

"Likes and dislikes have nothing to do with it."

"Go ahead."

He looked puzzled. "Go ahead and do what?"

"Say that you told me so. I know you've always been skeptical about DID. And in fact, Lester Gordon did have three alters, two of which were fully functioning. I just didn't handle the case very well. I was in over my head."

"I'll do nothing of the sort. I give you all the credit in the world for your good intentions. Hopefully you've learned some lessons from this."

"God, I hope so."

"What's the status of the case? Are you making any headway with the authorities?"

"I think so. It's pretty clear that he's disturbed. The only question is what to do with him."

"You spoke a moment ago about institutionalizing him."

"That would be the best course. And I feel obligated to find a solution, since I feel responsible. I screwed up."

"You're hardly responsible for him shooting the gallery owner."

"No, but I could have been more alert and followed the clues better. Anyway, I don't know what to do with him. The DA won't lift a finger to help. They'd just as soon throw him in jail."

"Well, the case has gotten a lot of publicity."

"True. So that's why I'm here today." She felt herself blushing again. "Would you help him?"

"Ah, I knew there was a catch." He gave her a paternal smile. "I think we could find a place for him, yes. But you're aware it's not a perfect situation. We don't have the resources—"

"I'd be really grateful. I couldn't even begin to thank you. All I ask is that you keep an eye on him. Please don't throw him into a psycho ward with rapists and people who are convinced they're Julius Caesar."

"I'll watch out for him."

"I'll continue to see him as a patient on a weekly basis, indefinitely. That should help with his adjustment."

"I'll bet he hasn't paid you a cent, has he?"

"No. He can't really afford it."

"God, you're a trip." He shook his head. "Go ahead and tell the DA he can come here. I'm not sure their office will go for it. I think it'll depend on how much pressure they're under to look tough on this."

"Thank you so much."

He handed her a box of tissues. "On top of everything else, I have to sit here and watch you cry?"

"I need to make this right. I won't forget you for this. Ever."

"Buy me a set of fishing lures when the time comes."

CHAPTER 44

Cheryl Weissberg was sweating as she pushed open the door of Assistant District Attorney Sherri Brancacci's office. The ADA sat behind her desk, facing Joel Needleman and Paul Hoffman.

"Sorry I'm late," said Weissberg as she took the empty chair, clutching a file folder.

Needleman looked at his watch. "Twenty minutes."

"I apologize. I took a cab, rather than rely on the subway, and we got caught in traffic."

"Of course." Needleman's irritation was visible. "Who would have thought there'd be traffic heading downtown at rush hour?"

"This shouldn't take long," said Brancacci, "so I suggest we get started. I assume everyone has the paperwork. You should have a copy of the plea agreement, Joel's psychiatric report on Lester Gordon, Dr. Jensen's affidavit of intent to care for the patient at Bellevue, and Dr. Weissberg's proffer of continued weekly therapy at her expense, accompanied by her patient assessment."

Needleman nodded.

"Got it," said Hoffman. "Do you know who the judge is going to be?"

"I'm pretty sure it will be Baruch," said the ADA.

"Perfect," said Hoffman. "He's slightly to the left of Karl Marx."

"I trust everyone has read the material," said Brancacci. "I asked for this meeting so that we could ensure the proceedings will go smoothly. I think everyone wants to wrap this up and put it behind them." She looked at the Public Defender. "Have you prepped your client, Mr. Hoffman?"

"Several times."

"I want to make sure he knows what to expect. We want to avoid any last-minute glitches."

"I think she's asking you if he's likely to come into the courtroom and cut off his ear," said Needleman.

"Joel, please." Brancacci shook her head. "Let's stay on track."

"He'll be fine," said Hoffman. "He understands the situation, and he knows he's getting off easy. We'll rehearse it again before the hearing."

"Good."

"When do you think we can get this on the docket?" asked Hoffman.

"If we're lucky, the week after next. I'm doing my best to expedite it."

"Good job," said Needleman. "This is almost as quick as those drive-through wedding chapels in Las Vegas."

Hoffman looked at the psychiatrist.

"How about you, doctor? Are you going to be able to contain your sarcasm when you testify?"

"I'm going to tell the truth," said Needleman. "I'll tell Baruch that your guy is a sociopath who needs to be taken off the street, otherwise he's likely to do this again. His sanity, or lack of it, isn't open to question." He gestured to Weissberg with his thumb. "She's the one you have to worry about. If the hearing starts to resemble a screening of *The Three Faces of Eve,* that's when you'll have real problems."

She glanced at the psychiatrist. "I gather you're a skeptic about DID."

"That's not the point," said Needleman. "I don't think it's been successfully used as a defense for decades. Baruch will be aware of the case law, so I advise you to go easy on it."

"This is going to be cut and dried," said Brancacci, trying to affect the sternness of a schoolyard monitor. "Joel is correct: let's keep the explanations to a minimum. We have everything worked out, so the hearing should be brief and straightforward." She looked at the trio arrayed in front of her desk. "Any questions or concerns? Anything you want to air?"

"I'm curious what you're going to tell Cantwell's family," said Needleman.

"Exactly what I'm going to tell the judge: this man is disturbed. He needs treatment. Putting him in prison wouldn't accomplish anything, and we have resources in the mental health system available to help him. We're in a position to do it, and it's the best possible outcome."

"I appreciate that," said Weissberg. "It's very compassionate of you."

"She's getting soft," said Needleman. "Either that, or she's a frustrated painter."

"I want to put this in the rear-view mirror," said the ADA. "The newspapers are fixated on it. Let's give this man the help he needs and move on. Any questions?"

The room was silent.

"Thank you for coming. As soon as I have the date for the hearing, I'll be in touch."

Everyone stood up, and Weissberg hung back as Needleman and Hoffman left the room.

"I want to thank you again," she said when she was alone with Brancacci. "I messed this up, and I'll feel guilty about it for a long time. I want you to know that I appreciate everything you've done."

"No worries. As I told you, I've been there. And it's the right thing to do."

"You're going to take a lot of crap for this," said Weissberg.

"So be it." Brancacci smiled. "Stick and stones may break my bones, but crap will never hurt me."

CHAPTER 45

It was a sunny June day in South Carolina. Breezes wafted through the center of Columbia, offering the last respite before the brutal heat of the summer. Cheryl Weissberg found the museum, paid her admission fee, and made her way toward the Theodore and Lillian Humphries Modern Art Collection.

The fresh white paint of the hallway walls reverberated off the pale marble floor. She stopped in the middle of the new wing and entered the Impressionist room. At the back of the gallery, isolated in an alcove, was a seascape. Weissberg approached the wall and noted the inscription: "*Dawn at Dieppe*, by Paul Signac (1863-1935). Donated by Father Gordon Humphries in memory of his parents, Theodore and Lillian Humphries."

She sat down on a leather sofa and gazed at the painting. Fishing boats were clustered in the harbor, their bare masts poking into the grayish light. The sun dominated the horizon, emitting brilliant bursts of yellow and orange. Off in the distance, whitecaps churned in the soft blue sea.

"It's beautiful, isn't it?"

Weissberg looked up, slightly startled: she had been so immersed in the canvas that she hadn't heard the woman enter the room. Her companion was middle-aged and neatly dressed in a brown tweed suit. She wore glasses, and her perfectly coifed brown hair framed a genial face. She looked like a librarian.

"It's remarkable," said Weissberg. "I have a copy of it at home, but this is the first time I've seen the original."

"I never get tired of looking at it." She sat down on the edge of the sofa. "Are you visiting Columbia?"

"Just for a few days, yes. The museum was actually one of the main reasons I came here."

"Well, that's wonderful." She extended her hand. "I'm Elizabeth Pattinger. I actually work here, and I was heading out to run some errands. But somehow I can never pass this room without stopping to look at this particular canvas."

"I can see why."

"It's a wonderful example of Signac. We don't have a precise date for it, but we assume it was done in the late 1890s. He was an avid sailor, and we do know that he anchored at many of the coastal ports in France during that period."

"I didn't realize that."

"It's an interesting fact, but not really surprising. I think all great art ultimately comes from personal experience. It almost has to."

"Quite true."

"I'm sorry, but I didn't get your name."

"Cheryl Weissberg. I live in New York City, and I thought a few days away from the rat race would do me some good."

"It's a pleasure meeting you. We're very glad you chose Columbia. And even happier that you came to see us." She rose and took one last look at the painting. "It always amazes me, no matter how many times I look at it. The colors are so bright and vivid that it really transports you to the edge of the water. It almost looks real."

"Yes." Weissberg smiled. "It almost does."

THE END

THANK YOU FOR READING!

If you enjoyed this book, I'd greatly appreciate it if you could leave an honest review on Amazon.

Your support really does make a difference.

OTHER BOOKS BY
MARK SPIVAK

Non-fiction:

Iconic Spirits: An Intoxicating History
Moonshine Nation: The Art of Creating Cornbread in a Bottle

Novels:

Friend of the Devil
The American Crusade
Impeachment

Visit Mark's Amazon author page:
amazon.com/author/markspivak

ABOUT THE AUTHOR

Mark Spivak is the award-winning author of two non-fiction books (*Iconic Spirits: An Intoxicating History*, and *Moonshine Nation: The Art of Creating Cornbread in a Bottle*) and three novels (*Friend of the Devil*, *The American Crusade*, and *Impeachment*). He is particularly fascinated with tales of human obsession and the extremes of the psyche.

Mark lives in Florida with his wife and his imaginary friends.

Visit Mark's website:
markspivakbooks.com

And his Amazon author page:
amazon.com/author/markspivak

Made in the USA
Monee, IL
03 April 2023

31193546R00196